Were they really going to do it in the middle of a sugarcane field?

Gage lowered himself to his knees and kissed the front of her panties.

Kayla stood naked except for the tiny scrap of fabric between her legs, a wedge of cloth drenched with desire and currently driving her mad, because the mouth that kissed the flimsy fabric could be kissing *her* if it was gone.

"Gage, please."

"Please what, Kayla. What do you want?"

"Take them off," she answered. "I've felt you doing this, exactly this, in my dreams. But now, with you here, I want to see it, and feel it, to know that this time it's real. I don't want any clothing between us."

His fingers slipped beneath the tiny straps at both hips, then slid the wet cloth away. The warm breeze from the levee kissed her heated intimate flesh to make her quiver all over.

"I want you inside me," she begged.

And then he was.

Blaze™

Dear Reader,

"I see dead people."

Got your attention, didn't I? Well, the movie *The Sixth Sense* got mine (and most of the world's too—it grossed over $600 million worldwide!). When Haley Joel Osment whispered those now famous four words, I admittedly had goose bumps marching down my arms...and an idea for a titillating book series firing up my brain.

What if, in order to have some semblance of a normal existence, a family was required to help ghosts cross over? The ghosts who had unfinished business, or couldn't find their way. And suppose the current mediums for this family were six twentysomething cousins, trying to live their own lives, while constantly on call to help those whose lives were gone? That's the basis for my first Harlequin Blaze miniseries, THE SIXTH SENSE. I hope it gets your attention, too.

Book two of the series, *Ghosts and Roses*, belongs to Gage Vicknair, a twenty-seven-year-old playboy who gets thrown into a game of beat-the-clock where he has to 1) stop a killer from sending another woman to the other side before her time, 2) help the killer's first victim to cross over and 3) learn how powerful sex can be when it's anything but meaningless. It's a good thing our boy Gage is up to it....

Please visit my Web site, www.kelleystjohn.com, to win fabulous vacation giveaways, learn the latest news about my recent and upcoming releases, and drop me a line. I love hearing from readers!

Enjoy!

Kelley St. John

GHOSTS
AND ROSES
Kelley St. John

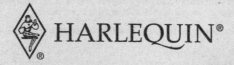

TORONTO • NEW YORK • LONDON
AMSTERDAM • PARIS • SYDNEY • HAMBURG
STOCKHOLM • ATHENS • TOKYO • MILAN • MADRID
PRAGUE • WARSAW • BUDAPEST • AUCKLAND

ISBN-13: 978-0-373-79341-9
ISBN-10:   0-373-79341-3

GHOSTS AND ROSES

Copyright © 2007 by Kelley St. John.

www.eHarlequin.com

Printed in U.S.A.

ABOUT THE AUTHOR

Kelley St. John's previous experience as a senior writer at NASA fueled her interest in writing action-packed suspense, although she also enjoys penning steamy romances and quirky women's fiction. Since 2000, St. John has obtained over fifty writing awards, including the National Readers' Choice Award, and was elected to the board of directors for Romance Writers of America. Visit her Web site, www.kelleystjohn.com, to learn the latest news about recent and upcoming releases and to register for fabulous vacation giveaways!

Books by Kelley St. John
HARLEQUIN BLAZE
325—KISS AND DWELL

To Brenda Chin, Editor Extraordinaire.

Thank you for loving the Vicknair family (and their ghostly sidekicks) as much as I do!

and

my heartfelt thanks to...

Criminal investigator Connie Rowe,
Dr. Michele Haynie Hughes, author Sabrah Agee
and my beloved Cajuns: Mom Z, Dea, Steve,
Teddy, Doris, Leigh and Kenny.

Any errors, as always, are all mine.

Introduction

GROWING UP in the Louisiana bayou lends itself to a natural familiarity with the staples of a Cajun heritage—vampires, voodoo and ghosts. The Vicknair family is quite familiar with the ghostly side of this equation. From the moment the family entered Louisiana, each member merged with the other side. Not the other side of the state line, or even the other side of St. Charles Parish. Oh, no, they straddle the boundary between the living and the dead. Their only means of living a seminormal life is to aid those who have difficulty crossing over, to help them fix what's wrong and make it right, so lost ghosts can find their way home.

The six Vicknair cousins—Nanette, Tristan, Gage, Monique, Dax and Jenee—currently serving medium duty understand the need to continue the family tradition and protect their secret. When a lavender-tinted envelope arrives on the infamous tea service in the Vicknair plantation's sitting room, they realize it's time to get down to business. Time to help a spirit. And woe to the cousin who ignores an assignment. While matriarch Adeline Vicknair may be dead, her feisty temper lives on, and when she assigns a spirit to one of her grandchildren, she wants it handled—or else.

Typically, assignments are dealt with in the same manner—one of the Vicknairs receives a letter, learns what the ghost needs in order to cross over, then helps the spirit achieve that goal. Every now and then, however, there's a kink thrown into the mix. During her last assignment, feisty Monique happened to fall in love with her spirit, and the rest of the cousins, particularly stickler Nanette, are still trying to grasp the reality that Monique's ghost didn't cross over; matter of fact, he's corporeal again and on this side with Monique.

Now Gage Vicknair is about to learn that being a medium can be dangerous, particularly when his assigned specter has been murdered…and the killer is only getting started.

Prologue

IN THE PAST four weeks, Lillian Bedeau had known someone was following her. She could sense it so clearly, that prickly sensation down the center of her spine, hair standing up at the back of her neck, goose bumps marching an eager path down her arms. Someone was there. When she went shopping for groceries, when she got the mail, when she dressed for bed at night. Someone was watching.

Thanks to a talented therapist, her nightmares had stopped five years ago. Visions of steel-gray eyes didn't wake her at night, didn't cause her to break out in a cold sweat. Didn't make her scream. But in the past month, the dreams had returned, the eyes more intense, the screams more chilling.

She'd known he was back; even though she hadn't seen him, she'd known. He was back and had found her, made her pay for sending him away…with a vicious thrust of a knife to her chest. Now every inhalation ripped at her lungs, and she could feel the lifeblood leaving her body with every pained step, but she wouldn't stop breathing, not yet. If she gave up now, she'd have no way to tell the others that he'd returned.

She'd tried her best to warn them, her four "sisters" from way back then. Only Chantelle was her sister by blood, but the four of them, Lillian, Chantelle, Makayla and Shelby, had bonded as tightly as sisters nonetheless. Raised in a small group home where they were the only girls, they'd been the only children he abused, a fact they'd learned at his trial. He never laid a finger on the boys.

For five long years, the girls were too afraid to tell anyone what he did to them at night, too scared of his promised retribution. But in the midst of their living nightmare, they'd found strength in each other, and in the roses.

The Seven Sisters orphanage was named for the Seven Sisters roses that bloomed on the grounds each year. It had been Makayla's idea for them to look to the roses for strength. The blooms were tiny individually, but they grew in clusters, so that together, they were strong enough to withstand the wrath of Louisiana's roughest storms. *That* had been the girls' goal—to be strong enough to withstand his wrath and make him pay.

To symbolize their bond, each of the girls had gotten a rose tattoo above her right ankle. They'd wanted a lasting symbol of finding their strength. Again, it'd been Makayla who had suggested the tattoos, and it'd been Makayla who had ultimately overcome her fear and sought help from their teacher, Ms. Rosa. Ms. Rosa had called the police that night, and then, with her by their sides, Lillian, Chantelle, Makayla and Shelby had endured the horrendous trial that had finally put him where he belonged: behind bars.

Lillian bit her lip to keep moving in spite of the pain shooting through every limb like shards of glass trying to push through her veins. He certainly wasn't behind bars now, and she couldn't fathom how he had got free. Wasn't the State supposed to inform them, warn them, if he were ever released? Or escaped?

She knew death was near now; the memories of the past, of everything she'd gone through with those four special sisters—children then, women now—filtered through her thoughts. Who else would he find? What if she didn't hang on long enough to warn them? If he had followed her throughout the day, then without meaning to, she'd led him straight to Makayla, and Makayla wouldn't have a clue she was in danger... Somehow she had forgotten everything, blocked it out.

Poor Makayla. She'd had the worst of it back then. Being the oldest and the strongest of the girls, she'd been the one he took most, the one whose spirit he'd most enjoyed trying to break. Lillian had tried to warn Makayla that she believed he was back, but for the past two weeks, Makayla hadn't returned Lillian's messages. When Lillian had called the small department store where Makayla worked and learned she'd quit without notice two weeks ago, she'd known something was wrong. Makayla wouldn't have quit her job on impulse; that wasn't the kind of person she was. And she didn't have any family, other than Lillian, Shelby and Chantelle, and she'd called none of them to let them know she was leaving town.

Following her instinct, Lillian had called the hospitals in New Orleans to see if her friend had been admitted, and one helpful nurse had suggested she try the homeless shelters. With a few phone calls, Lillian had learned that a woman who claimed to have no memory had arrived at the Magazine Street shelter two weeks earlier. She could only remember a name—Kayla. Lillian knew this woman was Makayla.

Lillian should have realized that he could have been following her when she'd visited the shelter earlier, not aware that it closed during the day. She should have told that nice girl who worked there, Jenee, her suspicion about Kayla's identity, that she could be Makayla Sparks and that she'd been molested, brutally and terribly, from the time she was nine until she turned fourteen. She should have told her about the horrible trial they'd all endured when Makayla was sixteen and Lillian a year younger. If Lillian had told the woman, perhaps Jenee could have helped. And perhaps Lillian wouldn't be where she was right now, struggling for her next breath, probably her last breath, without having warned her friend that, somehow, *he* had returned. Just as he'd said he would.

The knife that had pierced Lillian's chest had hit her like a one-two punch. One, shock. Two, defeat. But then she'd decided that he wouldn't win. She had to warn Makayla.

Her breathing became even more difficult, coming in rapid, sharp gasps, and her vision blurred as she stumbled down the dark alley that she prayed led to Magazine Street. Lillian groped at rough bricks and clots of mortar sticking out from the building's edge like short, gnarled teeth. If she didn't hold on tight, she'd fall again, and next time, she might not get up.

He probably thought she'd died at once, when he plunged the knife in and she'd fallen to the ground. How long had she been unconscious? She could hear plenty of noise from the street nearby, but that didn't mean anything. The Quarter was always noisy, whether in the middle of the day or the middle of night.

She squinted. *Focus.* It definitely wasn't the middle of the day. Too dark. Too dreary. Too scary. Middle of the night, then. Could she get to the shelter in time? Before she crumpled in this grungy alley—again? And if she did, would she ever wake up?

She didn't think so.

Was Makayla back at the shelter now?

Or had he already killed her?

Dizziness overpowered Lillian's senses, as well as a horrid nausea that desperately wanted to claim dominion over her shaking frame. Saliva pooled in her mouth and mixed with the metallic, bitter taste of blood. Would she make it back before she died? And would she ever stop seeing those flat, steel-gray eyes?

She had started trembling the minute she'd viewed those eyes, no longer a nightmare, but a reality. Lillian had noticed him staring at her from one aisle over at the French Market. He had worn a black hooded sweatshirt, even though the September heat called for short sleeves. She hadn't wanted to panic, hadn't wanted to assume that the figure in the dark shirt was him. The build was different, anyway. He'd looked younger than she remembered. Bigger. But those eyes had warned her that it *could* be him. The fact that he'd stopped on a dime when she'd noticed him was her second warning. And then, when she'd made the conscious decision to flee and retreated to the maze of alleys that would lead her back to the shelter, she'd heard his steps behind her, and the warning bells were like fire alarms.

That warning came too late, and he was there, hurting her and leaving her to die. But she wasn't dead yet, and she'd be damned if she'd give up without a fight.

Her hand pressed hard against her shirt, sticky and warm. Lillian wouldn't look down to see the result of his attack. If she did, she might give over to the nausea that had her trembling with every wobbly step.

The alley was void of life save a lone homeless man, propped against a silver trashcan with a brown-bagged bottle cradled against his chest. His stench nearly caused Lillian to hand over the reins to the nausea, but she didn't.

She had to be strong, had to fight a little longer. She had to get to the shelter, to warn Makayla and find help.

The man in the alley growled at her as she passed. Then he opened one eye and cocked a wiry brow at her hand against the sticky shirt before drifting back to sleep. Lillian growled, too, but hers was the result of her effort to get to the end of the alley. She recognized her location now, and she knew the shelter was close. Straight ahead. End of the alley, then across the street.

She could do it. She could, and she would.

Darkness cloaked the city. How late was it? What if the shelter had closed its doors for the night? What if Jenee had left? She sensed that the young woman could help her, could help Makayla, too. Lillian didn't know how she knew, but she did. She squinted past the pain and took the final steps from the pitch-black alley to the lighted street. Gasps of horror surrounded her as, without the building for support, she staggered forward. She wanted to speak, to warn Makayla, but all that came out were those sickly, eerie gasps.

"Oh, my God, somebody help her!" someone screamed as Lillian crumpled to the asphalt with a dull thud.

She opened her eyes, saw people gathering and watched a man grab a phone from his pocket.

"I'm calling 911," he said to the group.

"Police!" another voice yelled. "Help!"

And then, running across the street, Jenee surged forward. Dropping beside Lillian on the ground, she removed her outer shirt and replaced Lillian's hand with the fabric, then steadily applied pressure. She didn't yell or scream, but maintained a calm that Lillian desperately needed.

"Who did this to you?" Jenee asked, tears filling her eyes.

Lillian's voice cracked as she forced the words through

dry, parched lips. "Warn her." She tried to swallow, but her tongue refused to move. "Warn them all." Tears trickled down her cheeks from the agony of speech.

"Who?" Jenee repeated as sirens whistled in the distance. Lillian slowly closed her eyes.

1

KAYLA SMILED at the man entering the rose-filled courtyard and opened her arms in welcome invitation. He moved confidently, powerfully, his vivid blue eyes filled with intensity and a resolute goal—to please her, repeatedly.

He came to her each night, touching her body the way no man had ever touched her before, bringing her such exquisite sensations, such undeniable elation, that she felt empty when he was gone.

"I knew you'd come," she said, and the corner of his mouth crooked upward in that sexy grin that made her pulse jitter.

His shirt was the color of his eyes, Caribbean blue, and she licked her lips as he unbuttoned it and tossed it to the ground. The broad chest, sprinkled with light-brown hair, led to a built abdomen, also embellished with a thin sprinkling of hair that led to the top of his jeans, where his hands now rested against the waistband while he awaited her command.

"Take them off," she whispered. "Please. I want to see all of you." She did want to see him, but she wanted to feel him even more, deep within her, filling her, completing her. She yearned for this moment each day and wished it never had to end.

But she wouldn't think about the end now. Right now, he was here, and preparing to give her exactly what she needed. He knew how to please women, and he'd pleased many, Kayla realized. It was apparent in the way he moved, in the confidence of his stride, the assuredness in his eyes. But while he obviously knew his share of females, Kayla couldn't help but believe that she was different. She was special to this man, just as he was special to her. She could see it in his eyes, feel it in his touch, and when they became one, there wasn't any denying that their bonding was unique. It was real. It was meant to be.

He unfastened his jeans, then slowly slid the zipper down. Kayla's legs began to twitch in anticipation. She hated the fact that he was here and not inside of her. Yet. She nearly shouted for joy when the heavy denim hit the ground, and he stepped toward her.

The next move was hers, and she knew what to do. He wore black underwear, the sheerness boldly outlining his erection. He wouldn't remove the fabric that barely covered his glory; that was her job. And she loved it.

She leaned up and grasped the waistband, lifted it slightly to bring it over the end of his penis, then pulled the stretchy cloth down those muscled thighs and let it fall to the ground. He stepped even closer, and Kayla brought her mouth to the tip of his beautiful erection, licking one pearly drop of his desire away before he moved from her reach.

She looked up into those intense blue eyes and knew what she'd see—him shaking his head. He wanted to see her naked, and he wasn't giving her access to him until he had full access to her, too.

Kayla loved the way he made her feel—so strong, so bold, so ready for this, for making love, the way she couldn't remember making love in real life.

That niggling reminder, the whisper of a hint that this wasn't real, that she was merely creating what she wanted in her mind, caused Kayla to frown. She didn't know this man, not really, didn't even know his name. She wasn't even sure of her own name. She certainly didn't know whether he was real, or merely an intensely strong figment of her imagination.

But he sure seemed real.

He shook his head again, not allowing her to leave the dream until he'd completed his goal—pleasing her—and Kayla willingly let go of reality and let fantasy reign.

Sighing contentedly, she removed her nightclothes and panties.

His eyes were a smoky blue now, filled with lust and desire, and his smile showcased the wicked cleft in his chin. Kayla wanted to lick that sexy indentation, and she would. Soon.

He lowered himself to the ground beside her, and Kayla reveled in the heat of his body next to hers. Moving against him, she enjoyed the way they fitted so well together, the way his warmth seeped into her body and into her soul.

She licked the cleft in his chin while he moved his thigh between her legs. Rocking her hips to provide as much abrasion as possible between his flesh and her clitoris, Kayla knew that if he let her, she'd come merely from this, moving against him, feeling him this close, wanting him even closer.

"Please," she panted. "Don't make me wait any more. I need you. Please."

His mouth slid over hers and his tongue moved within her lips, then he rolled over on top of her, his legs pushing against hers and spreading them wide, preparing her for that hot, hard length to come inside.

The thick head of his penis pushed against her opening

and stayed there, while he broke the kiss and rose above her, those blue eyes staring into hers while he waited.

Didn't he understand that she was ready? That she was always ready for him?

No, he didn't. His questioning gaze told her that he was still mindful of her fears, that he didn't want to hurt her. But he would never hurt her. He only loved her, and she needed that love, that completion, more than she needed her next breath.

She couldn't wait. Wrapping her legs around his back, she rammed her hips upward to bring him, totally and completely and deeply, within her core.

Kayla rode the exquisite wave of desire, spiraling and burning and fighting for release. She matched him thrust for thrust, her breathing hard and heavy as she let go of all fear and gave him everything. His chest heaved above her, eyes focused on hers as her body tensed, then his mouth claimed hers, and her passion exploded in wild, convulsing spasms.

His hands grabbed her hips, and he pushed inside her, even harder, even farther than before, and his body tensed in his own powerful climax.

Kayla trembled with the after shudders, closing her eyes in exhaustion.

When she opened them, he was gone, and she was alone on her tiny cot in the shelter, while the other women in the room slept noisily, their raspy breaths and low snores filling the night.

She swallowed and tamped down on the urge to cry. How could she cry? He'd come to her again and fulfilled her need for intimacy, true intimacy and trust, with a man. She said a prayer of thanks that the blue-eyed man had given her a fantasy tonight...and that the gray-eyed monster hadn't delivered a nightmare.

"AREN'T YOU getting tired of meaningless sex?"

Gage Vicknair stood at the top of the levee and scanned the surface of Lake Pontchartrain, its murky brown water churning madly beneath the thick Louisiana humidity, while Monique's question churned just as madly in his mind.

Tired of sex? Gage Vicknair?

Not in this life.

But that wasn't what she'd asked, now, was it? She'd asked if he was tired of *meaningless* sex. *That* was the kicker, and that question had a different answer altogether. He was twenty-seven and, to his knowledge, he'd never experienced any other kind of sex *but* meaningless…in real life. But, for the past two weeks, he *had* glimpsed a deeper connection, yet only within his dreams.

And with a woman he'd never seen before.

Wouldn't you know it? At the point in his life when he'd decided he was actually ready to look for more, to give a woman more than merely a physical bond, he'd go and flip over a fantasy girl who existed only in his mind.

Laughter carried in the air from the partyers gearing up for a hot night at the Treasure Chest Casino, less than a block away from Gage's apartment on Williams Boulevard. And from the cars backed up around the Pontchartrain Center, the place would soon be hopping with tourists in town for the September RV show.

Long-nosed cigar boats pushed through the deep waters of the lake, and several elderly fishermen sat on white plastic buckets around the sloped bank, brown bamboo rods hovering above the gloomy water. A couple of pretty college girls dozed on striped beach towels, their bikini-clad bodies soaking up the last rays of the Friday sun.

His cell phone beeped the "Zydeco Stomp," and he

wasn't surprised at the ID displayed on the square gray screen. He flipped the phone open.

"Haven't you done enough damage for one day?"

"Oh, don't even go there." Monique's feistiness was in full force. "It should take more than an honest comment about your love life to get you pissed, but if you're wanting an apology, I'll give you one. I'm sorry." She paused for effect. "There, how was that?"

"It'll do in a crunch," Gage said, grinning. Heaven help him, he couldn't stay mad at her for long. Never had, not even when they were kids and she'd tried out her new school scissors on his hair while he was sleeping. Thank God she'd learned a bit more about haircutting since then, or Monique's Masterpieces would have flopped big-time. As it was, her salon was thriving. Then again, Gage gave her more business than anyone, since all of his previous lovers found their way to his sister's place to keep tabs on the "roving playboy." Their words, not his. But the description was accurate, and reminded him again of Monique's blunt comment.

Meaningless sex.

"I do mean that, by the way," she said. "I am sorry…"

"How come it sounds like a 'but' is coming?"

He nodded at two fishermen struggling to lug their buckets up the levee. A fat speckled trout on top of one of the mounds of fish flipped over with a jerk, its body slapping loudly against the additional mix of red fish and flounder filling the pail.

"Looks like you did okay," Gage observed.

One of the guys grinned, displaying a big gap where his two front teeth used to reside. "Sho' 'nuff."

Walking a short distance behind the men, a perky blond teen with a curvy body and a sexy smile sauntered up the levee, her tight T-shirt knotted beneath her breasts and her blue-jean short-shorts almost qualifying for indecent exposure. While the bikini-clad girls wore less, this one somehow managed to show, and tease, more. Slowing her pace to a crawl as she neared, she smiled at Gage.

"Hi there," she said, her voice a sexy whisper. Her diamond-embellished belly ring caught the sun and made Gage flinch.

All it'd take was a friendly hello, and he could put money on having her out of her shirt and shorts before the sun went down. But as Monique had pointed out, he'd had his share of meaningless sex, and he wasn't into jailbait. So he nodded politely, then turned his back to the flirty girl and let her go hit on someone who wasn't having a life-altering day, courtesy of his meddling sister.

And speaking of meddling Monique, he'd nearly forgotten she was on the other end of the line.

"You still there?"

"I was waiting to see what happened," she replied.

"What happened?" he repeated.

"Hel-lo there," she purred, mocking the teen's seductive tone before laughing into the phone.

"Watch it," he warned.

"Oh, all right. I'll stop," she said, huffing. "But the only reason I've been nagging you about your beyond-interesting love life is that I want you to have what I've got." She lowered her voice to a giddy whisper. "I'm so happy, Gage. Ryan is a dream come true."

"Actually," Gage corrected, "he's a ghost come alive, but 'dream come true' will work."

Monique, like Gage, their brother, Dax, and their cousins, Nan, Tristan and Jenee, had inherited the family's unique ability to communicate with the dead. Or, more specifically, to help ghosts who had trouble crossing over to the other side. Oddly enough, Gage had never seen the family obligation as anything out of the ordinary—since he'd been around Vicknair mediums since the day he was born—until Monique had fallen in love with her assigned specter. Even the Vicknairs were stunned that Ryan Chappelle had been sent back over to the land of the living to be with his soul mate, Monique.

"Ghost, dream, whatever." She giggled shamelessly. "Anyway, we're excited. That's why I called. I wanted to tell you that Ryan and I are at the airport. We're leaving for Las Vegas tonight, and if everything goes as planned, I'll be Monique Chappelle before midnight."

Gage swallowed hard. Monique hadn't known Ryan that long, but then again, he couldn't have stayed on this side if they weren't meant for each other. Still…Monique? His wild, vivacious and ready-for-anything sister? Married? To a former ghost?

"Gage?" Her voice sounded slightly worried.

"Yeah?"

"Say you're happy," she instructed.

"I'm happy." He was happy, because Monique was happy. But it was going to take some getting used to. And what about her assignments? Ghosts didn't take too well to waiting for help. "You're leaving town?"

"Don't worry," she said, evidently following his train of thought. "We'll come back if I start feeling ghosts, and I haven't had any burning sensations all day. I'm hoping I won't have any spirits calling until I'm safely back in Louisiana next week."

Monique usually sensed her ghosts a day before they came, so she was probably right. She and Ryan could go to Vegas, tie the knot and get back before she received another of Grandma Adeline's letters, as long as they were willing to cut the trip short if necessary.

Adeline Vicknair distributed ghostly assignments to each of the Vicknair mediums, and she could make their lives unpleasant if there was any delay.

Monique's skin burned when she had a specter coming. Gage, on the other hand, heard the dead ghost cry before he received a visit. Typically, he had about a day from when he first heard the ghost weeping until he actually met his specter, so he was usually at the Vicknair plantation waiting for his grandmother's letter when it materialized on her silver tea service. Once, however, after Hurricane Katrina had hit New Orleans, he hadn't been able to leave the emergency room at Ochsner Hospital. Being a trauma doctor, he simply couldn't just walk out on patients during a crisis. So, even though he heard the crying, he didn't leave.

The result had been horrendous.

Not only did he hear the ghost cry, he heard it wail. By the time he'd finally made it to the Vicknair plantation in St. Charles Parish, screams of agony had pierced his eardrums until he'd thought his head would explode.

Since that day, he'd never been late to receive a letter. Thankfully, New Orleans hadn't been hit with another hurricane like Katrina, which made it much easier for him to give his spirited grandmother the prompt response she expected.

"I told Dax that we're heading to Vegas," Monique added. "He's fine with it."

"Dax is typically fine with anything." Their brother wanted Monique's happiness as much as he did.

"Yeah, he is. Hey, would you mind telling Nan that

Ryan and I won't be there tomorrow to help with the house?" she asked, as though this weren't a huge request.

"Ah," Gage said.

"What?"

"Just realizing that I'd been waiting for the other shoe to drop, and there it is. The real reason for your call."

"I don't know what you're talking about," she lied through her teeth. He heard a flight departure announced in the background and wondered if his sister was literally standing at the threshold of the plane.

"Are they waiting on you to board?" he asked.

"No, that's another flight. We've got twenty more minutes before we can get on our plane." She cleared her throat. "So, you'll tell Nanette, then?"

"You didn't tell her that you're getting married?" Gage already knew the answer. There was no telling what Nan would do when she learned Monique had decided to marry her ghost. As the oldest cousin, Nan felt it was her duty to make sure the younger Vicknairs realized the magnitude of their responsibility to the family legacy, and to the spirits. She expected the rules to be followed, and she expected the other cousins to heed their assignments in a timely manner. Monique was not only notorious for breaking rules, but also for being late, which, quite frankly, drove Nan nuts.

Nan had made no secret of the fact that she was shocked the powers that be had allowed Ryan to remain on this side, soul mate or not, but she'd finally relented to the reality that the guy was here to stay. However, she'd had serious reservations about her cousin even dating the man.

"Not that I mind her knowing, but I didn't get a chance to tell her," Monique defended herself.

"You live with her," Gage said. "And more than that, I

don't. Yet you're asking me to let her know that, number one, you're missing a family workday on the house, and number two, you're buzzing off to Vegas to get hitched to a ghost."

"Are you saying you have a problem with Ryan and I getting married?" she asked.

Gage could almost see the lower edge of her heart-shaped lips pouting in what Cajuns classified as a major *bahbin*. Letting that *bahbin* pucker had gotten Monique damn near everything she'd wanted as a kid, and she knew that Gage wasn't immune to the effect.

Good thing he couldn't see her.

"You know I don't have a problem with it. And you also know that Nan will probably blow a gasket, and you'd rather it was me on the receiving end of her tantrum. You know Nan. She doesn't go for breaking, or even bending, the medium and spirit rules."

"I know, but like I've told her repeatedly, Ryan and I aren't breaking any rules. He has permission to stay on this side, and he's been living at the plantation—staying in my room, I might add—since he crossed back. She should be expecting us to tie the knot."

"Yet you didn't feel the urge to mention it." The last rays of sun glinted bright orange, before dipping beneath the horizon and leaving New Orleans, and Gage, in hazy dimness.

"Come on, Gage. Nan doesn't like change, particularly when it involves the spirits. She'll have to adjust to the idea, and I don't want to be around when she goes through that adjustment period. You know she'll take it better coming from you. And I didn't want her trying to talk me out of this, or even worse, trying to get approval from the powers that be on the other side for me to marry my soul mate. They wouldn't have let him stay here unless we were meant to be together. Surely they anticipated marriage in that equation," she spouted rapidly, as though she had already prepared this argument in her mind.

"Does he want to talk to me?" Ryan asked, his voice echoing in the distance of the line.

"No, I don't need to talk to him. And tell him two things for me, will you?" Pausing, Gage reconsidered and amended, "Make that three things."

"What?"

"One, take care of my sister. Two, congratulations. And three, he owes me big-time for taking on Nanette for you."

"Wouldn't I be the one who owes you?" Monique asked, her delight at his acceptance obvious.

"Oh, that's a given," Gage said. "But hey, if you're becoming one and all that, I figure it's a twofer deal."

"He says you owe him," Monique relayed to Ryan.

Ryan's deep laugh rumbled in the background. "Deal."

"It's a deal," she repeated. "Love you, Gage."

"You, too, sis. Be careful."

"I will." She hung up.

Gage pocketed his phone, checked his watch then walked toward his apartment. His shift at the hospital didn't start for another two hours, but he'd need every minute in order to get a shower then maneuver through Friday-night New Orleans traffic. If he was lucky, he'd get to the ER a few minutes early.

He crossed the courtyard that formed the center of his apartment complex and neared the kidney-shaped pond that housed a school of bold goldfish. Tall, decorative lampposts illuminated the peaceful area.

Gage paused and examined the familiar scenery. Something about the area looked different, *felt* different. He strained his ears, almost expecting a ghost's cry, but he heard nothing. Stepping closer, he studied the bright-orange shimmer of fish gliding beneath round lilypads. The fat fish darted in and out of the pads and swiftly swam through the water bubbling at the end of a rock fountain. Blooming shrubbery, mostly deep-pink roses, enclosed the area and offered privacy to those who wanted a few moments of serenity, whether standing at the pond's edge or sitting at the single wrought-iron bench at one side of the courtyard.

Gage looked at the fish, the bench, the shrubs. Something wasn't quite right, but he'd be damned if he could say what it was. Why did it feel so odd? And why did the memory of his fantasy woman suddenly fill his thoughts?

"Strange, isn't it?" Vernon Medders said.

Gage had been so enthralled that he hadn't heard the old gardener approaching. Leather-skinned and balding, Vernon Medders was a constant fixture around Lakeside Apartments. In exchange for rent, he tended to the complex's landscaping, particularly the courtyard, which he babied daily.

"What's strange?" Gage inquired.

"Them." The old man pointed to the shrubs. "Blooming again." He shrugged. "I don't mind it, since those are my favorite roses, but they're only supposed to bloom once a year, late spring to early summer, and they did their part back in June. Odd that they're blooming again in September, and they're just covered, too, aren't they?"

Gage studied the shrubs, completely saturated with clusters of dark-pink roses. *That* was what was so different. He'd walked past the courtyard yesterday and he hadn't noticed the roses. He'd have noticed such a rich, bold pink color, wouldn't he?

"Seem to have burst out overnight. Sure is odd, but I don't mind." Vernon smiled. "Really add another layer to the beauty of the place, don't they?"

"Yeah," Gage said. But it also added another layer to his unease. He had this vague sensation that it had something to do with the other side. The spirits often sent visual calling cards that they were coming, little things that signified a medium should be prepared. Typically, the hints would relate to the assignment, but Gage couldn't imagine what flowers blooming out of season could imply. He believed, however, that he would find out soon. And bizarrely enough, he suspected that it also had to do with his fantasy woman.

Wouldn't that be his luck? He'd found someone who'd shown him the beauty in sex, and she ended up being a ghost? Maybe he should've asked Monique for a few pointers on how she'd managed to keep a spirit on this side, just in case.

Gage strained his ears again. No crying. How long did he have before he found out whether these roses were meant for him?

Hell, he hoped he made it through his shift before Grandma Adeline sent a letter his way. Since he was about to take a week's vacation from the hospital, he really couldn't miss a night of work. And he hoped the ghost wouldn't be the woman of his dreams. He wouldn't mind seeing her again, but he'd prefer it if she was breathing at the time.

His cell phone rang again. "I'll see you later, Vern." He didn't have time to wonder about ghosts or roses or even sex with his fantasy woman. He had to get ready for work. Continuing toward his apartment, he answered the familiar ring. "Hello?"

"I got your message." It was Tiffany, his occasional weekend bed partner. "You sure you don't want to come over after your shift? You said you'd have a few hours before you were due at your family's Saturday thing."

Gage opened the door to his apartment while fighting the impulse to groan. He'd hoped Tiffany would take his cancellation as a sign to find someone else with whom to end her night. She was a Bourbon Street exotic dancer, and they typically got off work at about the same time, but ever since he'd started dreaming about his fantasy girl, he hadn't wanted anyone else, even always-ready-to-please Tiffany. In fact, he'd opted out of their traditional Friday-night tumble last week, too, because he couldn't get the other woman off his mind.

Plus, after Monique's observation earlier, Gage realized that he'd been subconsciously taking inventory of his relationships, or nonrelationships, and he no longer wanted merely to spend a few hours burning up the sheets. He didn't know how to explain that to Tiffany, who was all for burning sheets, anytime, anyplace.

Would he ever want that again?

"I'm beat, Tiff," he said, removing his shoes and socks, then unbuttoning his jeans and dropping them to the floor. "I'm working most of the night, then I want to get a few hours of sleep before I head over to the house in the morning. You understand?" God, he hoped she did. He entered his bathroom, then held the phone away from his ear long enough to whip his shirt over his head and start the shower.

"That's what you said last week," she reminded. "You know you want to get back to our Friday-night routine. I missed you—you missed me, too, didn't you? Besides, I'm sure I can keep your energy level pumping."

Gage swallowed. She sure as hell could keep him pumping, for quite some time, but at the moment he needed a little space from Tiff, and from the rest of his love interests, while he figured out why he felt so damn weird all of a sudden, and why the hell he was so entranced by a woman who only existed in his dreams.

"Yeah, well, I'm going to have to bail on you this time. I really do need to sleep." He adjusted the water temperature.

"Is that your shower I hear?" she asked. "You know, I could come over there now, and we could have a little fun before your shift, if you want. I'll wash your back, and you can wash mine."

His cock, obviously recognizing Tiffany's tone, steadily rose to the occasion. "Sorry," he managed. "No time tonight." He twisted the knobs controlling the water temperature. He needed it cooler. Much cooler. Cold.

"Oh, all right," she said, disappointment evident in each word. "Bye, Gage."

A vision of Tiffany's strawberry curls dangling around her shoulders, lips in a suggestive smile and ample chest heaving above him flashed vividly in Gage's mind. "Bye." He snapped the phone closed and tried to pinpoint the exact moment when he'd lost his mind. What guy wouldn't want no-holds-barred sex with Tiffany?

A guy like him, evidently, because the thought held no appeal whatsoever. He wanted sex, obviously, or at least his cock did. Still semihard from Tiffany's suggestive comment, it was ready to go full speed ahead. But the head above his neck wanted something else entirely.

Monique had been right, Gage realized, as he stepped beneath the cool water. He *was* tired of meaningless sex. He wanted something meaningful, the type of relationship he'd never had beyond his dreams. He'd be lying if he said the thought of having a real relationship had never crossed his mind—lately, it'd been hovering there fairly steadily, thanks to the fantasy girl—but hearing his sister say it out loud really drove the point home.

Gage wanted more.

He wanted a real woman who held the same mesmer-izing appeal as the woman in his dreams. But hell, how did you find that certain someone who made you forget about all other females and find genuine satisfaction in her, and her alone?

Satisfaction. *That* was what had been missing in Gage's life. He'd had sex, plenty of sex, yet he hadn't been satisfied. Physically, sure. Emotionally, not so much. Okay, emotionally, never. He wanted that tie to another human, to a woman who would make him feel…complete.

Gage turned the pressure control on the shower to produce a heavy stream of water, closing his eyes against the brunt of the flow.

He saw the image at once. Roses, a multitude of blooms filling the shrubbery surrounding the courtyard. This time Vernon Medders was nowhere to be seen, yet Gage wasn't alone.

She was exquisite, and, as always, she took his breath away. Long brown hair, silky and shiny, cascaded well past her shoulders and big chocolate eyes studied him as he neared. Her smile said that she'd been expecting him.

A soft breeze sent the mist from the fountain toward her, and moistened the thin fabric of her pale-pink gown, until she stood there with sheer, wet material touching her every-where, a mere hint of a covering over a body that was pure perfection.

He had to have her. He simply had to.

She opened her arms and motioned him forward, then smiled as he neared. "I knew you'd come," she whispered.

He knew somewhere deep in the back of his mind that he was in the shower, cool water running over his skin. But with her he was clothed in a shirt and jeans that her eyes told him she yearned to have removed. Gage wouldn't deny her the unspoken request.

She licked her lips as he unbuttoned his shirt and tossed it to the ground, and boldly studied his chest. Then her gaze traveled slowly down his abdomen, and lower.

Gage instinctively moved his hands to the waistband of his jeans, but he stopped there. This was no ordinary fantasy; there seemed to be more going on here, more than he could even grasp at the moment. He needed to know that this beautiful woman wanted…what he wanted.

"Take them off," she whispered. "Please. I want to see all of you."

Gage's pulse sputtered as he nodded, totally intent on giving her what she asked. Why was he so nervous about this? He knew his way around a woman's body; hell, he was known for his playboy status and wore the label like a badge of honor. But that didn't matter now, not with her. He didn't want merely to show her he was an experienced lover; he wanted to show this woman that he could give her more. That he could complete her, the way his soul whispered to him now that she could complete him.

He unfastened his jeans and slowly slid the zipper down, before pushing the fabric to the ground and stepping out of them. Again, he waited. She had to be the one to control this. It was up to her, after all. How Gage knew, he couldn't say, but he couldn't take her until she explicitly gave him permission.

He hoped she didn't wait long.

She moved toward him and grasped the waistband of his underwear, lowering her body as she pulled it to the ground. Her mouth was so close to his penis that her breath warmed the head, and then she brought that full, luscious mouth to the tip and licked.

While he thoroughly enjoyed her mouth on his cock, right now he wanted inside her, *if* she would allow it. He took a small step away, taking his penis from her mouth, and to his delight, she moaned for more.

Gage shook his head, visually informing her that this wasn't going to be a one-sided affair. He wanted to see her, all of her, the way she was seeing him.

As she removed the pink gown and her panties, Gage leisurely allowed his eyes to wander freely, examining the slender column of her throat, the cinnamon-tipped breasts and flat abdomen, the slight curve of her hips. He paused briefly at her glistening center before continuing down the length of her toned legs.

His throat tightened as he noticed something he hadn't seen before, a tattoo above her right ankle that appeared to be a small cluster of roses. Before he could get a better look, she took his hand and pulled him slowly to the ground, now covered with deep-pink rose petals, the exact same hue as the rose tattoo.

Gage lay beside her, the petals surrounding her beauty. Her hips moved against his thigh, and she was hot and moist against his leg. He wanted that heat, that moistness, to surround him.

"Please," she urged. "Don't make me wait any more. I need you. Please."

He couldn't wait much longer, either. His cock was so hard, so ready, that he simply couldn't hold back. He nudged the tip slightly into her heated core and held it there, then he rose above her and waited. He needed her to tell him that this was what she wanted. In an ordinary fantasy, Gage would push himself inside and know that the woman of his dreams wanted exactly that, but this was no ordinary fantasy—or just sex. It was more. Gage knew it in the very depths of his soul.

"Now!" Her legs wrapped around his back, and she took him, all of him, deep inside.

Did he *need* sex? No. He'd turned it down earlier because it no longer fulfilled his ultimate need. But did he *need* her? Yes, he realized, as she pumped her hips against him and pushed him toward losing control. Understanding now that she didn't want him to hold back, that she wanted him to give as freely, as powerfully, as she was giving, Gage grabbed her hips and rammed into her, determined to reach the very depth of her being, go so deeply that she would never doubt that he was the man who could fulfill as no other did.

Those deep-brown eyes told him that she would never, ever hold anything back from him. She'd give him everything, sexually and emotionally. And that's exactly what he needed from this woman…everything.

2

GAGE STARED at the whiteboard indicating occupied rooms in the ER. His shift would end in fifteen minutes, and they'd had no more than three beds filled at any given time throughout the night.

"Slow board." Hank Simone nodded toward the empty squares. "You know what that means."

"Yeah, it means I'm glad I'm about to get off work and start my vacation." Gage grinned at Hank, the newest intern in the trauma unit, then added, "But you're here another six hours, aren't you?"

"Hell, thanks for reminding me." Hank groaned, obviously dreading the impending increase in emergencies. A slow night in New Orleans typically meant at least twice the usual number of shootings, stabbings and barroom brawls for the next shift. Gage was actually happy he would be working on cleaning the grunge from the first floor of the Vicknair plantation in a matter of hours. Then again, going to the family estate also meant seeing Nanette and telling her about Monique's wedding.

"Maybe I should stay and help you after all," he said, only half joking.

"We've got a stabbing victim on the way in from the Quarter," the dispatch nurse announced. "Arrival estimated at ten minutes."

Gage listened to the grainy sound of the EMTs through the transmitter as they gave a rapid-fire injury assessment. The victim had a four-inch gaping laceration to the chest, a classic sucking chest wound. Gage's ears pricked as he realized the patient had tension pneumothorax and that the EMTs were performing needle decompression. Air had collapsed one lung and shoved the heart into the other side of the rib cage. "Looks like things will pick up sooner than we thought."

"Room two ready for arrival," a trauma nurse called out, nodding at Gage and Hank.

Then the pager at Gage's hip started beeping. He checked the number. "Damn."

"What?" Hank asked, as Gage grabbed the nearest phone.

"It's Jenee."

"The baby cousin?" Hank obviously paid more attention than Gage realized when he discussed his family.

"She's twenty-one," Gage said. "But yeah, that's her. It's the number to her cell phone, followed by 911. Why is she calling me with an emergency at four in the morning?"

"I hope she's okay, man." Hank moved toward the ER entrance, where the lights of an arriving ambulance filled the night sky with flashes of red.

"Gage?" Jenee answered after the first ring. "Thank God you called me back so fast. I called your cell, but didn't get an answer."

"No cells in the hospital, Jenee, you know that. What's wrong? Are you at the house?" he asked.

"No, I stayed at the shelter tonight. Kayla, the woman who lost her memory, was having a hard time. And I didn't send the 911 for me. It's for a lady who came to the shelter today. Evidently, she was trying to get back to us, but didn't make it. Somebody stabbed her, Gage. We're on our way to the hospital. I'm following the ambulance. I think we're nearly there, but I don't know how long she can hold on. You've got to help her."

Jenee had been drawn to this Kayla since the woman had arrived, alone and lost, at the homeless shelter where she regularly volunteered. Gage's youngest cousin hadn't been able to help the woman remember her past, nor had the doctors, but Jenee hadn't given up hope. Now another woman at the shelter had been stabbed. His cousin sounded as though she'd had a rough night.

"I'll do my best." Even as he spoke the words, Gage heard the familiar sound of a ghost's cry. This time, it was a faint whimper, definitely feminine, and seemed very near. He hung up the phone and moved toward the door and the approaching ambulance.

"God, don't let her be my next ghost," he whispered.

The ambulance doors opened, and the emergency medical technicians inside frowned and shook their heads over the woman, her clothing saturated in dark, nearly black blood.

"Sorry guys," one said, sighing thickly. "We did everything we could. Hell, I don't know how she didn't die before we got there."

Gage moved toward the vehicle and saw long blond hair cascading around a pained face. One of the EMTs moved his hands to her eyes and gently slid them closed, as footsteps approached, running toward the ambulance.

"God, no!" Jenee fell against Gage's side. "Oh, Gage!"

"I'm so sorry, baby," he whispered against her hair.

Then the woman in the bed sat up, her dark eyes opened and she reached for Gage.

His heart fired off rapidly in his chest.

She was alive.

She was sitting up.

She was—not getting any attention at all from the people moving around her body. They couldn't see what Gage saw, didn't feel her hand as she reached forward and brushed her fingertips down his cheek.

"You have to warn her, warn all of them." Her voice was a faint echo in the night. "Save them." She leaned back, her spirit joining with her still form once more, and Gage heard faint whimpering cries fill the night. He would see her again soon, he knew, as a spirit seeking his help in crossing.

He looked down and noticed her feet, one dirty and bare because she'd apparently lost a shoe somewhere along the way, and the other with a dingy sandal. But it wasn't the condition of her feet that caught Gage's attention; it was the small tattoo above her right ankle. Even covered in dirt and grime, there was no disguising the rose, the same one that he'd seen merely hours ago on his fantasy woman.

But this wasn't the same woman he'd seen in his dreams.

What did this mean? What was Gage supposed to determine from it? He was a firm believer that there was no such thing as coincidence, especially where the other side was concerned.

"It'll be okay." Gage stroked his hand up and down Jenee's spine while she cried. "I'll take care of you," he said, speaking to Jenee…and the dead woman.

EVER SINCE Kayla had arrived at the Magazine Street shelter, she'd spent the majority of her days feeling lost, confused, alone. In fact, the only time she had any real sense of belonging was in her dreams, with her handsome blue-eyed stranger. Unfortunately, she couldn't seem to summon him at will. He appeared almost every night, but she had no control over the matter, which didn't seem right, given he was *her* fantasy.

Or was he?

Kayla had discussed the possibility of the man being a part of her past with Jenee Vicknair, the volunteer at the shelter who had been so helpful, so kind to Kayla since she'd arrived there two weeks ago. But no matter how many times she talked about him, described him, struggled to put a name with the face, it didn't happen. She couldn't grasp anything that seemed tangible.

Obviously, he was more than a fantasy; he was real. She wouldn't see him so clearly, feel their lovemaking so intensely, if she hadn't made love with him before. But why hadn't he come looking for her?

The fact that she now thought of herself as *Kayla* was perplexing enough. Was that her real name? She didn't think so, but she was clueless as to what was. Yet when the shelter volunteers had asked her name upon her arrival at the old seven-story building, she'd given them that answer. What did it mean, that she couldn't remember her identity? And why did the prospect of remembering frighten her so much?

However, in spite of her uncertainties, each afternoon, when the shelter doors opened and Jenee welcomed her in, Kayla pushed past her fears of the unknown and found comfort. More than that, she found a friend, someone who made her feel more at ease with her bizarre situation and made her stay at the shelter bearable. Kayla could tell when she spoke with Jenee that she'd had that type of bond in the past. But who with? And how could she have forgotten them, when she could sense that their bond had been so strong?

Kayla wished she could put her finger on the answers, and she was grateful for the kindness Jenee showed her while she was trying to figure it all out. During the day, Kayla took to the streets of the French Quarter hoping to see someone, or something, familiar. Yesterday, she'd seen a man whose eyes made her stop and look again. Gray eyes. Cold eyes. Eyes that were eerily similar to the ones she saw in her nightmares. He hadn't even noticed her, his attention on a knife display at the French Market, but Kayla had noticed him, had almost *felt* him.

It hadn't been a good feeling.

She slid her arms beneath her thin pillow and turned her head toward the tiny windows lining the top of one wall. She didn't want to think of that gray-eyed monster again, and she wished she could force her blue-eyed stranger to return, to comfort her, love her, make her whole. But she couldn't, and that realization made her absolutely miserable. She needed him now. Always. Why couldn't he find her?

What if that was why she had blocked out her memories? Had something horrible happened to him, and he was no longer a part of her life? Was that why she couldn't hold on to him longer?

She bit her lower lip and focused on the darkness, lessening as morning arrived. Soon she'd have to leave the shelter again and take to the streets of the Quarter. Kayla really didn't want to go back out there again, where those gray eyes had been yesterday. What if he was still there? And what if he really was the monster that haunted her?

A heartrending sob echoed from a far corridor in the shelter, and Kayla strained her ears to listen. It didn't come from any of the women sleeping on the tiny cots filling the crowded room, nor did it come from the men's area on the other side of the warehouse-type building. This was a feminine cry, the cry of a woman suffering. Kayla couldn't just lie there and listen. Whoever it was needed help, needed her.

She pushed the scratchy blanket away and eased off the

cot, then silently crept past the other homeless women in the room. Her feet were cold on the floor, and she nearly went back to retrieve her shoes, but the weeping sounded so mournful, so sad, that she couldn't stop. Something terrible must have happened to make a person cry with such intensity.

A memory teased her senses. Crying, hurting, wanting to die. A sound very similar to the one she heard now. And then another memory, the recollection of a group of girls hugging each other, comforting each other through the pain. She missed those girls. She missed the sense of love, of support and the intense bond that they'd shared.

How could she feel so much toward them, and yet not recall their faces or names?

Moving down the hall that separated the sleeping quarters from the main area of the shelter, she noticed a faint light coming from the doorway to the kitchen. She entered the room and found Jenee Vicknair, wearing the same army-green T-shirt and khaki pants she'd had on last night, sitting at one of the worktables in the center of the room. Her arms were folded in front of her on the table, her head cradled within them. Long brown hair spilled freely down her back, and tears dripped just as freely over her right wrist.

"I used to do that," Kayla said softly.

Startled, Jenee raised her head, then squinted to see Kayla in the dim light generated by the single bulb above the stove. "Kayla," she whispered. "I woke you." Her brown eyes, usually filled with compassion and kindness, were red and watery. She rubbed the back of her hand beneath her nose and sniffed. "I'm sorry."

"I wasn't asleep." Kayla sat in the chair next to Jenee.

Tears continued to drip slowly from Jenee's bloodshot

eyes, while she breathed deeply, apparently trying to calm herself in the midst of an emotional storm. Kayla understood, and waited. There were times when conversation wasn't best for a person hurting. Kayla knew that, though she wasn't sure how she knew. Eventually, Jenee gave her a soft smile. Right now, she appeared much younger than twenty-one, reminding Kayla of a hurt child. Kayla somehow knew that look, too.

Then Jenee's eyes seemed to focus on Kayla. "You said you used to do that. What were you talking about?"

"Sit alone and cry to ease the pain."

Jenee blinked. "Are you remembering something about your past?"

Kayla shrugged. She truly appreciated Jenee's sincere interest in trying to help her find those missing pieces. "Nothing concrete, and the more I remember, the more I think it may be best not to remember at all."

"Don't rush it. I'm sure it will come when it's supposed to." Jenee sniffed again and what seemed the last of her tears toppled over the lower rim of her eyes. "Did you hear the ambulances during the night?"

Kayla nodded. "I hear them every night."

Ambulances, gunshots, street fights. New Orleans was known for all, particularly at night, and during her time at the shelter, Kayla'd become accustomed to the mingled sounds of violence in the darkness. The shelter volunteers had told her when she arrived that crime was a basic fact of existence in the city, but that she would be safe within the shelter. And she did feel safe here. Truthfully, she was more fearful of those gray eyes in her nightmares.

"Yeah, I guess you do," Jenee said. "But this time, they were directly outside the shelter, and I went to see what was wrong." She pushed her hair away from her face and held her hand against her forehead, then rubbed it as though trying to ease the tension away. "A woman was stabbed and evidently tried to get to the shelter for help." A heavy tear pushed forward and dripped down Jenee's cheek. "I tried to help her hang on, but she—didn't make it."

"I'm sorry," Kayla said. It seemed the only thing to say.

"I am, too. What's worse is that I recognized her. She came here yesterday. She was so young, no more than midtwenties, I'd say."

"She was homeless?" Kayla asked.

"No, I thought she was considering a donation. She even mentioned that she'd try to come back at night, when our guests arrived, to see how we fed and housed so many. I'm assuming she was trying to make it back here when she was stabbed."

"What was her name?"

Jenee shook her head. "I don't know. She didn't tell me yesterday, and according to my cousin, she didn't have any identification. He said she was probably robbed, and her ID was taken, too."

"Your cousin?"

"He's a trauma doctor and was working in the ER, but she died before the ambulance arrived at the hospital. He didn't have a chance to try to save her."

Kayla vaguely recalled Jenee mentioning the doctor in her family. It was a shame that her cousin couldn't save the woman who had obviously touched Jenee's heart. "Are you going to be okay?" Kayla asked, again sensing that bonding between females and knowing that she'd felt it before.

"Yeah, I will. And I really am sorry I woke you. Why don't you get a little more sleep before morning?" Jenee asked. "I'll be leaving when the breakfast volunteers arrive, but I'll be back this afternoon."

Kayla nodded, knowing Jenee would come back, even though Saturday wasn't her usual volunteer day. She always came back to make certain that Kayla was doing okay, and to see if anyone had come forward with insight to her past. Jenee was the main reason Kayla returned to Magazine Street each night. There were other shelters in the city, but this one had someone who really cared, and Kayla needed the familiarity of a friendly face.

She watched Jenee leave later, heading home to find comfort from her family. Kayla tried to force an image of her home, of some type of house or apartment, but nothing came.

What if nothing ever did?

3

GAGE'S HEART beat like Louisiana thunder as he ran his fingertips down her face and gazed into those chocolate-brown eyes. She was exquisite, beautiful, precious…and his. He'd searched for her for so long, had wished for her even longer, and finally, she was here, giving him everything he ever wanted, making him complete. In spite of his history with women and his typical confident approach to sex, each time with her, he trembled. The power of this was stronger than anything he'd ever experienced. The two of them didn't merely have sex—this, he realized, was making love.

He pressed his fingertips against her throat, felt her pulse racing madly, then slowly moved his palms down, caressing her as he progressed past her excited nipples, past her tense abdomen. Gage's own excitement escalated when he realized that he wasn't the only one trembling. Her body shuddered beneath his touch, and her hips rotated in eager anticipation. He slid his hands to her thighs and gently pushed her legs open, then lowered his mouth to kiss her clit, totally exposed and ready for his thorough perusal. He licked her there, tasting heaven, then prepared to give her an orgasm that would make her toes curl.

Agonizing sobs invaded the perfect moment. Gage shook his head, willing the painful cries to go away. Those brown eyes pleaded with him, full lips frowning at the corners. "Don't go," she whispered. "It won't take me long. I'm so close already. Please, don't go."

He didn't want to. He never wanted to leave her, truly, but the cries intensified, turning into a steady wail, and Gage had to battle the impulse to succumb to the sorrowful spirit's pull.

One time. If he could have her one time before he had to go, perhaps that would satisfy his hunger until he could return. He rose above her, pressed his hard cock against her wet opening, then looked into those chocolate eyes and waited for her to tell him, once again, that this was what she wanted, that he was what she wanted.

She licked her lips, nodded and...

She was gone.

Gage rolled over and nearly fell off the red settee in Grandma Adeline's infamous sitting room. With sudden clarity, he recalled where he was and why. Where? The Vicknair plantation, or more accurately, his grandmother's sitting room on the second floor of the vast home. Why? Because he suspected the woman who had died last night would be his next assignment, and he'd anticipated a letter from Adeline Vicknair declaring that fact when he'd arrived after his shift. The letter hadn't shown, and Gage had taken advantage of the opportunity to catch some much-needed sleep before it did.

"So, what was her name?"

Merely a few feet away, his oldest cousin studied him knowingly, as though her green eyes had witnessed the entire encounter. Wearing a worn black T-shirt and black painter's pants, Nanette sat cross-legged in a rose-printed wingback chair and sipped a cup of coffee. Her jet-black hair was in a high ponytail, another indication that she was ready for a Saturday of working on the house.

"We've got a couple of things to discuss before we get started today," she said, and indicated a pale-purple card balanced on one of her knees, "but first, tell me what female had you smiling like that. You looked like one of my ninth-graders, daydreaming through English. Who was she?"

"I don't know," Gage answered honestly, stretching on the settee. He rolled his head to one side and realized he'd slept with the armrest against his upper spine. Not good, particularly when he and his cousins had a hard day of manual labor ahead of them cleaning the first floor. The last rainstorm had sent yet another sludgy mess trickling through the plantation's shaky foundation, and the parish president, along with his renovation committee, were due to inspect the ground floor in a week.

Since Hurricane Katrina had taken its toll on the Vicknair plantation, the cousins had worked tirelessly to bring their beloved home up to the parish's standards for escaping demolition. True, the mansion hadn't nearly the majestic presence it had had before the hurricane, with many of its windows in need of repair, the eight columns across the front leaning slightly and the very foundation cracked from the pressure of the storm. But Gage knew the place could be the notable estate it'd been for over two hundred years, if they had enough time and money.

Nanette had obtained a detailed list of the minimum repairs needed to be done in order for the home to achieve historic landmark status and funding from the Louisiana Historical Society, but Charles Roussel, the parish president, was doing his damnedest to have the place condemned before the society got a chance to help. All of the Vicknairs knew Roussel's motives, and they had nothing to do with "removing a hazardous structure from the parish," as Roussel claimed. The weasel wanted the property for himself, but he was in for a fight. The Vicknairs weren't giving up their family heritage that easily. No way.

The plantation had escaped demolition last month because they had put on a new slate roof, but Roussel still deemed the place hazardous and had the committee coming to verify the fact next Saturday. Needless to say, Gage and his cousins would be busy with the house this week. In fact, Gage had requested the week's vacation from the hospital in order to make sure they passed inspection. But he knew that wouldn't be his only obligation to fulfill before next Saturday; he had a ghost on the way.

A ghost whose crying had pulled him out of a perfect dream about his ultimate fantasy woman and whose wails still echoed in his thoughts.

"You don't know her name? You mean I'm not the only one who fantasizes about sexy strangers?" Nan teased, placing her cup on a nearby table.

"Hardly," Gage admitted, though the woman in this dream didn't *feel* like a stranger. He'd made love to her daily for two weeks and felt so drawn to her, so connected to her, that he didn't even want anyone else. But he didn't want to talk about that with Nan. On the contrary, he wanted to find out about the purple card now in her hand. "What's that?"

It wasn't a letter, the typical method of communication between Adeline Vicknair and her grandchildren, but it was her signature color, pale lavender, and he could smell his grandmother's signature scent, too. Magnolias.

"Evidently, you now have a brother-in-law." Nan leaned forward and handed the card to Gage. "And the powers that be are apparently fine with the fact that he used to be a ghost."

Gage read the text. It always amused him that such otherworldly powers chose to relay their information in the form of a modern e-mail.

TO: Adeline Vicknair, Grand Matriarch of Vicknair Mediums
FROM: Lionelle Dewberry, Gatekeeper First Class
CC: Board of Directors, Realm-Entrance-Governing Squadron
SUBJECT: Case # 19-01-6418—Ryan Chappelle
Current Status—Applicant has been granted a second chance at life and love. Furthermore, applicant has married his soul mate, Monique Vicknair, with unanimous approval of Board.

"And how do you feel about this?" Gage sounded like a shrink, except he was the one on the couch.

Nan folded her arms and glared. "There isn't a hint of shock in your tone. You knew, didn't you?"

"She called last night, on her way to Vegas."

"And exactly when was she planning to tell me?"

"She wasn't. That's why she called."

"Your sister never ceases to amaze me." Nan's cheeks reddened slightly, but then she shook her head and laughed. "And neither do the spirits. Why would they announce her wedding to us this way?"

"Maybe they knew you'd need something from them saying it was okay for her to marry Ryan before you'd accept it without giving her grief," Gage said, probably giving her more honesty than she'd anticipated, but hell, he was tired, and he'd been yanked out of a very enticing dream by a ghost who still hadn't shown.

Nan's mouth quirked to the side. "I'm going to ignore that comment, smart-ass, for two reasons. One, you haven't slept more than four hours, I bet."

"What time is it?"

"Eight-thirty."

"You'd win that bet."

"Two," she continued, "you didn't have sex last night, did you?"

Damn, she knew him too well. "You'd win that one also."

"And three—"

"You said two."

"I added one." She didn't miss a beat. "Three, you're right. I wouldn't have anticipated the spirits sanctioning a marriage between a medium and a former spirit. I mean, really, we're not even supposed to touch ghosts, and Monique goes off and marries one."

"He isn't a spirit anymore, remember?"

"Yeah, and that part shocked me, too, but hey, who am I to say what they should and shouldn't do over there? I'm stuck on this side," Nan said.

"Stuck?" What was she talking about?

Nan waved him off. "Don't worry. I'm not planning to head to the other side anytime soon, but I tell you what, life on this end would be much more enjoyable if we could get this house up to par with the historical society, and if I could find somebody to make me smile the way you were grinning in that dream, and if Charles Roussel would damn well leave all of us alone."

"My bet is the parish president very much enjoys *not* leaving you alone," Gage said. "I saw the way Charles Roussel looked at you the last time he came out to complain about the house. And I thought I detected something zinging back in the other direction, too."

"You're losing your mind. The man wants to destroy our house. If anything was zinging, it was my temper," she snapped.

Gage chuckled. He'd known a mention of Roussel's name would get her mind off Monique's marriage, and the fact that he'd known about it before she did. Nan liked her role as the oldest cousin, and she particularly liked feeling she was in control of the Vicknair mediums. She didn't like discussing Charles Roussel. Gage really had sensed something zinging between them, but hey, if she wanted to deny it, he'd let her.

Assuming he'd effectively taken her mind off Monique, he placed the thick wedding announcement next to the silver tea service on the coffee table. The shiny tray sported a fancy pitcher and two equally fancy cups, but nothing else. He'd totally expected to wake and find a letter with information about the woman from the ambulance, the lady with the rose tattoo that was identical to his fantasy woman's. Would his spirit be able to tell him about her? Was there a possibility his fantasy lady really did exist, and in the land of the living?

You have to warn her, warn all of them. Save them.

Who did he need to save? And if it was so damn urgent, why hadn't she shown yet?

"Was the card the only thing on the tea service?" he asked.

Nanette nodded, apparently relieved they weren't discussing Charles Roussel anymore. "I figured that's why you came over after your shift, to get an assignment, but that card was it for now. You're hearing ghosts cry?"

"One ghost, and I'm fairly certain I know who she is."

"The woman who died last night?" At Gage's surprised expression, she elaborated, "Jenee told me about it, before she went to bed this morning."

"When'd she get here?" Gage had hated the way his youngest cousin had looked when she'd left the hospital, her face drenched with tears from viewing death head-on. It was something he saw every day, but that wasn't the case for Jenee, and she'd been terribly distraught at seeing the young woman die.

"She got here around six. She looked exhausted, poor thing. I know that had to be rough on her."

"It was. I tried to get her to come here with me when she left the hospital instead of going back to the shelter, but she said she didn't want to leave until the next group of volunteers arrived."

The front door of the plantation slammed loudly, then heavy feet pounded on the steps leading to the second floor. Within seconds, Tristan Vicknair's tall, muscled frame, clothed in a navy LaPlace Firefighter T-shirt and jeans, filled half of the double-door entrance to the room. At twenty-nine, he was the oldest male cousin of the lot and wore his second-in-command status like a badge of familial honor—not that he wouldn't have preferred the number-one position, but Nanette had beaten him to it by a year.

"You guys going to sit up here and shoot the breeze all day, or are you gonna help me clean up that mess? And where's the rest of our brood?" he asked.

"Dax is already downstairs working. I can't get him to *quit* working lately." Nan sounded concerned. "I think he's trying to keep his mind off his last ghost. I don't know what we're going to do about him getting so close to his spirits." She huffed out an exasperated breath. "The whole point is to get them to cross."

"Anybody tell Monique that?" Tristan asked.

Gage noted the smirk on Tristan's face and knew he was trying to push Nan's buttons. "Monique is in Vegas," he said, "and from the announcement Grandma Adeline sent this morning, she's got a ring on her finger."

At Tristan's satisfied grin, Gage realized he wasn't the

only one who thought Monique had found the perfect mate, even if he had been briefly in the land of the nonliving.

"Works for me," Tristan said. "I like the guy, and he's a damn good worker."

"Well, unfortunately Ryan won't be working on anything but his honeymoon for a while," Nan pointed out. "I have no idea how long they'll be gone, but we only have a week before Roussel sends someone out to check the first floor for contamination, and you *know* he'll come to oversee the inspection personally."

Gage suspected Roussel would come to the house to see more than the property, but he wouldn't mention it again. "I think we'll be able to clean it up okay without Ryan and Monique. And they're planning to stay a week in Vegas, by the way."

"Obviously, Gage knows more than I do." Nan's tone was peeved.

He grinned. "Only about my sister."

"And what about my sister?" Tristan asked. "Where's Jenee?"

"She didn't call you?"

Tristan's grin disappeared. "No, why?"

"She's fine," Nan quickly supplied. "In fact, she's upstairs sleeping in her room, but she had a rough night and probably won't be helping us with the first floor, at least not today."

"What happened?" Gage noted the worried crease in his cousin's forehead. As a firefighter, Tristan was protective of people in general, but when it came to his sister…

"While she was at the shelter last night, a woman was stabbed, and Jenee tried to help," Nan explained. "The woman was sent to Gage's hospital, but she was dead by the time the ambulance got there. Gage actually thinks she's going to be his new assignment, but no letter has shown yet. Anyway, Jenee went to the hospital and saw pretty much everything."

Gage watched as Tristan's mouth gaped, then he recovered and focused on the item that concerned him most, his sister. "Jenee witnessed a stabbing? Did it happen in the shelter? And why didn't she call me?"

Tristan had made no secret of the fact that he didn't think it was safe for Jenee to spend so much time downtown, in the heart of a high-crime area, at night. Gage felt the same way, though he did understand her desire to help others in need. It was something ingrained in the Vicknairs, probably due to the familial duty to help spirits. Gage suspected that this desire to help was the reason he was a doctor, Nan was a teacher, Tristan was a firefighter and Jenee was working toward a career in social work. But right now, her work was putting her near danger, and her big brother didn't like it.

"Jenee didn't witness the stabbing." Gage clarified. "The woman was stabbed somewhere near Magazine Street, then apparently tried to make it to the shelter for help, but ended up collapsing in the middle of a crowd of all-night partyers. Jenee heard the commotion outside and, naturally, tried to help, and called me because the victim was brought to Ochsner ER."

"And she *didn't* call me," Tristan repeated.

"She knew you were at the firehouse last night and didn't want to bother you," Nan said, trying to reassure him.

It didn't work.

"Hell, I'm her brother. I want to be bothered for something like that."

"Sorry about that," Jenee said from the doorway. Gage noticed that she wore the same clothes she'd had on last night, her bare feet the only difference from when he'd seen her at the hospital. "I really didn't have time for a lot of calls, and I needed to let Gage know she was on her way to the hospital."

"You're okay?" Tristan wrapped an arm around her and pulled her protectively against him.

"Yeah. Sad, but okay. And I am sorry I didn't call you."

"It's all right, but next time you're in trouble, I want a call, too, even if it's after the fact."

Gage nodded in agreement—if something like that had happened to Monique, he'd have wanted a phone call, too. He should have called Tristan himself, but he plain didn't think about it. He'd been too busy thinking about Jenee, and the dead woman and his upcoming assignment.

Unfortunately, nodding seemed to intensify the ghostly wails in his head. They grew to a near scream. His ghost would be here soon.

Nan stood from her chair and shot a glance at Gage. Evidently, his face reflected the noises overpowering his brain. "What is it?" she asked.

The wail grew louder and he winced, then focused on the silver tea service as though he could force the letter to appear. "I think my ghost is getting close."

"Then you stay here and wait while I get breakfast together. We'll bring you a plate," Nan offered.

"I'm going to hurry and take my shower," Jenee said. "Then I'll check back with you. If it's the woman from last night and she can't cross, I want to know why. Maybe I can help you with your assignment."

In this case, with a woman Jenee had seen die, Gage suspected all of the Vicknair cousins would want to help him, whenever he got the damn assignment and the wailing in his head finally ceased.

Nan turned to Tristan. "Go see if you can get Dax to take a break long enough to eat."

As soon as the last of the cousins disappeared from view, a lavender envelope appeared on the tea service. On the outside, in his grandmother's familiar swirling script, was a single name—*Gage*.

He grabbed the envelope, and the cries in his head immediately subsided. He ripped it open and withdrew the usual three sheets of paper composing a medium's assignment. The top one, on pale-purple stationery with a scalloped border, was his grandmother's letter. Its strong magnolia scent reminded him of her powerful bear hugs when he was little, when she had pulled him into her embrace and smothered him with "grandma kisses," while her heady perfume claimed all of the air around him.

Gage read the information at the top of the page.

Name of Deceased—Lillian Bedeau.

The face of the woman in the ambulance filled his mind. Gage was familiar with the look of death. Some faces showed horror, others peace and still others a determined fierceness, as though they were facing the unknown head-on with bold anticipation. The woman last night had looked fearful, but Gage suspected her fear was not for herself.

You have to warn her, warn all of them. Save them.
Gage continued reading.

Reason for Death—Stabbed while trying to save her friend.

The bottom of the page told Gage that he'd guessed right when he thought this ghost's requirement for crossing would be a tall order to fill.

Requirement for Passage—Saving Makayla Sparks.

Gage blinked, squinted at the words, then frowned. Who was Makayla Sparks? What kind of danger was she in? And save her from what? Death, Gage assumed. Tall order indeed. He eyed the ceiling. "Thanks," he mumbled to his grandmother, whom he knew was probably watching and listening.

A loose shutter flapped smartly against the side of the house, and there hadn't been a hint of wind this morning. "Don't worry," he said. "I'll do it. I just have to figure out how."

He moved on to the second sheet. As usual, it listed rules for dealing with the spirits. Gage knew them all, but since he was required to read every page in its entirety before his assignment officially began, he read them again. Then he tossed the sheet of rules to the side so he could view the final page, the official document directing his grandmother to assign Lillian Bedeau to one of her grandchildren.

TO: Adeline Vicknair, Grand Matriarch of Vicknair Mediums
FROM: Lionelle Dewberry, Gatekeeper First Class
CC: Board of Directors, Realm-Entrance-Governing Squadron
SUBJECT: Case # 19-01-6613—Lillian Bedeau
Current Status—Access Denied.
Required Rectification—Saving her childhood friend from the same killer who murdered her.
Time Allotted for Rectification—Five days.

FIVE DAYS to keep a killer from murdering a woman he'd never heard of, a woman who could be living in another country for all Gage knew. "Why didn't you give me a hard one?" he sarcastically asked the sculpted ceiling, and again, the shutter banged wickedly against the house. "Oh, you know I'll do my best, but don't you think a little more information is necessary? Like, who Makayla Sparks is, where she is and how I'm supposed to help my ghost save her?"

"I know all of that," a feminine voice said sharply from behind him. "And I'll tell you on the way. We don't have time to wait. He's looking for her now."

Gage turned to see the woman from the ambulance, her blond hair no longer matted, but long and glowing. Her entire body was glowing, in fact, in that same manner that all ghosts shimmered. And her eyes were the darkest black, another feature of those waiting to cross. Except Gage had never seen a ghost's eyes so determined, so anxious, so afraid.

"We have to hurry," she repeated, stepping toward the doorway. She wore the same pink blouse she'd had on last night, the same black capri pants, with the rose tattoo shimmering above her ankle. The difference was that there were no rips in the cloth where the knife had penetrated fabric and skin and muscle, and no dark stains of blood forming a liquid image of violence.

"Okay." He knew better than to make a ghost wait, even when a life wasn't at stake. "Where are we going?" he asked, practically running as he followed the lithe spirit down the stairs.

"Gage?" Jenee called, descending the stairway with her hair still shower-wet.

"My ghost," he said, indicating the area in front of him since he knew no one else could see her. "We've got to save someone."

"Tell her it's Kayla," the woman instructed. "Tell Jenee

the man who murdered me is going to murder Kayla, and we have to stop him."

"Kayla?" He quickly turned to Jenee. "That's the woman you've been helping at the shelter, right? The one who can't remember who she is?"

"What about her?" Jenee asked, panic in her eyes.

"She said the man who killed her is after Kayla."

"No!" Jenee bolted toward the front door. "I'm coming."

"No," Lillian commanded sharply. "*You're* the one who's supposed to help me save her. Tell her we'll bring Kayla here, but first we have to get there in time."

"I have to go alone," Gage shouted over his shoulder as he ran toward his truck, Lillian at his heels. "But we'll bring her back here." He slid into the driver's seat and looked into Lillian's fierce, black eyes. "We *will* get there in time."

"The shelter is closed, and she's alone. And he's there. I know he is." She blinked rapidly, as though holding back tears. "I know where she is. I see her. But I can't see him."

"We'll get there in time." Gage prayed it was true. He pressed the pedal to the floor and gravel and dust kicked up behind them as they spun away from the plantation down the long driveway, then quickly turned onto River Road.

"And I can't see Shelby, either," Lillian added.

"Shelby?"

"There were four of us," she whispered. "Four girls who testified against him back then. We were like sisters, all of us, and we went through it all together. I love them so much, and I can't let him hurt any of them. And he'll go after Makayla now. I know he will. That's what all of this is about—him making us pay, the way he said he would if he ever got out of prison. I know it's him. I recognized those eyes…when he stabbed me."

"Who?" Gage asked, speeding the truck around the winding curves that followed the levee's edge.

"Wayne Romero. He was the gardener at the Seven Sisters orphanage, where we lived back then. Me, my sister, Chantelle, Shelby Boudreaux and Makayla. Chantelle, Shelby and I lived at the Seven Sisters from the day we were born. Makayla was sent there after her parents died. She was a little older than the rest of us, and prettier. I think that's why he took her more."

Gage's stomach pitched. He didn't need clarification about that last sentence. He'd seen too many rape victims at the hospital, and far too many who were kids. *Were* being the operative word. After something like that happened to them, those sad little girls could no longer be classified as children. And now this pedophile was terrorizing his victims again, except this time, he wasn't stopping until they were dead.

"I can see my sister, and I can see Makayla, but I can't see Shelby at all," Lillian whispered. "Why can't I see her? And why won't they—" she gestured upward "—let me see him? It would help us find him. They know it would."

"I'll do my best to find all of them," Gage promised. "And we'll find him, too, and make him pay."

"Shelby's already gone. He found her and he killed her, too, I know it. I've hardly even talked to her this year, and she was having such a hard time," she said, obviously following the traditional impulse to blame oneself when a loved one had gone. "Why wasn't I sent to save her, too?"

"I honestly don't know."

She put her hand to her chest, above the spot where, only a day ago, her heart was beating. "We get together, the four of us, every Christmas," she said on a sob. "At Ms. Rosa's tiny house by the orphanage. Ms. Rosa's family donated the land for Seven Sisters, and Ms. Rosa's always been there for all of us, through the trial and ever since. Even if we didn't see each other all year, we knew we'd get back together at Ms. Rosa's for Christmas."

Lillian shook her head. "But I should have called Shelby more. I should have called her regularly, and Makayla, too, but—" she shrugged "—I don't know. You get busy with life, and you just don't spend the time you should staying in touch. Shelby has been going through a divorce and has had a rough time. She told me that last Christmas. I called her a few times after that, and we went out for coffee, talked about her and Phillip and what went wrong. It's hard to have a relationship after you've been *hurt,* you know? And now, she's gone."

Gage exhaled thickly. He had no idea why some were chosen to go early and others were allowed to live, and he never would understand. But if the other women were indeed in danger, he had to help them, too. He had to make sure the murderer didn't succeed in his plan to kill again.

"You've got a lot of faith in me, don't you, Adeline?" he asked.

"Yes, she does. And so does Makayla," Lillian replied.

"What do you mean?" He'd never met Makayla Sparks, or Kayla, as Jenee called her.

But Lillian didn't offer any further enlightenment. "You'll see. This was meant to be, you know. From long, long ago. Adeline told me."

"Told you what?"

She cleared her throat and ignored his question. "You'll have to be careful with Makayla. She doesn't remember her past."

"Why? What happened to make her forget?"

"He found her first," Lillian said. "Tried to kill her, but

Makayla was always the best fighter of the four of us. That's why he liked her so much back then. She put up the biggest fight, and it made him feel even more powerful to beat her down and get what he wanted. But this time, she wasn't a child anymore, and she fought like an adult. She stabbed him with a kitchen knife, then ran away."

"And that's when she forgot?"

Lillian nodded. "Adeline told me he broke into the house Makayla was renting. Like most of us, she moved around a lot, trying to make sure if he ever got out, he wouldn't be able to find her easily. But he did find her, and he broke in and tried to rape her in her kitchen. She grabbed a knife and stabbed him, then left. The next day, she showed up at the shelter and couldn't remember what happened in her kitchen, or anything else. Just blocked it all out. Protecting herself in a way, I guess."

Gage hadn't seen any cases of fugue amnesia—the type where the memory loss was triggered by a psychological event—but he certainly knew enough about it to realize that it could have happened if Kayla believed the past was repeating itself. She hadn't wanted to be victimized again, and she'd kept it from happening, any way she could. Good for her. But bad for him. He wasn't sure how to convince her to let him protect her, if she couldn't remember what he was protecting her from.

"She will," Lillian said. "You'll see."

Gage flinched. Obviously, the bonding between spirit and medium had started, and Lillian was taking advantage by reading his thoughts.

"She will trust you," Lillian repeated. "She knows you."

"You mean through Jenee?"

"She knows *of* you through Jenee, but that isn't how she knows you. She knows you from her dreams."

"What?"

"Up there." Lillian pointed toward the Poydras exit off the I-10. "Hurry. She isn't far away."

Gage hadn't even realized they'd entered the New Orleans city limits. Evidently, he'd been driving on auto-pilot while trying to process the mountain of information his ghost had supplied.

"You'll figure it out soon enough," Lillian said. "Just get her out of here, before he finds her and does the same thing to her that he did to me. I won't let that happen." She squinted. "I see her, getting on a streetcar. I know where she is. Turn right."

Gage set his jaw and followed her instructions. He wasn't willing to let the killer achieve his goal, either. If he didn't save Makayla, Lillian couldn't cross over. More importantly, if he didn't save Makayla and the other two girls who were in danger, he'd never forgive himself. The light turned green, and he punched the gas, then smelled the putrid scent of burning rubber as his tires cut into the asphalt and his truck surged forward. There was no time to waste; he had to stop a murderer before he sent another innocent to the other side.

4

WITH HER ATTENTION darting recklessly from one passenger to another, Kayla transferred from the Magazine streetcar to the Canal route. She made certain to stay within crowds as she traveled around the city, and she also made certain to survey all eyes looking her way. Those cold gray slits she'd viewed yesterday at the Quarter were out there somewhere.

Who was he? Was she simply letting her imagination run wild after learning of the woman's stabbing outside the shelter last night?

No, she didn't think so. Hearing about the stabbing, about the woman who died, had brought back memories…about a knife and a man, a vicious man. Kayla could almost taste her fear, and her determination—he wasn't going to hurt her again. No matter what it took, she wouldn't let him hurt her again.

Her thoughts swiftly moved back to the knife, not the typical type of weapon you'd think a killer would use, but a smaller knife with a serrated edge, a kitchen knife, and in this apparition, the blade was in her hand.

Kayla shuddered. Did that happen? Had she actually had a knife in her hand with the intention of defending herself against that…that awful man? It was the gray-eyed monster who'd been after her in that dream; she had no doubt about it.

The man of her nightmares had hurt her; she could sense it in her soul, but she didn't mind that she'd forgotten those particular memories. If he'd done what she thought he'd done, she didn't want to remember.

Ever.

Kayla boarded the Canal streetcar and quickly moved to the center of the crowd, standing so she could still see out of the windows, but wasn't totally visible to those outside. While the brightness of day kept most predators at bay, Kayla wasn't fool enough to believe that she'd be safe alone. She'd do her best to stay hidden in the masses.

The Canal streetcar was much more crowded than the Magazine one and was filled not only with the typical New Orleans commuters, but also with tourists seeing the downtown attractions. Their attention wasn't as focused as the locals; they were still awed by the city. The locals knew better. The city was intriguing, but it wasn't a playground by any means. A woman could die in the middle of the night without anyone noticing.

She could die in the middle of the day, and no one would even know her name.

The thought made her shudder.

A big, burly man next to her leaned close, his breath foul and the stench surrounding him even worse. "Surely you ain't cold in N'awlins? Or is it me making you quiver?" He grinned, bits of tobacco dotting his discolored teeth.

Kayla swallowed back the urge to toss her breakfast and leaned away from him on the noisy car, but she didn't have much space for a retreat. Additional passengers had boarded at the North Peters stop, and she simply had to endure the disgusting male a little longer.

Why couldn't she recognize just one person in the crowd? This morning, when she'd seen Jenee crying, she'd recalled a whisper of a memory, of being surrounded by friends—female friends?—or maybe even relatives. Sisters? She recalled them giving her support, but she was the one who kept them together; Kayla knew that instinctively. She could hear herself speaking to them.

We have to be strong, strong like the roses.

Kayla thought of the rose tattoo above her ankle, currently hidden beneath her jeans. What did that mean, strong like the roses? And who was she talking to? Sisters? Friends? Or other girls that the gray-eyed man had hurt?

She chewed her lower lip and bit back her frustration. How could she protect herself from the guy if she couldn't remember anything but those terrifying gray eyes? Or those mesmerizing blue ones?

Kayla hated having to leave the shelter during the day. She tried her best to remain busy, and to make her limited supply of money last. Jenee had given her some cash, and the shelter had provided her with streetcar and food vouchers, and the necessary clothing she needed to get by. In fact, the Magazine Street shelter and Jenee Vicknair had been nothing short of a godsend for the past two weeks. But still, Kayla needed to know the truth. Where did she come from? And what made her forget?

Buildings blurred as the streetcar passed them in a flurry, then the scene settled into focus when the vehicle stopped. Kayla nearly cheered when the foul-smelling man got off. He winked at her before exiting, and she pretended not to notice, looking away. And froze. She had planned to get off the car, too, at the next stop, and use one of the vouchers to find something to eat at Riverwalk. Now she aborted that idea completely.

She saw *him,* standing there in the center of the crowd gathering to board the car, and moving toward the door.

Icy fear clawed her spine, made her entire body shake in panic. He wore a hooded shirt, his head bowed slightly as he wedged his way into the midst of those loading into the car, but Kayla knew what was hidden beneath that navy hood. Cold gray eyes. Yesterday's sweatshirt had been similar, but black, and had invoked the same raised brows and shrugs from those around him. A hooded sweatshirt in September in New Orleans. The man obviously didn't mind drawing attention, and he had Kayla's now. Luckily, he didn't appear to have seen her yet, his head still bent toward the ground, which meant…she had a little time.

She squirmed between the men and women lining the aisle toward the back of the car. She didn't have long, only a few seconds, and if she timed it wrong, she'd be on a streetcar with a guy who, she suspected, knew her past, and had even been a part of it. A horrible part. That gnawing, daunting fear consumed her now, and she wasn't about to stay on this car and analyze it with him merely feet away. He lifted the lower edge of his sweatshirt to withdraw money for fare, and something at his waistband caught the sun. A knife? Gun?

"Excuse me." She used her shoulder to barrel past a man whose belly consumed the aisle. "Sorry, I need to get off here." She squeezed past a woman holding her toddler. The little boy smiled as she passed, and Kayla said a silent prayer that he and his mother would get off this car safely, the same way she was doing right now.

With more relief than she'd thought possible, she pushed through the last bit of crowd at the back of the streetcar and stepped out, just as the sound of the brakes disengaging filled her ears and the car pulled away.

Kayla blew out a heated breath, looked at the rear window of the car and saw *him,* his palms pressed against the glass and his face hidden in the shadow of that hood. He balled one hand and pounded his fist, then turned toward the front of the car.

The brakes screeched again, and to Kayla's horror, the streetcar began to slow.

No! She whirled and was dismayed to find that the crowd that had emerged from the car had already dispersed into several nearby shops and restaurants. With no way to hide, she ran. Reaching the nearest side street, a brick-lined alley, she glanced back toward the trolley and saw him jumping off, then rolling to the ground from the abruptness of his exit. He scrambled to his feet, and Kayla bolted down the alley.

"Help me!" she screamed, as an old man in a white chef's apron opened a metal door leading to the alley. He looked at Kayla, then behind her, where she had no doubt the hooded man followed. "Please!" she yelled. The man slammed the door.

She ran past a Dumpster, trying to put some distance between her and the hooded stranger.

Stranger? No, Kayla didn't think so. But all she knew for certain was that he was chasing her, and if he caught her...

Kayla couldn't think about that. She had to run, had to keep moving, had to get away.

"What are you doing, old man?" she heard a man yell behind her. Had the cook returned to help? The distinctive sounds of a fight ensued, grunts and growls and groans echoing down the alleyway, then the metal door slamming shut again. Kayla slowed to suck in a ragged breath and looked back. The hooded man was on the ground with something protruding from his right thigh. The image brought a rush of memory—a man with a knife protruding from his chest, her hand on the knife.

"Argh!" he yelled, and to Kayla's horror, he stood and started running toward her.

She jerked around and tripped, falling over a wooden crate and twisting her ankle. A small cry burst out, but she got up and continued, running as best as she could, her ankle protesting with every step…and her predator nearing with every second.

She reached the end of the alley and turned down the next, dismayed to find that it was yet another alley, God help her. Her breathing came in short, sharp gasps and her side pinched fiercely. The new alley had several side passages branching off the main path, and—praying she wasn't making a mistake—Kayla chose one and entered it at a frantic pace. Too late she saw that the alley was partially covered by awnings, and the majority of the way was in thick, dark shadow.

Pulling on her last ounce of courage, she decided she couldn't retreat. This was it, win or lose. She couldn't go back. Perhaps the darkness would shield her from his view. Perhaps she had actually found the only path away from…

She slammed against a thick wall and her breath left her body in a mighty whoosh. Kayla's head spun as her face was forced against the unyielding barrier. Not a wall, she now realized, as the strong pounding of her captor's heart thudded against her ear and two bands of pure muscle imprisoned her against his frame.

She fought to get away, kicking her legs wildly and doing her best to get her knee to his groin, but the more she tried to get free, the tighter his grip became.

"Let me go!" she yelled, but the sound was muffled by the expanse of his chest. Kayla whimpered, and the noise made her feel even more pitiful. He had her, and she had walked—run—right into his trap. Now she was going to die in a dark, New Orleans alley, and no one would even care.

"Be quiet," he growled, moving backward, deeper into the alley, and pulling her along. Her feet dragged against the gritty asphalt, her arms trapped at her sides.

The two words, more of a command than a reprimand, evoked another memory. Kayla as a young teen, small for her age, and utterly helpless against the brawny man overpowering her. Everything was dark, creepily dark. Her legs kicked, fingers clawed, but nothing would stop him. He was relentless, determined, evil.

Be quiet. Stop fighting, dammit. You know this is what you want.

The reality of the image, of what had obviously—definitely—occurred in her past, hurt almost as much as what was happening now. She'd die before she let him do it again.

Adrenaline pumped fiercely through her veins, and her resolve intensified. One way or another, she was getting away from this monster. Kayla curled her fingers and pushed her nails into his sides with as much force as she could muster. It didn't even slow him down. Then she slung one foot out and caught her heel against the corner of something metal. A Dumpster? A door? She didn't know, but she used the leverage to jerk him off balance, then shifted her weight, putting all of it on her good ankle, and sent her other leg straight up, the knee connecting forcefully with his groin.

"Dammit, what the—"

The bands of steel encircling her loosened momentarily. Kayla managed to turn her body away from him, but still he wouldn't let go. He relentlessly pulled her toward the opposite end of the alley. Now what should she do? A hint of sunlight illuminated the area and she saw his tan forearm, pressing against her chest as he yanked her down the alley. Kayla leaned over and chomped on it. *That* would make him release her. Or so she thought. To her absolute horror, the arm tightened, so much that breathing became difficult.

"Stop it," he ordered.

And *that's* when several things that she'd missed in her moment of panic became evident. One, her assailant wasn't wearing a hooded sweatshirt. In fact, his arms were bare, due to his short-sleeved shirt. Two, he hadn't tried to attack her with a knife or a gun or anything else. He was fighting her, but not to hurt her. He seemed to be trying to get her out of the alley. And three—and most importantly— someone else was now in the alley. A dark shadow moving quickly, in spite of his noticeable limp.

The arms that surrounded her took advantage of her reduced resistance, scooping her up and hauling her mercilessly down the short distance remaining in the alley. Before Kayla had a chance to protest, her captor shoved her into the driver's side of a big black truck, pushed her across the seat, climbed in and gunned it…seconds before the dark, hooded figure emerged from the alley.

5

LILLIAN HAD SAID Kayla was a fighter, but damn. Thank God she hadn't achieved a direct hit to his crotch, or he'd have gone down like a rock. She'd gotten close enough to make him suck air, but not close enough that Gage had to worry about procreation. The gouges in his sides and the bite on his arm were nothing to sneeze at, either. He knew without looking that she'd broken the skin, and there was no doubt he'd have a nice little scar as a reminder of this encounter for years to come. Hell, it's a wonder she hadn't hit bone.

But he didn't blame her. On the contrary, he admired the hell out of her. The woman had been victimized in the past, and she wasn't going down without a fight. Good for her. He wished more of the women he saw in the ER had that primal instinct. Maybe if more predators expected that kind of battle, they wouldn't think women, particularly petite women like this one, were such easy prey.

He stole a look in his rearview mirror and saw the hooded guy round the corner, lift an arm and...

"Get down!" Gage shoved Makayla—*Kayla*—to the floor as the rear window shattered.

Lillian screamed from the backseat. From all indications, the bullet and the resulting shards of glass had gone directly through her, not that it mattered anymore, but it had obviously scared the hell out of her. Makayla, however, remained balled up on the floor without making a sound. It appeared that she had finally realized that the man *without* the gun was the one to put her trust in, for the time being.

He spotted the ramp to I-10 and put his truck's maneuverability to the test, taking the curve at forty-five miles per hour in an effort to get out of sight before the creep found a vehicle of his own.

Wind whipped through the vacant space that used to be his truck's rear window, and Lillian gripped the back of the front seat, her hands and body glowing a little brighter, probably due to her fear.

"Is she okay? He didn't hit her, did he?"

Gage watched Makayla's back move with a rapid but steady intake of breath. He knew only one bullet had hit the car, and it had exited through the roof. However, whether she'd been physically hit or not, Makayla Sparks could definitely be suffering from the attack. "Are you okay?" he asked.

"Come on, Makayla. Please be okay," Lillian pleaded from the backseat. "Say you're all right, please."

"Are—you—okay?" Gage repeated, knowing the woman on the floor couldn't hear the ghost in the backseat. Good thing he was used to spirit and nonspirit communication. And good thing he was used to dealing with emergency situations. In the ER, remaining calm rather than panicking could determine whether a life was saved or lost. And Gage wasn't into losing.

"Yes." Her reply was barely audible over the roar of the truck.

"Are you sure?" he asked, noticing she made no attempt to get up from the floor.

"Yes," she said, a little louder this time, but she still made no effort to look his direction.

He decided now was as good a time as any to attempt some sort of introduction. "My name is Gage Vicknair. I'm Jenee's cousin, the ER doctor. I believe you know her from the shelter, right?"

No answer.

"I'm not going to hurt you, Kayla," he added, using the name she'd gone by in the shelter, and the name Jenee had always used when referring to her.

"Makayla is smart," Lillian said. "She determined you weren't going to hurt her back in the alley, or you'd never have gotten her in this truck. But bless her heart, she's so confused. She can't remember—" Lillian gasped. "Oh, dear."

Gage promptly looked in the mirror, but saw no sign of anyone following them. Knowing he couldn't speak directly to Lillian without further confusing Makayla, he looked pointedly at the spirit and waited for her to tell him what was going on.

"It's Chantelle," she said. "My sister. I can see her, feel her. She's at the hospital and about to identify my body. I can't let her go in alone." Her lower lip trembled. "I know she can't see or hear me, but she'll feel me if I'm there, won't she?"

Gage nodded. He truly believed the dead were watching over those who had to go through the horrible experience of losing a loved one. He'd often sensed them around grieving families in the hospital.

"And later, you'll need to get to her, too. Wayne Romero hasn't come after Chantelle yet, but he will. He's trying to kill all of us, just as he said he would." The wind whipped her glistening blond hair madly around her shoulders, creating a silky blur around her illuminated face. "I need to go to her."

Gage nodded. "Go."

Then she was gone.

"Go where?"

He kept his hands steady on the wheel, but turned to view the woman who'd now lifted her head…and Gage's heart stilled within his chest. He knew her.

The woman from his dreams.

"You." Her mouth formed the word, though Gage didn't hear a sound, either due to the velocity of the wind, or because she merely mouthed the syllable, but there was no denying the look in her eyes. She recognized him, too.

Gage was certain if they'd ever met in person, he'd have remembered. But the only time he'd ever seen this woman was in his mind. Even disheveled from her ordeal, there was no masking her exquisite beauty, or the immediate response Gage's body felt from merely looking at her. He'd made love to her repeatedly in his fantasies. Now she was here.

She edged up on the seat, then reached out her hand and placed a shaky fingertip to his cheek, slowly easing it along his jaw and to his mouth. Her eyes were wide with disbelief, her mouth slightly open as she touched his lower lip. "You're here. Finally."

The tires drifted across the rough edge of the road, and Gage swerved to bring the truck back between the lines. Then the Gramercy exit, only a short distance ahead, surprised him; he hadn't realized they were this close to the plantation. He sharply turned the wheel to get off the interstate. The action pitched her closer. Much closer. One hand now braced his thigh; the other gripped his arm.

"I'm not dreaming," she whispered, those chocolate eyes feeding the desire that had started with this morning's dream.

Gage stopped the truck at the end of the exit ramp and swallowed thickly. What the hell was happening? He didn't understand how he could've so clearly visualized someone he'd never met. "No, you're not dreaming, and neither am I."

She tilted her head as though processing his words. The move pushed her hair to one side, showcasing her delicate ear, elegant jawline, arched brows, straight nose, kissable lips. The face of an angel, yet only minutes ago, she'd been nothing shy of a hellion when she attacked him in that alley.

"You know me, don't you?" she asked, focusing on his eyes. "You know who I am."

His mind replayed everything he'd learned in med school about fugue amnesia. If she wanted to remember, he should let her. And it didn't hurt to prompt the patient with the facts of her past, as long as he didn't create additional shock.

Surely her name wouldn't shock her.

"You're Makayla Sparks," he said, then turned the truck toward River Road. He needed to keep moving toward the plantation. She was bound to have more questions, and he wanted Jenee nearby to help him answer them. His cousin had befriended Makayla at the shelter; maybe she could help Gage tell her about her past, beyond the fact that he had been making love to her on a regular basis in his dreams.

"Makayla," she repeated, trying out the name. Her hands still held on to him, whether for support or balance, or just because she wanted to, Gage didn't care. It felt good, very good, to have her so close. Only, the intimate contact sparked the memory of her running her hands all over him, caressing him with her fingers, her palms, her mouth. How could he know so much about her, the way she looked in the heat of climax, the sweet sounds she made, the way she kissed, the feel of her lips and the taste of her sweet, hot center? He knew it all, intimately, yet he'd never even experienced her touch...until now.

"That's not right." She frowned. "I mean, I don't doubt that is my given name, but—" she shook her head again "—I don't want to be called that anymore. Makayla was helpless and ended up getting hurt."

Gage nodded, understanding setting in. She *did* remember some of her past, about being abused. But did she remember the abuser? "Kayla, then?"

"Yes, Kayla." Then she lifted her hand from his thigh and gently touched the reddened spot on his forearm where her teeth had broken the flesh. Images of her touching him, naked body on naked body, overpowered his thoughts. "I'm so sorry for biting you."

It took Gage a moment to remember that she was talking about biting him today, in the alley, rather than every night in his bed. "It's not as bad as it looks."

"That's good, because it looks bad." She turned to view the shattered window, and the glass all over the backseat. "Oh, look at your truck."

He loved the way her mouth shaped the words, loved the way her hair shifted around her face due to the wind in the cab, loved…everything about her. "It's not your fault," he said, mentally reminding himself that they were still talking. "And we'll get the guy responsible, eventually. Then he'll pay for the damage to the truck, and for everything else he's done to hurt you. I swear it." And he meant it.

Gage had been determined to make the guy pay for murdering Lillian and for abusing her and her friends when they were children, but now that he knew his fantasy woman, Kayla, had been one of the abused, and that the maniac had nearly gotten his hands on her again today, Gage wasn't going to let anything stop him from protecting her.

"I know we will," she said. "When I thought he was the

one who had me in that alley—" She paused. "I kneed you, too. Did I hurt you?" Her eyes moved from his face to the center of his thighs. Gage wished he hadn't seen where her attention had headed, since that part of his anatomy was already on red alert from being this close to her. Finally.

"No, you didn't hurt me." He managed a smile, even though the area she was currently examining was trying its best to get noticed…and succeeding. "You, um, missed the mark."

"I don't see how," she said without any hint of humor in her tone.

Gage held his grin in check. At least she'd changed the subject and wasn't talking about the abuse, or the abuser, not that they would be able to stay off that subject long, since Gage planned on making sure the guy was caught. But for now, she was riding with him in his truck. Even with a shattered back window and a bullet hole in the roof, the urge to grin crept back in, and this time, he let the smile slip free.

"Are you laughing at me?" she demanded.

"Never," he denied. "I'm just glad I got to you before he did, that's all."

Her brow knitted again. "I remember you, you know."

"I'm afraid that's not—"

"We're lovers, aren't we?"

Shocked, Gage shook his head. "No, we aren't." He'd never made love to her in real life, though he was sure thinking about it now.

"How could I have dreamed it?" Her voice was barely louder than a whisper. "I saw us so clearly, and we were making love. And your eyes, the way you looked at me, I saw that, remembered it, ached for it."

She'd dreamed it? The powers that be could do a lot more than he'd realized if they'd controlled both of their dreams…with each other. But why? "I don't know if you'll believe this or not," he said, nearing the last curve before the Vicknair plantation, "but I dreamed about you, too. And I dreamed of making love to you, too." He decided not to add that it was the best he'd ever had, the most intense, the most emotional, the most memorable, and that since touching her, he didn't want another woman.

Were they destined to make love in reality? But they barely knew each other, had only met today, in the midst of danger and near death. Not exactly Gage's usual way of wooing a woman.

He pulled the truck down the gravel driveway leading to his family's estate. Mature magnolias lined both sides of the road and formed a dark-green canopy above them. The new slate roof captured the sun and gleamed brilliantly, its gray-blue textured tiles blending with the sky to make the top of the home appear never to end. Gage loved the look and was immensely proud of the fact that he and his cousins were responsible for it turning out so well. Unfortunately, the roof was the only part of the exterior that had been restored. In stark contrast, the columns leaned slightly, the siding was peeling and holey, and many of the windows were patched with either wood or plastic—or both. But they were taking care of it all, one piece at a time. The place, right now, wasn't anything to brag about, but Gage loved it.

He turned to see Kayla's reaction, and her face told him all he wanted to know. Her eyes were wide, her mouth slightly open in awe. "It's incredible," she said. "How wonderful it must be to live in a place like this."

"Yeah, it was. I lived here during med school, but after I took the ER job at Ochsner, I got an apartment closer to the city." He shrugged. "It's easier."

"I think I'd drive the extra miles," she said, not looking at Gage as she continued to take in the structure. Sugarcane fields surrounded both sides and the back of the house, and the lofty reeds, nearly ready for the grinding season, were a good seven feet tall.

Gage's chest swelled. There was something to be said for seeing your home through another's eyes, particularly the chocolate eyes that had dominated his dreams and now his reality.

"Was it because I was scared?" she asked, twisting in the seat to look directly at Gage.

His confusion must have been evident, because she didn't wait for a response before continuing.

"Is that why we've only dreamed of making love? Have I been afraid since he raped me?"

Hell. She thought the two of them had dated, and that she hadn't been willing to let him get close. That would make sense, if the two of them had actually met before today.

But it wasn't the truth.

"We weren't lovers, Kayla." How could he explain the fact that she'd recognized him, dreamed about him, when they'd never met? Simple. He had to tell her about the ghosts, and Lillian, and, well, everything. As a doctor, he knew that telling her something that might shock her wasn't the best thing for amnesia, but as a man, he couldn't lie to her about their intimacy, or lack thereof.

"I know we weren't, because I wouldn't let you," she said. "But I've thought of you ever since the day I entered the shelter. I've seen your eyes and could feel you in my mind, holding me, comforting me, making love to me. *You* got me through the loneliness, through that terrifying void. I knew eventually I'd find you, and that somehow I'd see that warmth, that love, in your blue eyes again."

"Kayla, I don't know how to explain this, but even though I have dreamed of you, too, we've never met, not before today."

She shook her head. "That's not possible."

"I know it doesn't seem possible, but it's true. I can't explain what's happening, either, but I'm hoping we can figure it out together."

"But you have dreamed of me, that way?" she asked, and Gage hated that he was causing her further confusion. She'd spent the past two weeks at the shelter not knowing who she was, and he wasn't making things better by telling her that even her dreams of him weren't real. He sure had felt something in those fantasies, and he suspected what she felt toward him was equally strong.

"Yes, I have dreamed of you that way," he said. "But we've never met."

"We've never met," she repeated softly, then swallowed and continued. "Even when I couldn't see you completely, I could see your eyes, and you made me feel safe. How could I have felt so safe with you if I didn't already know you?"

"I honestly don't know," he said.

"I also knew I'd see him again, and those cold, evil gray eyes. I don't remember his name, but I remember those eyes, and I remember what he did." She looked at Gage. "Tell me his name. You know it, don't you?"

Gage didn't see any reason to withhold information from her, particularly if she already remembered the abuse. Knowledge was power. "Wayne Romero."

Her face tensed and her body shook as she tried to control the response to the name. "No," she whispered.

"Hell." Gage pulled the truck to a stop before the house, thinking he'd messed up.

"I could never see the face, not clearly, not until now.

Mr. Romero. The gardener, with those horrible gray eyes." She visibly swallowed. "He was so evil. We were so scared of him back then…."

"We?" Gage asked, realizing that her memory of Romero had prompted additional memories. Did she remember Lillian now? If she did, telling her what was happening now, about Lillian and Romero and the ghosts, would be a little easier. Well, as easy as it could be, considering he'd have to tell Kayla that Wayne Romero had murdered her friend.

"Me," she said, "and the other girls at the orphanage. I remember how we lived in fear of him and of the nights— God, how I hated the nights. He was the gardener there, at the orphanage, and he took us at night. And if we said anything, he said he'd kill us all."

Kayla bit her lip. "Eventually, I didn't care about his threats. I went for help, and then we put him in prison, where he belonged." She paused, then added, "Why is he still out there? He hurt me, and he hurt the others, too. I remember hearing their muffled screams."

Gage hated the thought of Kayla and her friends being hurt. It made him sick, made him want to hit something hard—preferably Romero. "He was in prison, but he got out somehow. I learned he was trying to hurt you, and I went to find you. So far, that's all I know. But we'll figure it out. I'll get my family to help, and of course, the police have to know something."

"You think he escaped?" she asked.

"I don't know."

"That wasn't the first time he tried to kill me, since he got out. He came after me, and he tried to rape me again. And I stabbed him." She didn't sound shocked by this revelation.

Gage's mind raced as he realized what Kayla needed in order to cope with her past, what had helped her to remember, and to remember with acceptance rather than shock or fear.

Him.

She needed *him* to get through this ordeal. And he needed her…period.

The urge to reach out to her, to hold her and keep her safe, was almost overwhelming. He felt so much for this woman, yet they had just met, and he'd have to keep reminding himself of the fact, even if they'd been more to each other already in their minds.

And in his heart.

What about hers? Did she feel nearly the intensity toward him that he felt toward her already? And if they did get together physically, would it be as incredible as it had been in his mind? Could it be? Because he'd never had anything like that before, where he felt more than the union of bodies, but also the union of souls.

She stared silently at the plantation, then whispered, "That's why I blocked everything out, isn't it? He was going to rape me again?"

"I believe so. Evidently, you believed you were safe from him, and then he returned. It's natural that you defended yourself, and natural that you protected your mind from reliving the pain of the past."

"But I've been remembering bits and pieces," she said.

"Another way that this type of amnesia typically works," Gage explained. "You remember things gradually, until your mind is comfortable in the fact that you can handle the memories. Then you remember the forgotten events."

"I still don't remember that day when I stabbed him,"

she admitted. "I just remember the knife in my hand and the way it felt."

"You may never remember everything about that day." Gage knew that while most patients with fugue amnesia usually remembered the majority of their lives, many never remembered the psychological event that caused the amnesia. "That's common, and if you've recalled your life prior to that day, then I'd say you've probably remembered everything you can."

"But today I did remember the past, what he did back then, because my mind knew I could handle it now?" she asked.

"That's the way it works."

"And I could handle it…because of you." Her knowing gaze said that she suspected the same thing that Gage did. *He'd* given her the strength to confront her past.

Then her eyes widened. "Oh, no. What about the others? Did he find them, too?" Her voice rose in panic. "We have to warn them. Lillian and Chantelle and Shelby—the girls who lived in the orphanage with me. We all sent him to prison. We all testified. He'll be after them, too. We have to tell them that he's out there again."

"We will." Gage dreaded having to tell her about Lillian. Why *had* the guy been released from prison? And how soon could Gage make sure he was back where he belonged? Behind bars, and away from Kayla Sparks. He wouldn't let him hurt her again. In fact, if he had his way, he wouldn't let anyone ever hurt her again.

Jenee bolted out the front door of the plantation. "Gage!" she yelled, running toward the truck then yanking the passenger door open. "Kayla, thank God you're okay," she said, relief washing over her features. "I'm so glad you found her, Gage." Then her eyes moved to the back of the cab, and she gasped. "What happened?"

"That's what happens when a bullet and a sheet of glass have a meeting of minds," he said.

"Gage told me a guy was after you." Jenee hugged Kayla. "I take it he got there in time?"

"Yeah, he did. But I kind of kneed him and bit him before I realized he was the good guy." Kayla looked apologetically at Gage. "I *am* sorry about it."

"Dare I ask where you kneed him?"

"If you're wanting specifics, about two centimeters to the right of the mark," Gage answered.

Jenee smirked. "Well, I'm glad you got there in time. So, does that mean your assignment is complete then?"

Gage hadn't thought about it, but Jenee was right; if he'd effectively completed his assignment, saving Makayla Sparks, then Lillian would have crossed over. But she hadn't, which meant…Kayla was still in danger. Hell. "No, my assignment isn't over."

"Assignment?" Kayla asked.

Jenee's mouth flattened as she realized her error. "I wasn't thinking. Gage hasn't had a chance to tell you how he knew you were in danger, or how he found you, and—well, it's probably going to be a bit of a shock."

"Which is why I haven't said anything yet," Gage said pointedly.

Kayla looked from cousin to cousin. "I don't want you hiding anything from me. I mean it. I've been in the dark too long."

"You're right," Gage agreed. "And I'll tell you everything tonight, but I need to wait for someone else to get here to help me. Is that okay?" He wanted Lillian's input when he talked to Kayla about her murder.

"As long as you promise to tell me tonight."

"Deal."

"That guy apparently knows that you've been staying at the shelter, so I think you should stay here until we make sure he's behind bars," Jenee said.

Kayla nodded. "Nothing against the shelter, but I really don't want to go back now that I've gotten my memory back," she said, then corrected, "or most of it back."

"You've remembered your past?" Jenee asked.

Kayla nodded again, but didn't offer additional information.

"She's been through a lot today." Gage hoped Jenee would take the hint that they needed to let Kayla tell them everything on her own time.

Jenee smiled sympathetically. "We'll have time to talk later, since you're staying here." She turned to Gage. "And you need to stay here, too, not only to help us with the house, but also to keep her safe."

"I agree." As if leaving were an option. He wouldn't leave Kayla.

"Come on inside, and we can try to figure everything out." Jenee backed away from the truck so Kayla could exit.

Kayla waited for Jenee to move out of earshot, then turned toward Gage. "I'm glad you're staying," she whispered. "Whether we really knew each other before or not, I feel—safe—when you're near."

"I won't let him hurt you again, Kayla. I swear it."

Walking behind Kayla and Jenee to the house, Gage wondered about his desire to protect this woman. It was more than his typical professional response to take care of someone in need. In fact, he'd equate the desire to shield her from harm to the type of emotion he'd experience for a member of his family. But she wasn't family; she wasn't even really a lover.

So why did he feel so much? And toward a woman who

would have a hard time trusting men, due to her abuse. As a doctor, Gage understood that fear more than most men. He'd seen women at the hospital who'd been traumatized by rape, and he'd heard them vow never to let a man touch them again. Some stuck to that vow. Others, with patience, tenderness and love, eventually trusted the opposite sex again, and even learned to enjoy their bodies again.

Kayla already trusted him; he could see it in her eyes. But that trust was based on dreams.

If the two of them actually tried to make love, would that trust carry over into reality? Could the real thing be anywhere near as incredible as the fantasy?

6

KAYLA'S SKIN bristled as she entered the plantation. A real home. It'd been two weeks since she'd left her own home, not really a home but her current rental house. Since her parents had died, the closest thing she'd had to a home with a real family was her time with Ms. Rosa and Lillian, Chantelle and Shelby. While she treasured her relationship with all of them, she still knew it wasn't the same as what the Vicknairs shared here in this house, a place that, according to Jenee, had been in their family for generations.

Kayla hadn't even lived in the same location long enough to start thinking of it as a true home. She'd been too fearful of Romero returning to stay in one place. And now, here she was with her fantasy man in his home. A real home where a real family lived.

She could sense the difference between this place and the shelter, and her previous house for that matter, immediately. This house had a history, had meaning to the people who lived within its walls. It gave Kayla a peace of mind that she hadn't had during her time at the shelter. The shelter served its purpose, gave people a place to eat and sleep, but it was cold and distant. In complete contrast, this house was warm and inviting.

Jenee had described the Vicknair plantation and her family's determination to save it from destruction in many of their conversations over the past two weeks. Kayla merely had to see the look of love in Gage's eyes as he viewed the place to understand why. This home bonded the Vicknairs, uniting them as a family.

She glanced at Gage and saw those same intense blue eyes studying her, watching her every reaction as she took it all in. She wanted to touch him, to move beside him and feel the warmth of his arms around her. How could she already feel so much for this home, merely because it was *his* family's home? Kayla didn't know, but she did. She felt drawn to Gage, and because of that, she felt drawn to this vast home that was his heritage.

Even though it had obviously seen better days, the Vicknair plantation's very walls were alive with the past. A curved staircase lined one wall of the foyer, but several of the spindles were missing and the steps were in dire need of refinishing or replacement. On both sides of the foyer, thick sheets of paint-splattered plastic closed off the majority of the first floor, and beyond the sheets, loud clattering and grumbling male voices filled the air.

"Tristan, my brother, and Gage's brother, Dax, are working on the first floor," Jenee explained.

Gage quickly updated Jenee on what had happened in the Quarter and how they'd got away from Romero, and Kayla took advantage of the opportunity to further survey her new surroundings.

A short hallway led to the back of the house and the kitchen, judging from the smell of sausage, onions and peppers drifting from that area.

The door to the kitchen swung open, and a striking woman stepped into the hall. Her hair was pulled high on her head and the resulting ponytail fell across one shoulder to sleekly blend with her black T-shirt. She smiled, pushing high cheekbones even higher and transforming her heart-shaped face into cover-girl material. She favored Jenee, but where Jenee's hair was light brown, hers was black as night, and where Jenee's facial features were soft and sweet, hers were more classically sculpted. Kayla imagined Jenee would be described as pretty, but this woman would be classified as beautiful— and sexy. A slight difference, but a difference nonetheless.

"You're Kayla?" she asked.

"Yes."

"I'm Nan Vicknair, the oldest of the bunch." She wiped her hands on the front of black workpants rolled up to her calves in thick, uneven cuffs. Her feet were bare and red-tipped toes caught the light as she moved down the hall. "We've been waiting to hear what happened. I'm so glad Gage found you." She turned toward Gage. "So you got there in time?"

"Barely, but yes."

"But your assignment isn't over?" she asked, and her smile faded, while she glanced back toward the kitchen. "What does that mean?"

"How do you know it isn't over?" Kayla heard the bewilderment in Gage's tone. "No, don't tell me," he said, indicating Kayla with a jerk of his head. "We'll talk about it in a minute, after we've had a chance to get Kayla settled in. And I'm going to need your help, everyone's help, in trying to get information on the guy who's after her."

Nodding, Nan pivoted away from Gage and focused on Kayla. "Did Jenee tell you that we want you to stay here for a while? We want to keep you safe until that guy is caught." She paused. "Jenee told me about your memory loss. Do you know who he is yet? Can you remember him?"

Kayla wondered how Jenee's family knew so much

already, when she'd only been approached by the hooded stranger this morning. If Jenee had known for the past two weeks who Kayla was, wouldn't she have said something? She was certain that Jenee had been as mystified as she was about why she'd forgotten the past and why no one had come forward to claim her. "I remember him now. His name is Wayne Romero, and he abused me and three other girls when we were children. We helped put him in jail, but evidently he got out." She swallowed. "Back then, at the trial, he swore he'd make us pay, that he'd get out and come after us, and that next time he wouldn't stop until we were all dead. That's what he's trying to do now."

"Romero shot at them," Jenee informed her. "Busted out the back window of Gage's truck and put a hole in the roof."

Nan gasped. "Oh, Gage, I'm *so* glad you found her in time."

"Gage still hasn't told me how he knew that Romero was after me, or where to find me," Kayla said. At first, she hadn't given much thought to how he'd found her in that alley; she was just glad that he had. But now she was beginning to resent being kept in the dark. Kayla hated the dark.

"You haven't told her how you found her?" Nan asked Gage.

"I haven't had the chance," he replied, and the intensity on his face seemed to tell Nan that she should choose her words carefully.

Why? What were they hiding?

Kayla surveyed the man whose eyes had captivated her and comforted her every night for the past two weeks. She doubted many women passed Gage Vicknair on the street without giving him a second glance, and a thorough one at that. He wasn't overly tall, a couple of inches shy of six feet, but he had an athletic, muscular build that emanated physical strength, strength that she'd personally witnessed today, when he'd caught her in that alley. His skin had a golden, earthy tone, more indicative of a surfer than a trauma doctor, and his sun-streaked, spiky hair also gave him the appearance of a man who enjoyed the outdoors. He smiled reassuringly at her, and white teeth gleamed in the midst of that rugged, tan face. "Don't worry. We'll explain everything soon."

Kayla nodded. She wanted to know what he was keeping from her, but she trusted him to tell her eventually. Less than an hour ago, he'd risked his life to save her, and Kayla had no doubt that he'd do it again. How could she not trust him completely?

"Gage is right. We will do everything we can to keep you safe," Nanette said, and again glanced back toward the kitchen. Then she turned to Gage. "But I think you should know that we've got—company—in the kitchen. I assume it's your assignment, though there's no way we can tell for sure."

"When did she get here?" Jenee asked.

"Right after you went outside." Nan gave Jenee a shrug as though this matter were totally out of her control. "Evidently she cooks when she's anxious. Looks like she's making jambalaya."

So, Gage's *assignment* was a woman? What did that mean? Kayla noted his reaction to this news. His brow puckered and his mouth frowned slightly at the edges.

"It's okay. We haven't got time to waste anyway, so we should go ahead and let Kayla know what's happening." He took a deep breath, let it out.

"Listen, I know you're getting a lot thrown at you today, but as long as Romero is still out there, we're going to have to move as quickly as possible. We do have someone who will help us, but it's going to come as a bit of a shock to you when you learn who it is, and I'm afraid the truth may upset you." He paused. "God, Kayla, you've been through a lot, and I don't want to cause you to…"

"Run again?" she finished. "Forget everything again because I can't handle it?"

He nodded.

Kayla worked to choose the right words. She didn't remember most of the attack at her house, but she knew one thing—she had been alone and she had been afraid. She wasn't afraid now, and she definitely wasn't alone. She had Gage Vicknair, and amazingly enough, with him by her side, she knew she could handle anything. "You're going to be with me, right?" she asked and prayed he understood the depth behind the question. It wasn't something she could completely analyze right now, this intense feeling toward this man she'd just met.

"Yes I'll be with you." He stepped in front of her and held out his hand. "Come on."

Kayla hadn't had a lot of physical contact in the past two weeks, so she was ill-prepared for her body's instant reaction when he interlaced his fingers tenderly with hers. A comforting sensation, of being held, of being safe, made her throat close, and her eyes start to burn.

He stopped a few feet shy of the kitchen. The hallway was narrow, forcing the two of them to stand close. Heat radiated from his side and she wanted to turn and face him head-on so her entire body could experience the incredible warmth.

"This is probably going to be difficult for you to understand. I guess the best way to explain it is to show you."

"I'm ready," she said.

He pushed the swinging door open, and Kayla realized that she'd lied; she wasn't ready after all.

Water ran noisily from the faucet to the sink, which

wouldn't have been anything out of the ordinary, except it didn't flow steadily from the spout. Instead, it splattered wildly midstream, as though something was disrupting the flow, but Kayla saw nothing in its way. Then the knob on the faucet turned on its own accord to shut off the stream and a blue-and-white checked towel lifted above the sink and danced in midair.

When the towel fell back to the counter, Kayla collapsed into the nearest chair. As she sat down, a cutting board slid along the counter, then a knife pulled itself free from its chopping block before attacking a bulging yellow onion.

The potent scent of peppers, onions and sausage, sizzling in a black iron pot on the stove, combined with the bizarre images, made Kayla light-headed.

"What's happening?"

As if the knife had heard her, it dropped to the floor with a loud clang.

"Are you okay?" Gage asked, but Kayla realized he wasn't looking at her. He was looking at the area where the knife had fallen.

"Is who okay?" Kayla could barely whisper.

"My assignment."

The kitchen door swung open and Nan and Jenee bounded through. "What was that?" Nan asked, then eyed the knife on the floor. She started toward it, then stopped when it levitated upward and dropped into the sink.

Gage indicated the chair across from Kayla, and it eased back from the table.

Kayla felt her pulse in her throat and her head *and* her heart. Her entire body throbbed with trepidation. Gage's assignment was... "A ghost?"

Jenee nodded, while Kayla stared at the chair across from her. The woman in the kitchen, Gage's assignment, was dead.

A ghost. And she was supposed to help them find Romero. Kayla believed in ghosts—most everyone who lived in Louisiana did—but she had never experienced one in person.

"Are you okay?" Gage asked her, concern in every word.

Kayla nodded. She *was* okay—shocked, but okay.

"You want to explain what we do?" Nan said to Gage. "Or do you want me to?"

"You go ahead," he replied, moving to sit beside Kayla at the table. Again, just knowing he was here made her feel as though she could handle whatever Nanette had to say.

Nanette cleared her throat and looked apologetic. "It's tough for others to grasp at first...but basically, we help the dead who have trouble crossing over. You could say it's our family heritage."

Gage gave Kayla an easy smile. "I had planned to tell you gradually, but we only have five days for my current assignment to cross, and I believe I'm going to need your help, since it appears we'll need to find and stop Romero in order for that to happen."

"Your assignment," Kayla repeated. "She's a ghost, and she's sitting in that chair?" She pointed to the chair across from her at the table. "And before she can cross, you have to stop Romero."

"Actually, before she can cross, I have to save you from Romero," Gage clarified.

Kayla didn't understand that, either, since he already had saved her from Romero. But right now, that wasn't what seemed most important. "What does she have to do with me?"

Gage cleared his throat. "This is Lillian," he said, motioning to the chair. "Lillian Bedeau."

"Lillian?" Kayla shook her head. "No!" She immediately recalled the little girl who'd shared a room with her, Chantelle and Shelby at the orphanage, the way they had confided in each other. She pictured Lillian, with long blond hair in an ill-fitting pale-pink nightgown and bare feet. Her eyes were big and round and sad, and, in this memory, she was crying. She was so sad. And Kayla was, too.

Kayla's mind fast-forwarded to the day of the trial. She and Lillian were the oldest, and they'd helped Chantelle and Shelby stay strong through the horrible ordeal of putting Wayne Romero behind bars. They did it together, testified and told the truth and watched them take him away for good.

And they'd all listened to his promise, growled with venom.

I'll get out, and you'll all pay. I'll hunt you down, and I'll kill you. Every one of you. Wait and see.

Kayla shuddered at that memory. Then she thought of Lillian last Christmas, when the girls had all got together at Ms. Rosa's. She looked forward to those Christmas bonding sessions, and to the sporadic calls from Lillian, Chantelle and Shelby throughout the year. When they met at Christmas, it was as if they had always been together.

Kayla had thought it would always be that way.

But Lillian was in that chair across the table. And Kayla didn't have to wonder who had put her there.

"He murdered you. Oh, Lillian!" She reached across the table and thought she sensed a presence, a pressure, patting her hand.

"She says that she doesn't want you to be sad right now," Gage said. "She isn't hurting anymore, and she just wants you to stay safe, and to help keep Chantelle and Shelby safe, too."

Kayla couldn't speak. Her throat had closed in completely and her chest was so tight she could barely breathe.

"Kayla? She wants to know if you're okay."

"Lillian?" Kayla whispered. "You aren't hurting?"

"No." Gage reassured her. "She isn't. But she's worried about you, and the others, and she isn't crossing until she knows that all of you are safe."

"Chantelle and Shelby?" Kayla said. "He's after them, too, isn't he? Where are they?"

Ms. Rosa's mother, the woman who'd started the Seven Sisters orphanage, was so old back then and honestly had no idea about the evil man who abused them all. She'd trusted everyone and had sincerely wanted to provide a better life for children without families. In her mind, Romero was simply the landscaping guy who'd volunteered his time at the orphanage. She'd actually been grateful for his help.

"Lillian saw Chantelle today, and she wants me to go get her and bring her here, until we can make certain Romero is back behind bars, where he belongs. I'll bring Shelby here, too, as soon as we find her."

"So you don't know if Shelby is okay?" Kayla asked. "Or if he's already gotten to her, too?" Her memory of the little freckle-faced girl who'd turned into a pretty auburn-haired woman caused her voice to crack. "Shelby," she whispered.

"We're going to try to find her, and we're going to take care of you and Chantelle," Gage promised. "But we also have to find Romero. This won't be over until we do."

"Lillian," Kayla said, swallowing thickly. "I'm so sorry. All of you testified because of me. If I hadn't asked you to, then maybe none of this…"

Gage shook his head. "No, Kayla. She said she won't let you take the blame for any of this. If you hadn't turned him in, then he would have killed all of you back then, eventually. He wouldn't have let you leave the orphanage and risk letting the authorities find out about what he'd done. She says that you're the only reason she ever lived any kind of normal life, and she can only feel grateful for that," Gage relayed. "And she said for you to be strong now, the way you taught all of them to be strong." Confusion etched Gage's features, and he added, "She said to be strong, like the roses?"

Tears falling freely, Kayla scooted back from the table, leaned down and lifted the hem of her jeans to reveal a tiny rose tattoo above her ankle. The girls had gotten the tattoos to remind them that they were as strong as those roses, and that even after everything Romero put them through, they would survive. And they had, until now. Now Lillian was dead, and Romero was intent on sending the rest of them to join her.

"That's a beautiful tattoo." Jenee crouched down to look at Kayla's ankle.

"It's the Seven Sisters rose," Kayla explained. "It's different than most other roses, because it blooms in clusters. The tiny roses are so tightly grown together that they appear as one. At the orphanage, the bushes were filled with them, so that the entire walls looked like they were covered. Because they all gathered together, they seemed bigger than they were. That's the way we wanted to be, when we finally exposed Romero, bigger than we were."

Jenee leaned closer. "Kayla, I had no idea about your past when you were at the shelter. If I had known, I wouldn't have let you stay there. I'd have brought you back here sooner. I didn't realize that Lillian was your friend, either, until Gage got his assignment this morning. I swear, I had no idea you were in danger."

"I know." She managed an understanding smile.

"Kayla," Gage said, urgency in his voice. "This is hard to explain, but Lillian—all ghosts—can see those that they were close to on this side. That's how I found you this morning. She saw you. Right now, she sees Chantelle, and she's on her way home. We're afraid Romero may go after her next, so I have to go, to get to her before he does."

"I want to come."

He shook his head. "No. I don't want to take you any- where near him. He can't see Lillian, and she'll be able to keep an eye on Chantelle and help me get to her quickly, but I don't want to put you in danger again." Gage touched her hand, and the warmth of his flesh against hers gave Kayla strength. "Jenee and Nan will be with you until I get back, and Tristan and Dax are here, too. You're safe here."

He stood, then turned to Nan. "Lillian said the police have talked to Chantelle about her murder, so maybe we can get some additional information about where they think Romero is from her when she gets here. But in the meantime, can you guys start searching the Internet, making calls—whatever—and find out how the hell he got out of prison?"

"Sure," Nan and Jenee answered in unison.

"And, Nan, my truck isn't in the best of shape. Are your keys in your car?"

"Yeah, take it," she told him. "We'll get another room ready. This place may be falling apart, but at least it's big and has room for plenty."

He stopped at the back door to look at Kayla again before he exited the kitchen. "I promise, we'll be back soon, and we'll bring Chantelle. And then we will find Romero." Then he—and Lillian, Kayla assumed—left the plantation.

Nan peeked out the kitchen window and watched them leave. "Well, if he needs to get somewhere quick, that car will do the trick." The phone rang, and she answered it. "Hello?"

"Don't worry, Gage will help Lillian cross over," Jenee whispered, while Nan spoke to whomever was on the other end. "And he'll keep you and Chantelle safe."

"And Shelby," Kayla said. "We still have to find Shelby, too. Bless her heart. She's the only one of us who married. She was young, but she truly loved Phillip, and he loved her." Kayla frowned. "But the past was too much for her, and she couldn't get over what Romero did. She ended up divorcing Phillip." She shook her head. "I hope Romero didn't find her, too."

"I'm hoping that, as well." Jenee's face showed she wasn't so certain he hadn't. Kayla wondered, too. If Lillian could indeed sense people she was close to on this side, why had she been able to find Kayla and Chantelle, but not Shelby?

Lillian. Kayla couldn't quite grasp that she was gone. "Jenee?"

"Yes?"

"How did he kill her? It was with a knife, wasn't it? He tried to use a knife on me at my house, and back then, I remember when he hurt us, he sometimes held a knife to our throats. We were blindfolded, always, and sometimes, he held a knife to our throats when he…" Her voice trailed off, and she just couldn't finish.

Jenee wrapped an arm around her as she spoke. "Yes." She took a breath and added, "I'm so sorry, Kayla, but the woman who was stabbed outside the shelter…"

Kayla's trembling hand covered her mouth. No. "That was Lillian? The woman you tried to save? So, she was trying to get to the shelter? To me?"

"He had already found her, Kayla," Jenee said, her voice soft and soothing. "It wasn't your fault. He was following her already, I'm sure, and then he followed her there. He wouldn't have been at the shelter first. How would he have known you were there?"

"But she died trying to get to me, didn't she?"

"Because she wanted to warn you, and the others, as well. It wasn't your fault what happened, Kayla. You have to believe that," Jenee insisted.

Nan hung up the phone. "That was Gage. He wants us to also check the Internet for an address for Shelby. Her last name is Montana now, according to Lillian."

Kayla nodded. "That was her husband's name. Montana. Phillip Montana. She kept his name after the divorce because, well, I think she still loves him."

"I'll go get Nan's laptop," Jenee said, quickly leaving the kitchen.

"You all help ghosts to cross?" Kayla asked, trying to get her emotions under control.

Nan nodded. "It's part of our legacy. As far as we know, ever since the Vicknairs moved to St. Charles Parish and built this place, our family has taken assignments from the other side. Instructions on what we need to do to help ghosts cross." She shrugged. "That's why we're all so intent on saving our home. This house helps ghosts cross over, and we're not all that certain whether we'll still have a means of communicating with the spirits if it's destroyed."

"Do you often have to stop killers in order to help a ghost cross?"

"Never before, as far as I know," Nan admitted. "But trust me, Gage won't be doing this alone. We'll all help, and we'll work with the police, or whomever else we need to work with, to make sure we stop this guy. I promise you, the Vicknairs aren't going to let Lillian down. We'll help her get through, and we'll keep all of you safe." She nodded her belief that they could accomplish this task. "And Gage will protect you."

Jenee returned with a black backpack slung over one arm and withdrew Nan's computer. She waited for it to boot up, then madly clicked the keys to enter Romero's information in a search engine. "Oh." Jenee leaned forward as she scanned the results of her search. "We've got something."

"Did you find him?" Kayla moved closer so she could also see the information.

"There's only one mention of Wayne Romero on this search engine." Jenee selected the link.

The image that displayed was an archived issue of the *Times-Picayune*. An article detailed the trial of Wayne Romero, and mentioned that several girls from the Seven Sisters orphanage had testified against the establishment's gardener to achieve a conviction.

"That's all?" Kayla asked. "Nothing more recent?"

"There's only the one result," Jenee said. "I'll keep looking, but first, let me try to find Shelby so we can get an address for Gage." She clicked on more keys, then looked up at Nan. "She lives in Metairie."

"You found her that easily?" Nan asked.

"There's only one Shelby Montana listed, and it came right up—why?" Jenee asked, writing Shelby's information on a small notepad.

But Kayla knew why Nan sounded concerned.

"If you found her that easily, then Romero would've found her easily, too." Kayla's stomach pitched. A few minutes ago, the scents in the kitchen had had her craving jambalaya; now, those same scents, combined with the fear clawing at her insides, made her feel sick. Had he already found Shelby?

Jenee ripped the paper from the pad and handed it to Nan. "Call Gage. Chantelle lives in Kenner, not far from Metairie. Get him to go by Shelby's place, too, and bring her back here." Then she entered another name. *Chantelle Bedeau.*

As quickly as Shelby's, Chantelle's address displayed on the screen. "Romero probably has Chantelle's address, too," Jenee said, dismayed. "Tell Gage they need to get to her before she gets home, if they can."

Nan already had Gage on the line and relayed all of the information, spouting addresses as quickly as she could. "And, Gage," she added, "be careful. Please."

She hung up the phone and turned to Jenee and Kayla. "He said Lillian sees Chantelle. She's in her car and a couple of miles ahead of them. Gage said he'll get to her before she gets home. My Camaro's not a new car, but it's a fast one. He'll catch her."

"I hope you're right," Kayla said.

"Then they're going to head to Shelby's apartment. But he said Lillian's been trying to sense Shelby, and she still hasn't felt anything." Nan's voice was somber, and Kayla knew why.

"She's dead, isn't she?" Kayla asked. "He's already gotten to her."

"I don't know."

"But the way all of this works," Kayla continued, trying to put the pieces together about the Vicknair family and the spirits they helped, "if Shelby were alive, then Lillian would feel her, right?"

"The way we understand it, spirits can sense people on this side," Nan said.

"Well, not all people," Jenee clarified, "but those that had a strong influence on their lives, either positively or negatively."

"Wouldn't—I mean, if she feels people who had a strong influence on her life, and if that includes a negative influence—wouldn't she be able to sense Romero, too?"

Jenee looked at Nan, and the older cousin shrugged. "I

would have thought she'd feel him, too, but, as we learned not long ago with my cousin Monique, we've still got a lot to learn about spirits and the other side."

"What happened with Monique?"

"She got married," Jenee said. "And she happened to marry a spirit."

"Former spirit," Nan corrected.

"That's possible?" Kayla asked.

"Well, I sure didn't think so," Nan admitted. "But yeah, apparently it is."

Kayla clasped her hands in front of her on the table, and instantly remembered the way Gage had held her hand, and her response to his touch.

"So everything Gage knew about me, and him finding me, protecting me, all of that," she said. "He did all of that because of what Lillian told him?"

"He knew you were in danger, and that he had to get to you," Jenee said matter-of-factly. "And you're right, he knew about it because of Lillian."

Kayla wanted to know more, such as, how she had dreamed of him for the past two weeks, and how he had dreamed of her. And how she could have been so intimate with him in her dreams, if she'd never physically touched him until today. Or why she felt so complete when he was near.

But those questions weren't meant to be answered by Gage's cousins; they could only be answered by the man himself—if he managed to make it back to the plantation safely with her friends.

7

KAYLA'S HEART thundered violently in her chest as she ran from the hooded figure. He was big, yet agile, and faster than any man had a right to be. And he was intent on catching her, hurting her, making her pay.

Her lungs pushed air out, sucked it in, as she struggled to stay ahead of the hunter chasing his prey. Chasing her. She couldn't let him catch her, because he would kill her this time. She knew it, sensed it, anticipated it…unless she got away.

Move, Kayla!

Her heartbeat roared in her ears, pulse pumped so hard it made her skin burn, as she struggled to use every ounce of strength she possessed to find a way out of the darkness, to find the light, to find…Gage.

His arms claimed her with acute possession, and those mesmerizing blue eyes told her that he was here, that he would take care of her, that he would make that horrid hooded figure go away.

"Please," she pleaded, and he scooped her in his arms, as though that were exactly where she belonged…and it was.

They were no longer in the alley. They were in the Vicknair plantation, and it was completely restored to its former glory—pristine and powerful and perfect, like the man who shared its name.

He placed her reverently on his bed, then silently, lovingly, removed her clothes.

Kayla's body tingled in anticipation as she watched him remove his shirt, his jeans, everything, until he stood before her, beautifully naked and boldly aroused. For her.

He didn't move toward the bed. Instead, he stood there, moonlight illuminating his beautiful features, his face signaling his intention to wait until she was ready, until she said yes.

"Yes," she whispered, reaching for him. "I need you. Please."

His blue eyes grew stormy, and he climbed on the bed, then slowly, tenderly, made love to her, until she wept from the sheer joy of finally having him where he belonged, inside her, completing her, blocking out the horrible past and giving her a glimpse of the future....

GAGE SAT at the kitchen table and forced his eyes to focus on Nan's computer. It was two in the morning and he was exhausted, plain and simple, but he really wanted to find more on Romero before he went to sleep. He only had five days; he had to make the most of them.

He was used to long hours—hell, he worked twenty-four-hour shifts on a regular basis at the hospital—but the responsibility of trying to protect Kayla, and now Chantelle, from a killer had upped his usual stress level exponentially. He dealt with life and death every day, yet, typically, the advances of modern medicine and the patient's existing condition were the major factors determining whether he could save a life.

But in this situation, whether Kayla and Chantelle lived and whether Lillian Bedeau crossed over, totally depended on his decisions over the next five days. Make that four days, since technically, day one was over.

No pressure.

Add to that the fact that he'd been two long weeks without sex, and that he'd dreamed nightly about it with a woman who was currently asleep upstairs in the bedroom next to his, and Gage knew this went way beyond what he dealt with on a daily basis in the ER.

Thank goodness Kayla and Chantelle were open to the idea of ghosts. At least he didn't have to deal with trying to convince them that what he said was the truth. Chantelle hadn't batted an eye when he'd told her that Lillian was with him. She had sensed her sister's presence and was touched beyond measure to have some means of communicating with Lillian via Gage. She'd suspected someone had been following her and had even mentioned Wayne Romero to the police when they'd asked her if she knew of anyone who would want to harm Lillian. According to Chantelle, the detective assigned to the case, Detective Ingram, was checking into Romero's current location in the prison system and would let her know. Which was good, because Gage wanted—needed—to know, too.

Gage, Chantelle and Lillian had then proceeded to Shelby's apartment, but it had been empty. What's more, there were at least five newspapers crammed in the box beside her door. Five papers meant she hadn't been home in at least five days. And the neighbor had said he'd seen her leave with a suitcase.

Where was she? Dare he even hope that she was still breathing, since Lillian couldn't sense her at all? Was it possible that Romero had already murdered her, too? Gage wasn't going to give up until he knew for sure. Somehow, he had to find Shelby. Or find her body.

He read the article from the *Times-Picayune* several more times, hoping to find a piece of pertinent information that he might have missed, but the only thing that seemed to be of any help was a mention of the prison where Romero had been taken after the trial. Gage had hit another brick wall and, at this point, was too tired to try to find another search method. "Hell."

The kitchen door creaked softly behind him. Gage turned to see Kayla, her doe eyes wide and her mouth slightly opened, probably from finding him cursing in the kitchen in the middle of the night. She had on one of those pajama sets that Nan, Jenee and Monique always bought each other for Christmas, but Gage had never seen any of theirs in that shade of pale pink, or that sheer.

Her nipples pressed against the fabric in tight little points, and the only way any male wouldn't have noticed was if he were dead. Gage wasn't dead. They were the color of cinnamon, the exact color they had been in his dreams, which made him wonder if everything else about his dreams would be the same, and they were showcased beautifully by the shimmering pastel fabric. Gage blinked past the impulse to take his gaze lower.

"I tried to wait up and see Chantelle," she said, "but I couldn't keep my eyes open. She's here now?"

"Yeah, and she's doing okay, all things considered."

"She and Lillian were so close. I know today was really hard for her. I should have stayed up."

"You've been through a lot." Understatement of the year, but he'd leave it at that. He waited for her to say more, but she didn't. She just stood there, watching him. "Is something wrong?" He'd assumed the ordeal she'd been through would have her sleeping well into tomorrow morning. What had woken her? "Did you have another nightmare?"

"It started that way." She gradually moved to the seat

next to him at the table, and Gage fought his body's typical response to a half-clothed female, and its unique response to Kayla. Everything about this woman did more to him, made him feel more, sense more, want more.

But she wasn't ready for that. She'd been through too much, and he wanted her to continue trusting him and let him protect her. There was no way he'd stop protecting her, ever. "Started that way?" he asked, that protective nature kicking in, thankfully, and overpowering his baser needs.

"Yes. I was back in the alley and running from him, from Romero, but—" She stopped and tilted her head as though remembering the nightmare.

"But?" Gage prompted.

"Something was different about the hooded man in that alley."

"What do you mean by different?" He wasn't sure he really wanted to know. If she was thinking back to the abuse, did he really want to hear about it? The thought of Romero, or anyone else, hurting her made Gage livid with rage.

"I didn't realize at the time that that guy in the alley could be Romero, because I still couldn't totally remember him. But now that I do, when I compare the guy in the alley to the guy in my memory, he seems different." She frowned. "Bigger, and more…agile, I guess? He moved like a young man, but Romero was older."

"You don't think it was him?" Gage was baffled.

"I *think* it was," she clarified. "But I'm just surprised at how he moved."

"I've seen the effects of adrenaline pumping through the system and an older man could easily appear to be more agile if he had a surplus pumping through his veins. No doubt seeing you fleeing that streetcar gave him that surplus."

"I guess you're right," Kayla said. "Are you trying to locate Shelby now?" She indicated the computer.

"No. We went to her apartment, but she hasn't been there in a few days. Lillian gave me the name of her ex-husband, Phillip Montana, and I plan to call him first thing in the morning and ask if he's heard from her, or if he knows where she is. But right now, I'm trying to find out more about Romero, while we're waiting for information from the police."

"How?"

"Louisiana has an inmate-search feature for all prisoners in the state, so I looked him up. The system has records of the prisons where inmates are housed, whether they've been paroled, released, escaped, you name it."

"And?"

"He isn't even in the system. I saw in the old article from the *Times-Picayune* that he was originally in the state pen in Angola, but there's no record of him there now."

"What does that mean?" She leaned closer to view the screen, and gave Gage an enticing whiff of floral shampoo, or soap or something. The scooped neck of her top slipped lower as she peered at the monitor, and Gage received an all-too-tempting view of her breasts, not overly large, but shapely, exactly the way he'd seen them in his dreams.

He fought the desire to pull her on his lap and push that sheer material out of the way, then do everything that he'd already done to her in his mind....

But that wasn't what she needed; he knew that, so, swallowing hard, he pulled his mind back to her question. "It means that he isn't in Louisiana anymore. According to the site, I can call the Department of Corrections and ask if he has been transferred, but..."

"But?"

"But according to the procedures outlined here for victims, all of you should have been contacted if he was released, or escaped or even transferred." Gage looked at those chocolate eyes. "No one contacted any of you, right? Or do you not remember?"

"No," she said. "And I remember almost everything now. Well, right up until when he broke into my apartment. Everything about the actual incident is a blur, besides the feel of the knife in my hand, but everything before that is fairly clear."

"Then I can't figure out why he isn't listed here. I suppose we'll have to wait for the detective who talked to Chantelle, Detective Ingram, to get back to us with the information. Surely he'll know what happened with Romero."

"When did he say he'd call?" she asked.

"He said she should hear something tomorrow."

She nodded, chewing her lower lip. Something was on her mind, but she wasn't telling him, and Gage couldn't stand that worried look on her pretty face.

"What's wrong?"

"My dreams," she said hesitantly. "My dreams of you. Tonight started with the nightmare, with trying to run away from Romero in that alley, but then, at the end, it ended up with the two of us…together."

"I've had those dreams, too." He chose not to say more.

"What does it mean, that we've dreamed of each other like that, when we never saw each other before today? Has that—well, has that happened to you before?"

Gage shook his head. "No, never. But maybe we dreamed about each other because you're the person that Lillian is supposed to save, and I'm supposed to help her do that so she can cross."

"You already have saved me," she pointed out.

He inhaled, let it out. How much should he tell her?

"Gage," she said, and he really liked the way his name sounded on her lips.

"Yeah?"

"You're keeping something from me. What is it? Tell me."

Kayla was tougher than she looked, that was for sure, as if he could doubt it after he'd seen her scrap in that alley. And she wanted to know. "Lillian's requirement for crossing is to save you."

"Right. You told me that."

"So if she had accomplished that goal by having me get to you in that alley before Romero did, then she would have crossed over. But she didn't."

"That's because of Chantelle and Shelby. She's helping you take care of them, too."

"That's not the way our assignments work. A spirit crosses when a requirement for rectification has been fulfilled. They don't wait around for anything, or anyone, else."

Realization finally dawned. "He's going to come after me again, you mean?"

"I just know that she's supposed to save you, and what I did today didn't accomplish that, not in the eyes of the powers that be."

"And that's why you're keeping an eye on me here."

"Yes." Gage nodded.

"I may not have said it yet," she whispered, "but I truly appreciate everything you're doing for all of us."

"That's what our family does." He attempted to make it sound cavalier. He really didn't need to let her know the effect she had on him, particularly at this very moment, when he wanted to kiss her more than he wanted to breathe.

"There's more to it than that," she said, and it wasn't a

question. She knew exactly how she affected him, and he couldn't deny it, so he remained silent, his jaw clenched tight as he waited for her to finish this conversation and go back to bed.

Her bed.

"We're going to be very busy over the next few days, trying to find Shelby and Romero, and trying to help Lillian cross," he said. "You really should get some more sleep."

"I can't."

"Why not?" he asked.

"Truthfully?" Her eyes glistened. "I woke up, and I was afraid."

"Afraid of Romero?"

She shook her head. "No, that wasn't it this time. I woke up and realized I was alone. During all of my time in the shelter, I was in a room with at least twenty other women. Someone was always nearby, so…"

"If anyone tried to harm you, someone was there," Gage finished.

She nodded, and the tears pushed over the rims of her eyes and trickled down her cheeks.

Gage reached for her and gently pulled her out of her chair and onto his lap. "Are you okay with this?" he asked, holding her close and moving his hand protectively up and down her spine.

"Yes." Her voice was barely more than a whisper.

"Listen." He fought the urge to grow hard with her this close. "You don't have to sleep alone. If you want—"

"I do," she said, before he completed his offer. "I want to sleep with you, but—"

This time Gage interrupted and completed the difficult sentence. "But only sleep. Nothing more. Just so you'll feel safe, and know that I'll be there to protect you through the nightmares, and through anything else. I won't let anyone hurt you, Kayla."

"I believe you." She moved her hand to his chin and touched him softly. "I do believe you." Then she placed her head on his shoulder, the warmth of her body seeping into his skin, and into his soul. "You helped me through the past two weeks, whether you were actually there or not. And I can't tell you what that meant to me." She sat back up, and the movement caused the strap of her top to slide off her right shoulder.

Gage tenderly slid the strap back in place. The feel of her skin beneath his finger was intoxicating—soft and silky, and very nice. She visibly swallowed, and Gage wanted to kiss the delicate pulse in her slender neck. But he didn't, not yet. He wanted to take this slowly. She'd been through so much, and she needed a man she could believe, a man she could trust, whom she could give herself to…and love. She needed a man who could give her all of that, and more.

Gage vowed to be that man—in his heart, he already was.

8

GAGE BLINKED at the sunlight spilling brilliantly into his apartment. No, not his apartment, he realized, but his old room in the plantation, and the light forcing him awake wasn't from the sun; it was from a bulb. Had he fallen asleep with the light on?

Kayla's soft body pressed flush to his side and she hummed contentedly with each breath against his chest. He recalled leading Kayla to his room and gently tucking her into bed beside him, and he knew that the only light then had been from the moon. And the only person who would have turned on the overhead light was sleeping in his arms.

Why?

Gage thought he knew. Damn Wayne Romero. Was she so scared that she not only couldn't sleep alone, but she couldn't sleep in the dark, either?

She nuzzled his chest, then lazily opened her eyes and stretched. "I can't remember the last time I slept so peacefully. Thank you."

He'd slept well, too, amazingly well, considering it was the first time he'd spent an entire night with a female doing something other than having sex. He smiled down at her, and pondered whether to ask about the light. Fortunately, he didn't have to.

"I…turned on the light after you went to sleep," she

said, and one corner of her mouth dipped down. "Did it bother you?"

"I was so tired that it didn't matter at all, but I did notice it when I woke. You want to let me know why you turned it on, or would you rather not talk about it?"

Kayla rolled to her back and tucked the sheet beneath her arms, looking away from him as she spoke. "He always blindfolded us." Her voice was as soft as a child's. "I've never slept in the dark since. Even at the Magazine Street shelter, there were two night lights in the room where we slept. Then I couldn't remember why I was so afraid of the dark, but now I do."

His rage toward Romero was blinding. The man had destroyed her childhood, and now he was trying to take away the rest of her life, as well.

Gage wasn't going to let that happen.

Apparently wanting to change the subject, she smoothed her hands over the comforter and looked up at him. "Thanks for letting me sleep with you."

He smiled. "I can't recall any woman ever thanking me before, particularly when all we did was sleep."

"How many women have you taken to bed where all you did was sleep?"

Gage knew his answer was about to expose him but good. "None."

She remained silent for a moment, then the corners of her mouth eased upward. "Why is that?"

"I don't think we've got time to discuss it right now." He tried to avoid the conversation.

She was on to him. "I told you why I sleep with the light on," she reminded. "Now I want to know why you've never slept—only slept—with a woman."

"Were you an attorney before you showed up at

Jenee's shelter?" he asked, stalling, and again, she was on to him.

"I worked in retail. And I still want an answer. Why am I the first woman you've slept with?"

He gave up. This was going to tell her way more than he wanted to reveal at the moment, but he couldn't refuse her. "Sex is physical—it's enjoyable and fun and damn near necessary to me for me to function," he admitted. "But sleeping with someone, and holding them while they dream, that's…"

"What?" she asked, her brown eyes intense.

"Emotional, personal and extremely intimate." Before she could respond, he added, "I'm going to take a shower and then get started on those phone calls to the Department of Corrections and to Shelby's ex-husband." He climbed from the bed and her attention immediately shifted. His body wasn't the only thing standing upright, and she boldly eyed his cock, hard as a rock and straining against the gray gym shorts he'd worn to bed.

She didn't say a word as he crossed the room, though the flush on her face said that his erection definitely had an effect on her. Whether she was aroused or embarrassed Gage couldn't tell. He paused at the door to the bathroom, then turned to see her still eyeing him from the bed. "Are you okay? I mean, while I take a shower, will you be okay?"

"I'm fine. I only get scared at night, but I would like something, if it's okay by you."

"Name it."

"I need a shower, too." Pushing the comforter and sheet aside, she slid her bare feet to the floor, stood and walked to him, then traced her fingertips down his jaw, his neck and slowly down his chest and abdomen. She stopped at the band of his shorts, where his dick pressed against the fabric and a damp spot proved the powerful effect she was having.

"Kayla, two days ago, you'd never seen me before." Gage tried to remind her that taking things too fast was a bad idea, a very bad idea.

"I had seen you," she countered. "And you saw me, too. It may have been our dreams, but if your dreams were like mine, they were so real. I could feel you, and I trusted you. I still do."

He swallowed hard. It was so confusing, this over-whelming urge to cradle her in his arms, carry her to the bed and make love to her the way he had so many times in his mind. But Gage had another method for putting the brakes on, and he decided that now was the time to use it, to force her to think longer before giving him…exactly what he wanted. "I don't have any protection here."

She blinked a couple of times, then her brow creased. "Nothing?"

Gage shook his head. "I haven't lived here in three years."

"Dax lives here, doesn't he? Surely he has something."

Whether she realized it or not, her voice quivered with her words, and her pulse raced madly at her throat. While Gage thought she believed she wanted him completely in the most intimate way, he knew that she was far more ter-rified than she was letting on. And he wanted her, but only when she trusted him enough to relax and enjoy it.

Now wasn't the right time, no matter how much his cock begged to differ.

"I'll get something for us to use later," he said, "but not from Dax, and not now. You're scared, Kayla. I can see it, and I don't want you to be scared when we're together. I'd possibly hurt you without even realizing it, and I couldn't live with myself if I did."

"But I want—I need…" Her lower lip trembled, and

Gage couldn't resist the urge to finally taste her sweetness. He brushed his mouth against hers in the softest of kisses.

"I'm going to give you what you need," he said smoothly. "Are you okay with that?"

"Yes." There was no quiver in her voice this time, nothing but absolute certainty.

He smiled. She was obviously aroused; her taut nipples, pressing against the sheer fabric of her pajama top, emphasized the fact. Gage sat on the edge of the tub and turned on the water, then took her hand and gently pulled her toward him. "Here," he said, moving her fingertips into the flow of the stream. "Is that warm enough for you?"

She swallowed, nodded.

"I want to give you what you need," he said again, "but if I make you uncomfortable at all, or if you simply decide you don't want what I'm offering, you tell me to stop. Understood?"

"But you said you don't have protection."

"I don't, and *that* isn't what I'm offering." He ran his hands under the hem of her shirt. "Raise your arms for me, Kayla."

She did, and he slid the fabric up and over her body, then dropped it to the floor. Her breasts pushed forward, and he pressed a whisper-soft kiss to each nipple, relishing her sharp intake of breath as he did. Her body was very responsive, in spite of her fear. Bringing Kayla Sparks to orgasm was something he very much wanted to do, but doing it without scaring her would take every bit of willpower he possessed. He couldn't do this quickly. He had to keep things slow and make sure she wanted everything before he gave it. Gage had never put so much thought into every move, every touch.

"These, too?" He ran a fingertip beneath the elastic of her pajama shorts.

"Yes."

He eased the filmy shorts down her legs, letting his fingers caress the smooth skin the entire way down.

"What about *your* shorts?" she asked.

"Up to you." He stood to give her the option of stripping him naked or leaving him clothed.

Her eyes turned the color of dark chocolate, and her hands moved to his hips. She pulled the shorts down slowly, gasping audibly when his erection was freed.

Gage decided to lighten the mood, anything to keep her from being scared. "I'm kind of glad you decided to take them off. Would've been rather odd showering with them on."

He pushed aside the pale-blue curtain that enclosed the tub and shower, then motioned for her to step inside. As she did, he admired the gentle curve of her bottom, the way her legs had precisely the right amount of muscle and the right amount of feminine curve. He wanted to kiss those legs, and lots of other places, too, when she was ready. And he suspected she was getting closer and closer to ready.

Gage followed her into the shower and slid the curtain closed behind him, then took the washcloth from the rack and a thick bar of apple-scented soap from the dish. "You first, or me?"

"You can go ahead." She kept her eyes on his face.

"Okay." He lathered the cloth, running the soap under the water, then twirling it within the rag until the result was a foamy thickness. Then he pressed the sudsy fabric to her cheek and waited. "Close your eyes, Kayla."

She didn't. In fact, her eyes looked up at him in horror, and he realized what he'd done. "No, honey, *don't* close your eyes," he corrected. "I just didn't want to get soap in them."

"Oh," she whispered, and then, to Gage's surprise, her

lids slid closed. "Okay," she said, but he noticed that her jaw was tense.

He washed her face soothingly, taking tender care, then rinsed it just as carefully. "You can open them now."

She stared at him, and the trust in her gaze was undeniable. It had been the smallest of things to do, closing her eyes while he washed her face, but for Kayla Sparks, a woman who had been in the dark for so many years, it was monumental.

KAYLA'S HEART thudded madly as Gage pressed the cloth to her throat, then slowly eased it behind each ear, across her nape, over her shoulders. She'd never, ever, done anything like this before, and she was both elated and terrified. Throughout her adulthood, she'd worked hard to overcome the fears that Romero had instilled in her when she was a child, but she realized with absolute clarity now just how many she hadn't conquered.

She'd wanted to go to college, but she'd barely finished high school after what had happened. It reminded her too much of the classes she took at the Seven Sisters. Ms. Rosa taught her back then, and Romero often stood near the windows, supposedly working on the shrubbery, but in truth watching the girls he terrorized each night.

She'd wanted to have a successful job, but that was difficult when she didn't stay in one place very long. Constantly changing her address and employment didn't make for the ideal career situation. It simply wasn't possible.

And the big fear due to Romero…her fear of relationships and of men in general. She'd never let any man get too close, and certainly had never told any man about what had happened in her past. But Gage already knew. And more than that, he'd already been close to her in her

dreams. She wanted him, but she couldn't deny his accu-
sation that she was too scared to let him really touch her.
The truth was, he was right. She'd tried for nearly an hour
to go to sleep next to him in the dark, but had finally given
up and turned on the light. The fact that she needed it made
her miserable, and made Kayla realize that she was still
very much afraid.

She hated Romero for doing this to her.

She chewed her lower lip and watched Gage, mesmerized by the tender manner in which he washed her
abdomen, and then lowered to his knees and lathered the
cloth again. He lifted her feet, and Kayla was absolutely
shocked at the pleasure that filled her when he lathered her
ankles, her feet, her toes.

The spiraling intensity of desire strengthened with each
teasing pass of the cloth. He started back up her legs,
moving the soapy rag up one inner thigh in tiny little
circles, while his fingers mimicked the technique on the
other. And then he stood, placed the cloth back on the
small silver rack in the wall and began to rinse her, thoroughly, completely, with his hands.

"Almost done," he said. Kayla's entire body felt as if it
would melt, or explode, at his command. He turned her
away from him and put his back to the spray, so that her
body was barely misted by the heated stream. Wrapping
his arms around her, he lathered his hands with soap, his
long fingers curling around the bar, while Kayla watched,
spellbound. Then he placed the bar back on the dish and,
to Kayla's absolute delight, moved his hands between her
legs. Gage pressed his fingertips softly against her folds,
rubbing gently and massaging her thoroughly. The desire
built steadily, stronger and stronger.

She sucked in a deep breath of air and prepared to let

go, but suddenly he took those talented hands away. "No," she whispered.

"I need to rinse you now." He stepped farther into the stream, bringing her along into the water, so the intimate flesh, tingling from his touch, was drenched with the hot water trickling down her body, teasing her intimately—but teasing wasn't nearly enough.

"Please," she said.

"You're not afraid, Kayla?"

"No." And she wasn't. In fact, she'd never wanted anything more than…

He pushed her forward again, and his erection brashly nudged her bottom. She imagined it hard and hot and deep within her, and this time, the thought didn't frighten her.

He eased one finger into her tight center and Kayla cried out immediately. "Kayla?"

"Don't—stop."

Obeying her command, his thumb circled over her clitoris. Kayla lost herself in the feeling of his finger, in and out, slowly and steadily, and the pad of his thumb, applying more pressure and increasing the friction, flicking over her clit while the water's spray trickled over her, adding another element to the rising heat that had her spiraling, burning, reaching for something that was so desperately close.

"Come on, baby," he urged, his breath warm against her ear as he nudged her wet hair out of the way and bit her lobe. "Let go for me, Kayla. Ride it, baby, and set it free. You need this, honey. Take it."

Her hips bucked wildly, but he never withdrew the hand, two fingers pushing deep within her now and the pad of his thumb pressing harder, moving faster, stronger, pushing her to the edge, pushing her…

Kayla's heels bore down against the bottom of the tub,

her hips surged forward, pressing her clit harder against his thumb as her vagina pulsed fiercely around his fingers, and she spun out of control.

His arms tightened around her and she let her body collapse against his sturdy frame. Who would have thought it would be this good?

The erection pushing against her bottom reminded her of what Gage had done, giving her exactly what she needed, as he'd promised, but taking nothing in return. His body craved release, too, and she wasn't about to be a selfish lover.

She turned to face him and said, "Thank you," for the third time this morning.

He grinned, and kissed the top of her head, then pulled her to him and held her close. Have mercy, this man was heavenly. And he'd just taken her there. Now it was time for him to see stars, too.

She leaned away from him and smiled. "Your turn."

"Kayla, I really don't think—" he started, but she stopped him with a kiss.

"Please don't."

"Don't?"

"Think." Then she took the bar of soap and lathered her hands. She could have used the washcloth, but she'd never had the courage to touch a man before, had never even been close enough to a man to try. She'd always been too afraid that all of them were like Romero, but she knew, deep in her heart, that this man was different. More than that, she knew in her soul that Gage Vicknair was meant for her, to help her get past the pain, and rid her of her fears. She'd felt that before she ever met him, when she saw those beautiful eyes in her dreams. And now, he was here and had given her an exquisite orgasm that had her feeling as though she could take on the world.

She wanted to do the same for him.

While his body had been beautiful to look at this morning, and to feel against her while she slept, that was nothing compared to actually touching his flesh beneath her fingers. Kayla slid her soapy hands across the broad expanse of his chest, taking extra time to run a fingertip over each dark male nipple. Then she moved her hands up his shoulders and down his arms, stroking his biceps as she passed and pressing her body against him. Water sprayed over his shoulders to douse her face. She pulled him out of the stream and licked the water away, smiling when his eyes focused on her mouth and her tongue.

He kissed her then, and her mind went numb. His hands wrapped around to cup her bottom and center her against his hard length. Kayla wished he had protection, because right now, at this very moment, she felt no fear. None at all. And she wanted him more than she'd ever wanted anything.

His tongue teased her lower lip, then eased inside her mouth with sweet dancing thrusts that had her hips moving in direct correlation. She moaned, then, before she had a chance to realize what he was doing, she felt Gage's fingers slide across her thigh to her center and thoroughly explore, with quick circular strokes that, in no time at all, had her climaxing again.

She shuddered through it, then looked up at Gage in absolute amazement. "I said it was your turn."

"And I decided I wanted you to have another turn first." He gave her an impish grin.

"You're terrible," she said, then shook her head. "No, Gage, you aren't. You're incredible."

She reached for the soap again. "You said you'd give me what I needed, right?"

"I did, and I will."

"Well, right now," she stated, pressing her soapy hands against his thighs, and then sliding one to his penis and the other to his balls, "I need this." Kayla lowered to her knees and ran her soapy hands over his manhood, then she cupped her palms to capture warm water and rinsed him clean. His penis was so big that she wasn't sure she could do what she planned, but she wanted to try.

"Kayla, you don't have to—" He stopped talking when her mouth closed over the head, then she eased down over him, taking as much as she could before sliding back up, her tongue licking the tip.

She pulled back and kissed him there, then looked up. "I want to. But I'm not sure if I know how."

"Trust me," he said hoarsely. "You're doing everything right."

She smiled at him, believed him, and then proved that, once again, Gage Vicknair had given her nothing short of the truth.

9

"WHERE'S KAYLA?" Chantelle asked when Gage entered the kitchen Sunday morning. Her blond hair hung in loose ringlets over the back of her chair. He glanced at her again, amazed at how her face mirrored her sister's, though Lillian's now shimmered with a ghostly glow. He hoped Chantelle's wouldn't do the same anytime soon.

"I believe she's drying her hair." He tried to sound as though he didn't know it to be a fact, since he'd just left her smiling smugly as she got ready in the bathroom. She'd thanked him yet again, when their shower had ended with both of them extremely satisfied, and Gage was beginning to understand her gratitude. Each time they touched, she was moving further away from her past, and Gage was thrilled to be a part of helping her heal the emotional scars caused by Romero. "She should be down soon."

"Why don't you tell my sister that you know exactly where Makayla—I mean, Kayla—is, and that she's happier than she's been in years?" Lillian asked, whisking batter in a glass mixing bowl. "She really needed that, you know."

Gage was extremely thankful that the other occupants in the kitchen, Nanette and Chantelle, couldn't hear his ghost. He stepped closer to Lillian and whispered, "Tell me you didn't watch us." He sure as hell had never anticipated one of his assignments watching him in the throes of lovemaking, and he sure wouldn't have wanted anyone seeing what had transpired this morning between him and Kayla. Not because he was ashamed of anything, far from it, but that would horrify and humiliate her, and he wasn't about to let anyone do that, not even her old friend.

Lillian shook her head. "Of course not. I simply sensed that both of you were immensely...pleased. And unless I really misinterpreted the sensations, I'd say Kayla was pleased at least a couple of times."

Lillian used a ladle to spoon several circles of batter onto a skillet. "I'm so happy for her. She deserves this. She deserves you. We all deserved to have that eventually— normal lives with normal relationships, and happiness."

"I'm sorry that he took your life from you," Gage said. "I wish I could have stopped him before that happened."

"I know. But it wasn't meant for me to stay here longer. It'll be better on the other side. I know it will. But I also know I won't be able to let this side go until I'm sure my sister and Shelby and Kayla will be safe from him. I don't want them going through what I went through, and I can't stand the thought of him getting what he wants—all of us dead." She frowned. "I don't understand it—I've tried to sense Romero, I swear I have, but—"

"Nothing?" Gage was totally baffled by why Lillian Bedeau wouldn't feel the presence of her killer, or at least sense his hatred toward her and the others that had put him in prison.

How could they stop him if they couldn't find him?

"Not a thing."

"What are you two talking about over there?" Nan asked. With her computer in front of her, she sat across from Chantelle and peered over the screen at Gage. "Anything happen last night that we should know about?"

Nanette could typically tell by looking at Gage whether he'd recently had sex. It used to bother him, how well she could read people, particularly him, but now he was used to it. "Nothing you need to know about, Nan."

She smirked. "Uh-huh."

Chantelle swiveled in her chair and stared at the stove, where her sister was busily cooking. "Doesn't seem fair that you're fixing all of that for us, and you can't eat."

"Tell her I'm not hungry, and that I want to do this. She knows how much I love to cook," Lillian said.

Gage relayed the message, and Chantelle nodded.

"You were a good cook. I mean, you *are* a good cook." She frowned. "Lillian?"

Lillian chewed her lower lip. "She's having a hard time—I can feel it. Can you take over here for a sec?"

"Sure." Gage grabbed a spatula and lifted the edge of a pancake, not quite golden yet. He watched as Lillian moved to her sister and wrapped an arm around her.

A heavy tear trickled down Chantelle's cheek. "I'm going to miss you when you cross over," she whispered, obviously realizing her sister was with her now.

Lillian, glowing a little brighter, glanced back at Gage. "Tell her I'll keep an eye on her, and that I'll expect her to go for her dream."

"She says that she'll watch over you, and that she wants you to achieve your dream." Gage checked the pancakes again and turned them over.

"My dream? Oh, Lillian, you mean my wanting to be a writer?" Chantelle questioned, shaking her head as more tears fell. "You know I've always been scared to show my work to anyone."

Nanette straightened in her chair. "I always tell my students to reach for their dreams. Obviously, Lillian wants you to do the same." She paused, then added, "She won't be able to communicate with you like this when she crosses over, Chantelle. So if she's telling you what she wants for you, you need to understand that it's important to her to let you know before she crosses. When Gage completes his assignment and Kayla is safe, Lillian won't get a final chance to tell you goodbye. Take advantage of your time with her now."

"Chantelle wrote stories all the time when we were growing up at Seven Sisters. It helped her cope with—everything." Lillian kissed the top of her sister's head, then returned to the stove, motioning Gage out of the way. "A lot of her writing was about the pain we went through, but she really can tell a great story, and if she sets her mind to it, I know she could sell them. I'm afraid we've all pushed our dreams aside because of our fears, and I don't want her doing that."

Gage thought of Kayla, pushing past her fears this morning when she let him bring her to orgasm. "Lillian wants you to try, to submit your stories and see what happens," Gage said, moving to the table. "It's important to her to know that you will go for your dream, particularly since Romero cut short all of her chances to reach her dreams."

Chantelle visibly pulled herself together and looked toward the stove. "I'll try, okay, sis?"

Lillian blinked back her tears. "Fair enough," she said, which Gage repeated.

Nan clicked the computer keys. "I can't find anything else on Romero, and we haven't heard from Detective Ingram. Chantelle said he is supposed to call her cellular when he gets more information. Did you find anything last night after we went to bed?"

"Nothing except the article you'd already located. I did

find an inmate-search feature at the Louisiana Department of Corrections site, though."

"And?"

"He's not there."

"What do you mean, he's not there?" Nanette asked.

"They don't have him on record at all," Gage said. "But I think if he transferred to another prison, his record would have moved to that prison. The detective should be able to tell us whether that was the case, when he calls."

"You think he was transferred?" Nan asked. "But he's obviously out now. Do you think he was paroled, or escaped? Because it seems like if someone with his history escaped, they'd tell folks. And surely the victims would be informed."

"I don't know what happened, but the corrections department office should be open now. I'll go ahead and give them a call before Kayla comes down. And I need to call Shelby Montana's ex, too. Phillip Montana may know something about where she is now."

"Yeah, he'd be the one to ask," Chantelle said. "They divorced, but they still talk. Isn't that right, Lillian?" She looked in the direction of the stove as though expecting to hear her sister's reply. At the silence, her face crumpled.

"Oh, Lillian, I wish I could talk to you, really."

Lillian looked at Gage. "Tell her that she can talk to me through you, and that I'll always be with her, even after I cross. I can, can't I? Still see her from the other side?"

Gage nodded. He did believe those on the other side kept an eye on their living loved ones, and he knew for certain that his Grandma Adeline did.

"Tell her I'm still with her, and tell her that she needs to be strong now, and to find Shelby."

Gage relayed Lillian's instructions, then watched as Chantelle sniffed through her tears. This situation had to be tough for her, even tougher because she knew her sister's killer was still out there somewhere. But Lillian was right. Chantelle would need to be strong now; they all needed to be strong now, to find and protect Shelby.

He dialed the state corrections department and inquired about Wayne Romero. By the time Gage hung up, Chantelle's face was dry.

"Well?" Nan asked.

"They said that he probably transferred, and while they should have record of it in the computer, it isn't there, so they're checking into it and are going to call me back. Evidently, sometimes things like that slip through the cracks—they forget to make the computer updates on transfers."

"Kind of a big thing to forget, don't you think?" Nan looked annoyed.

Gage nodded, and used the number Chantelle had provided to dial Shelby's ex-husband.

Phillip Montana answered on the first ring. Since Chantelle knew their relationship to be amicable, Gage leveled with the man and informed him that his ex-wife was possibly in danger from Romero. Montana wasted no time telling Gage that Shelby had checked into a rehab clinic in Slidell only a week ago, and that she was still there. He also informed Gage that he'd kill Wayne Romero himself, given the opportunity.

"Do you know how long she'll be at the clinic?" Gage asked.

"It varies," Phillip said. "I have no idea." He hesitated, then added, "Listen—I know she has a hard time dealing with her past, but I want her to let me help her work through it, instead of shutting me out. Anyway, if you see her before I do, tell her to be careful, and tell her that I love her."

Gage felt for the guy. "Can we call her while she's there?"

"No calls. That's part of the therapy, cleansing her mind

of the outside world, and all the fears that go with it. Shelby's life has been filled with fear, thanks to Romero. You can go to the clinic, though, and ask to see her. They take visitors Monday through Saturday from two until four, but the staff there will have to approve you to visit, and then Shelby can always veto seeing you. Believe me, she's done that plenty when I show. Says she doesn't want me to see her that way." He sighed heavily into the phone.

"Thanks." Gage hung up, then turned toward the women waiting at the table. "She's in a rehab clinic in Slidell, and he isn't sure how long she'll be there. They don't have Sunday visiting hours, but I can go tomorrow afternoon and see if she'll let me talk to her."

"Why can't I feel her?" Lillian asked, loading several plates with steaming pancakes.

"I don't know," Gage said.

"Don't know what?" Nan asked, reminding Gage that they hadn't heard Lillian's question.

"Why Lillian hasn't been able to sense Shelby, the way she sensed the others."

Nan frowned. "My first thought would be that, well…"

"That she's dead?" Chantelle finished.

"Honestly, yes," Nan admitted. "That's what I thought."

"I'm going to find her, see if I can see her at that clinic," Lillian said. "I should be able to do that, right?"

"I think so," Gage said.

Lillian smiled at Chantelle, who was oblivious to her sister's tender gesture, then disappeared.

"What is it?" Chantelle looked around. "She left, didn't she?"

"Lillian is going to try to see Shelby at the clinic. She'll let us know what's going on." He moved to get the next batch of pancakes off the griddle.

"Where do you think he is now?" Chantelle asked. "Romero? What do you think he's doing now, and how can we find him?"

"My guess is that he has spent whatever time he's been out of prison trying to find each of you," Gage said honestly. "He obviously found Kayla first, and attempted to hurt her again in her home, but she defended herself." He sent up a silent prayer of thanks.

"And then you think he went to Lillian? That maybe he's trying to find us based on our age?" Chantelle asked, and Gage pondered the possibility. He hadn't really thought of it that way, but it made some sense. Romero had started with the oldest girl, Kayla, then had moved to the next one in line, Lillian. Next would be Chantelle; more than likely, he had already located her home and was perhaps even watching it now.

"Yeah, that may be exactly what he's doing," Gage agreed as the kitchen door eased open and Kayla entered. She wore a white blouse and khaki shorts, part of the clothes that had been raided from Jenee's closet for her. Personally, he liked the look she'd had on when he left, her body barely covered in a rose-colored lace bra and matching panties. His cock twitched at the thought of that sexy ensemble hiding beneath the top and shorts.

Unlike the frightened woman he'd found in the alley yesterday, she was the picture of contentment, and her soft smile and admiring eyes zeroed immediately in on Gage. He wanted to have her again, give her another orgasm that made her forget the past and relish the present, and he wanted to do it right now. Unfortunately, his most observant cousin, as well as Kayla's childhood friend, were watching their every move, so he'd have to wait.

But he didn't plan to wait long.

"Kayla." Chantelle surged from her seat and quickly embraced Kayla in a hug that forced the air out of her lungs. "He—he murdered Lillian."

"I know," Kayla whispered, holding her friend. "I'm so sorry, Chantelle. She was trying to get to me at the shelter, and he found her."

Chantelle shook her head. "No, it wasn't your fault. He was following her. He'd have gotten her no matter what—but, still, oh, Kayla, I can't believe she's gone."

"I know." Kayla had a look of intense determination, and Gage understood it immediately. She wanted Romero to pay. Gage wanted the same thing.

"I'm so glad you're okay." Chantelle lowered her voice, but not enough that Gage couldn't hear. "Kayla, he—Romero—he didn't hurt you yesterday, did he? Gage said he didn't, but, I didn't know if…"

"If I was hiding the truth?" Kayla asked softly.

Chantelle nodded.

She shook her head. "No, I'm not hiding anything anymore. I'm not hiding period."

Worry creased Chantelle's forehead. "Do you think we'll be able to stop him? I mean, he already—got to Lillian."

This time, Kayla pulled Chantelle into a tight embrace, and her voice quivered as she spoke. "I'm so sorry, Chantelle."

Chantelle's face was hidden from Gage's view, cradled against Kayla's shoulder, but she sniffed loudly. "I didn't want her to see me cry while she was here. I mean, it's good that I'm getting to say goodbye before she crosses, but still, she's gone. And she died in pain."

Gage watched Kayla, her hand running up and down Chantelle's spine as she sought to comfort her friend. Kayla had to realize that she was still in danger, but she wasn't worried about herself; on the contrary, she was taking care of her friend as though Chantelle were the one whom Lillian had to save.

"Lillian isn't here?" Kayla asked. "Where is she?"

"We found out that Shelby is in a rehab clinic in Slidell, so Lillian went to try to find her," Chantelle said.

"When did she—" Kayla began, then stopped as Dax barreled through the door to the kitchen, his long, dark hair in dire need of a cut, his eyes bloodshot and his face in the early stages of a beard. Or in the late stages of a need for a shave. He was beyond looking scruffy and heading toward full-blown grunge, nothing like the clean-cut youngest Vicknair that all the cousins knew and loved.

Nanette held her fork in the air and pointed it at him as she spoke. "You didn't sleep again last night, did you? Did you work on the first floor all night?"

"Guilty as charged." Dax smiled, reminding Gage that his tenderhearted little brother was hiding somewhere in the mess of the man invading the kitchen. "And I would've kept going, but I smelled pancakes. And for the record, the work should be done in another day or so. I may call that committee and ask them to come check us out a day earlier than they planned, just to prove we're not intimidated by them."

Within seconds, Dax was seated at the table, maple syrup and melted butter nearly overflowing from his plate as he stuffed his face, an enormous glass of orange juice sitting at the ready.

"Chantelle, Kayla, this is Dax," Nan said, waving her hand toward him. "He's the most well-mannered of the cousins, in case you can't tell."

At that, Dax raised his head and snarled. "Tell me about that guy we were searching for last night," he said. "I searched the Internet and the prison databases, but found nothing. Did you get anything else?" Evidently, when Dax had taken a break from working on the house, he'd also tried to get info on Romero. A typical Vicknair, trying to help with the spirits, at the same time as he tried to save their beloved home.

"Nothing else," Gage said. "But we're hoping the detective working on Lillian's murder will have something."

"I hope he does, too," Dax said. "One, so your spirit can cross and the other women won't be in danger from that creep, and two, because I've got to go back to the day job tomorrow, and you'll need to run the show on the first-floor repairs. We're ahead of the game, but it's not completely there."

"What happened to Tristan?" Nan asked Dax.

"Got called in," Dax answered between syrupy bites. "They needed his help with a fire at one of those swamp houses in Manchak." He took a big sip of orange juice, and Gage wondered exactly how long his brother had gone without eating. Poor Dax: he still had it bad for his last ghost, Celeste. She'd stayed on this side long enough to help a young spirit cross over, but once the little girl had gone, so had Celeste…with Dax's heart.

"I'd thought that we would visit Shelby today," Gage said. "Or at least do something toward finding Romero, but we can't see her until tomorrow, and until I hear back from the state corrections department about where Romero transferred or hear something from Detective Ingram, I don't know what else to do, so I'm good to help today."

"Me, too," Nan added. "And I'm sure Jenee will, after she gets back from serving breakfast at the shelter."

"I feel like I should be doing something to help Lillian." Chantelle looked frustrated. "Or Shelby."

"You can't see Shelby today," Gage said. "And Lillian

will stay at the rehab clinic to keep an eye on her." He knew most people handled grief better when they kept their minds and bodies busy.

"You could help us out here, if you want, while we're waiting for the information to surface."

She looked somber, but nodded. "I'll help, too," Kayla said.

Nan finished her pancakes. "I'll find Chantelle and Kayla some old clothes to wear. No way do you want to get in that sludge wearing anything nice."

"That's right, nothing nice." Dax's words were slow and slurred.

"When's the last time you slept?" Gage asked, changing his tone in one fell swoop from concerned brother to determined doctor.

"Friday?" Dax questioned. "Thursday?"

Gage pulled Dax from the chair and guided him out of the kitchen. "You're not any good to us as tired as you are, and don't worry, you aren't shirking on your familial duty, either. I didn't help at all yesterday."

"From what I hear, you were saving Kayla from being murdered and getting shot at in the process. I saw your truck. It looks like hell."

"Yeah, well, I didn't do crap around here, and I'm not about to let you one-up me. So sleep and let me catch up." He pushed open the door to the hall and gently shoved his little brother through. "Can you handle the stairs?"

"Hell, I'm tired, not drunk."

"Good. Then take them on, find your room, or whatever room you come to first, and sleep."

"Doctor's orders?" Dax asked.

"Doctor's orders." Gage watched him start up the stairs. "Hell, I didn't even know he was still down here when I went to bed. I thought he'd called it a night long before. He's really got it bad for that ghost."

"I'm going to see what kind of clothes Nan found for us." Chantelle got up from the table. "And, Gage, thank you. Thank you for helping me talk with Lillian, and thank you for bringing me here to your family and to safety, until we catch Romero. I—I'm not ready to die yet." She paused. "Truthfully, I'm not ready to let Lillian go, either." She started down the hall.

Letting the kitchen door bounce back into place, Gage crossed the kitchen and sat across from Kayla. "She's having a hard time."

"I know. And I don't know how to make it better," she said, moving her fork around the edge of her pancakes, but not making any effort to take a bite.

"I think the main thing you can do—we can do—is to be here for her, and let her make her way through grieving for Lillian. Maybe working on the house today will help."

"I hope so." She lifted a small bite of pancake to her mouth and slowly chewed.

Mesmerized, he watched her swirl another tiny piece in the syrup, then slide it in her mouth.

"Gage?" she questioned.

"Yes."

"Is it wrong that so much is happening to my friends, and I am so sad about Lillian and scared for Chantelle and Shelby, and me, but still…"

"Still, what?" he asked, but he knew.

"Still I want you." She lowered her eyes to look at her plate. "I really liked that, you know. What you did to me. Tasting you."

"I liked it, too. And it's normal to turn to each other for comfort, emotionally and physically." He hesitated, wondering how to convey the power of his feelings. "Trust me, what we did this morning, and what we're thinking about now, or at least what I'm thinking about now, isn't wrong."

"I'm thinking about it, too." Her eyes lifted and Gage was drawn to the sincerity within them. She licked syrup from her lips. "How long are we going to wait?"

He couldn't remember being so aroused by watching somebody eat pancakes. One way or another, he'd have condoms before the day ended. She was ready, and Gage wanted to show her how wonderful making love could be, when it was, indeed, making love. "Tonight."

She'd obviously noticed his attention. "Want to taste?" she asked, cutting a bigger bite this time and holding the fork in midair.

Without answering, he scooted his chair closer, then placed his hand on her wrist and lowered the fork to the plate. He moved his mouth to hers, and slowly slid his tongue across her lower lip to taste the sweetness of the syrup. She moaned, pushing her mouth against his and opening it in invitation.

Gage explored her thoroughly, taking his tongue inside and teasing hers. The sugary sweetness of the syrup tantalized his palate and the exquisite sweetness of Kayla Sparks tantalized his soul.

He deftly slid the top button of her blouse open, and the second, then moved his hand inside to feel the beat of her heart, racing madly beneath his fingertips. Her head eased back and Gage broke the kiss to feast on her exposed neck, while his hand skimmed the lacy edge of her bra and cupped her breast.

"Oh," she whispered.

"Oh, yes?" he asked, only willing to go as far as she wanted.

"Yes."

His hand moved beneath the silky fabric of her bra and found the hardened pearl of her nipple. He rolled it between his thumb and forefinger, then lightly pinched it while she gasped.

"Yes?" he repeated. It was important to make sure, to verify, that this was what she wanted. That *he* was what she wanted. She was so fragile right now, no matter how strong she appeared on the surface, and he planned to be a part of what healed her, not of what harmed her. So each step of the way, each call of how far to go, was hers to make.

"Yes," she said on a breathy exhalation that caused his jeans to suddenly lose all room at the crotch.

"What do you want, Kayla?"

"I want you to make me—" She peeked over his shoulder toward the door, which both of them knew could swing open at any moment.

"I don't think it'll take me long to get you there," he promised. "You want to come, don't you?" Gage asked, his hand out of her bra now and easing toward the center of her thighs. He palmed her womanhood, pressing his fingers against the center of her shorts, and finding them warm and damp. She was so responsive to his touch, so ready to learn how to give her body completely, without fear, to him.

"Yes," she said, letting her legs drift apart as he moved his hand slightly, then slid his fingers inside.

"Yes?" he asked, fingering her clit.

"Oh, yes."

With one finger, he circled the sensitive nub, then slid down her slick folds to dip inside her hot, wet center. She leaned her head back farther, her shirt still open from where he'd teased her breast, and the rose-colored bra pushed aside, so that one perfect cinnamon nipple was exposed…and accessible.

Gage kissed it softly, licking the sensitive nub before gently pulling it with his teeth, while he moved his finger over her clitoris in tight little circles, increasing the friction with each touch, then sucking her nipple deep into his mouth. His tongue moved over the hard point in direct correlation with his finger over her clit, flicking and sucking and nibbling and circling…until her entire body stiffened beneath his touch, and then her release came, soaking her panties, her shorts and his hand.

Gage marveled at the sight of Kayla setting her desire free. He kissed her hard, wanting to possess her, to make her his own. Never had he wanted a woman so much. Never had he stopped before he also reached sexual fulfillment. But right now, with Kayla's trembling body within his arms, Gage felt anything but unfulfilled. On the contrary, he couldn't remember a moment in his life when he had felt so wonderfully, totally and completely satisfied.

10

KAYLA SAT alone in one of the rocking chairs on the plantation's porch while everyone else cleaned up after the long day. She'd taken the hottest shower she could stand in an effort to help her body relax, yet muscles that she hadn't even known existed still ached in protest of nine straight hours spent helping Gage's family shovel mud and debris from the first floor. Dax and Tristan had made a huge dent in the gunk yesterday, but there had still been plenty to do today. The entire home was barely standing, but she hadn't realized how much worse the bottom floor was until she'd stepped beyond those plastic sheets and viewed firsthand the damage done by Katrina and the smaller storms that had followed.

Though Gage and his cousins believed all contamination had been removed with their initial cleaning after Katrina, they still insisted that everyone don face masks, helmets and hazmat suits to shield them against the possibility of toxic mold, which was what the parish president, Charles Roussel, and his committee members would check for next Saturday.

Wearing the protective suit had quickly increased her body temperature, as did the physical exertion involved with the cleaning, and Kayla literally felt drained from the effort. Drained physically, but moved emotionally. Gage's family loved their home so much that they weren't willing to let the place go without a fight. Their family bond was the type of thing Kayla had experienced briefly, and missed sorely throughout most of her childhood.

With some effort, she recalled the short nine years that she'd had with her parents before they died. Happy memories prevailed, of vacations to the beach, laughing with her father as they tried out the new waterslide at the city park, sitting with her mother on the curb in front of their home and waiting for the ice cream truck to pass. She could almost taste her trademark purchase, banana-flavored ice cream in the shape of a big yellow smiley face. She and her mother would order one and share it, laughing when it dribbled down their arms as they licked their way to the stick.

Her eyes welling up, Kayla decided to leave the seclusion of the porch. With so many people around, it wouldn't be secluded for long, and she really didn't want to have to explain why she was crying. Plus, the Vicknair family was on a natural high from the results of their day's labor. The first floor actually looked more like the inside of a home now, instead of a riverbank, and they were pleased with the progress. Chantelle, on the other hand, had also retreated from the family, saying she was tired and wanted to rest in her room. Kayla knew her friend well enough to know that she'd simply needed time alone, to think about all that had happened, and deal with the fact that Lillian was gone.

Kayla needed time alone, too, to think about Lillian, her parents and…Gage. He was inside the house, not far from her at all, and yet she still yearned for him to be closer. It amazed her how it felt as if he was already a part of her, as though they belonged together, and without him, her life simply would never be complete. It made her feel warm inside, the way she'd felt in his arms this morning, when he'd held her in the kitchen. But it also terrified her. How could she be so close to someone she'd just met?

A warm, early evening breeze from the Mississippi River blew over the levee and softly whistled as it stirred the magnolia branches lining the driveway to the plantation. A tiny opening led to a narrow path through the cane, and Kayla proceeded down it, surrounded by thick reeds on both sides.

She inhaled the smell of the cane around her. The scent, sugary and sweet, should have lifted her spirit; instead, it only reminded her of how much she had missed out on during those teen years, when the Vicknair kids were probably all helping with the cane harvest, enjoying time with their family on the plantation…having normal lives.

Her formative years had been filled with the fear of a man who abused her on a regular basis. She had her friends, and she had Ms. Rosa. But even with all of them, it wasn't the same as a real family.

Blinking back her tears, she moved deeper into the field. The tall reeds completely enclosed her, and she welcomed the reprieve from the real world, where a killer still loomed, determined to make her pay for his incarceration. Kayla found herself at an opening in the field, where a small circle of cane lay flat against the ground. Puzzled, she stopped walking and stared at the area, a tiny cove within the soaring cane.

"Heavy rains do that, make the stalks lean over in spots."

Startled, Kayla turned toward the husky voice and saw Gage. Wearing a bright turquoise T-shirt and well-worn jeans with a hole in one thigh, he looked, in a word, perfect.

As dismal as she'd felt only moments ago, she suddenly felt better. Much better. She imagined the sight of Dr. Gage

Vicknair made lots of women feel better, whether they were sick or sad or not.

His broad chest, his slim hips, his muscled thighs— Kayla remembered all of those intriguing features from their shower this morning, and her center tingled at the sudden rush of heat from the memory.

"Your eyes are incredible." She hadn't meant to state the obvious, but the turquoise shirt intensified the vivid blue, and she simply couldn't resist the chance to tell him.

He grinned. "You always say exactly what you're thinking?"

"No." In fact, she was rather shocked that she had. "Usually, I keep what I'm thinking inside."

"But not with me?"

"Evidently not. Or at least not when your eyes are making my breath catch."

"According to the all-knowing Nanette, my eyes change colors, or at least shades of blue, based on what I'm wearing."

"You've never checked it out yourself?"

He laughed. "Nope. If I stood around looking in the mirror to see what color my eyes were for a given outfit, I'd be a bit concerned."

She grinned at that. No, Gage Vicknair wasn't the vain type, but then again, why should he be? He didn't have any reason to worry about his appearance. "Well, today they're turquoise, almost electric."

"Electric," he repeated. "Sounds dangerous."

"Oh, they're dangerous," she said, enjoying the flirtatious banter between them. She was so comfortable with him, felt so right with him. Relaxed.

He moved closer, and she noticed a thick blanket draped over his right arm.

"What's that for?"

Gage unfolded it and fanned it over the fallen cane. Then he turned to Kayla, stepped so close that the heat of his body seeped into her flesh, and ran his hands smoothly up and down her arms. "I saw you walk into the field, and I decided to follow," he murmured, his words feathering against her ear as he nuzzled her neck.

"That doesn't explain why you brought the blanket."

He softly kissed her ear, then lifted his head to look at her. Have mercy, those eyes *were* dangerous.

"Let's just say I knew about the hidden alcoves within the cane, and I thought we might make the most of one of them."

There was no denying the lust in his mesmerizing gaze, and Kayla's insides quivered.

"Here?" she asked.

"Not necessarily everything," he said. "Unless that's what you want, Kayla. That's what I'm offering now, whatever you want."

She took a deep breath of sweet, cane-scented air, and decided that Gage Vicknair had given her nothing short of the truth, about anything, and she would give him no less. "I want you."

"You want…" He waited for her to complete the sentence, and Kayla didn't waiver.

"I want everything, now, here, with you. But—"

"But?"

"But I've never been with a man that way. I mean, I've had a man take my body, but I've never given it. And, I won't lie—I'm scared. I want to make love with you, Gage, and I don't want to wait anymore. But you may have to, you know, take it easy with me, the first time."

He smoothed his hands over her hair, then cradled her face within his palms. The tender gesture had her eyes watering, and she wondered if she would be able to follow through with what she'd started. She did want him, but she didn't want to be so emotional about it that she cried throughout their first time. Nonetheless, her tears began to fall.

"Kayla." His voice was so soothing and kind that her tears came even faster. "We don't have to, honey."

She shook her head. "Please. No. I don't want to stop, I want this. And I don't know why I'm crying. Maybe because I can't believe that this is real, that you are real. I dreamed of you, and in my dreams, I gave myself completely. That's what I want, to give myself completely to you."

He slid the pads of his thumbs down her cheeks to brush the tears away. "Are you sure?"

She nodded. She couldn't remember ever being more sure of anything.

"I'd planned on our first time being in a bed, but this *is* even more private than the house. Plus, there's the adventure factor…"

"I'll say there is," she said, smiling through her tears, and very much wanting adventure with Gage Vicknair. Then she tilted her head in question, and prayed he had the right answer. "What about protection?"

"Remember your long shower?"

She nodded. Part of the reason she'd stayed in there long enough to turn prunish was because she thought he might eventually join her. It hadn't happened, and she'd nearly given in to the urge to bring herself to climax within the hot water, but she'd resisted. She wanted to come, but she wanted to come with Gage. "Yeah, I remember."

"While you were in there, I took a trip to the store. We're taken care of, darling, for as much as you want."

As much as you want. She really liked the sound of that. Kayla hadn't ever really *wanted* a man. She'd wanted to experience what other women talked about, that desire to have a man touch her, caress her, make her scream in pleasure. But every time she thought about giving herself to a man, *pain* was what she remembered.

She wanted to erase those memories and make new ones in their place, right now, with Gage. As if sensing her thoughts, he pulled her so close that there was no denying the bulge in his pants, or the heat between her legs. His hands shimmied beneath the hem of her brown tank top and gently caressed her abdomen, her waist, and then her back, until her body melted against his.

"You feel so good, Kayla, soft and smooth and warm."

She eased away from him and lifted her arms, waiting for him to slide her shirt over her head. Then she moved against him again, reveling in the heat, in the power, of his big male body against her smaller female one. This was the way being held by a man should feel, safe and secure and incredibly arousing. She was definitely aroused now, from the ache in her nipples, brushing against the soft fabric of his shirt, to the dampness between her thighs.

She glanced at the quilt, lumpy from the cane reeds beneath it. "That doesn't look all that comfortable."

"It isn't," he admitted, "but it'll add to the adventure, and to the memory we're about to make together."

It isn't. How did he know?

"You've done this before?" she asked, then immediately wished she hadn't. He'd already stated that he didn't fare well when he went too long without sex, and she didn't really want to know the details of his sexual escapades.

Kayla frowned. That wasn't totally true. She *did* want to know, at least about this, because it was their first time, and she didn't want it to be a repetition of something he'd done before.

Gage placed a knuckle under her chin and tilted her head

to look directly into her eyes. "I've never done this before," he said. "I just know that cane isn't exactly something I'd think of as mattress-soft, but I promise you'll enjoy it anyway. However, if you'd rather go back to the house and to my bedroom…"

"No," she whispered. An entire army couldn't get her to leave this cane field now, not until she'd experienced *everything* with Gage.

"Good," he mumbled, occupied with palming her breasts and running his thumb over the hardened points.

The action sent an arrow of desire straight to her uterus, and she shivered.

"Cold?"

"No." She was on fire, for him.

"You didn't wear a bra," he said, his hands still paying homage to her breasts in the most amazing way.

"There's one in my top." She gasped as he unbuttoned her jeans and eased them down her hips. "A shelf bra…made into it." Kayla struggled with her words, since her mind was dizzy with the friction of her jeans and his hands sliding down her legs and the breeze from the levee teasing her wet center.

"I'm guessing Jenee picked it out." He guided her to step out of the jeans and onto the blanket. Her feet wobbled on the cloth-covered cane, and he caught her hips to steady her.

"Yeah, Jenee did." He put her jeans on top of her shirt, then lowered to his knees and kissed the front of her panties.

"Remind me to thank her." His voice was a husky growl, and Kayla felt lightheaded as he kissed her navel, nibbling a slow path down the lower portion of her belly to the top of her panties, and then, while she moaned her agreement, to her clitoris.

"Gage?" She stood naked except for the tiny scrap of

fabric between her legs, a wedge of cloth drenched with desire and currently driving her mad, because the mouth that kissed the flimsy fabric could be kissing *her* if it was gone. Now that she was giving herself to him completely, she didn't want anything less from him.

"Yeah?" he asked, his mouth moving against the sensitive area between her inner thigh and her labia. She eased her legs wider to give him better access, and her hands gripped his hair, holding him *there,* where she wanted him so desperately.

"Please."

"Please what, Kayla? What do you want?"

"Take them off," she answered. "I've felt you doing this, exactly this, in my dreams. But now, with you here, I want to see it and feel it, to know that this time, it's real. That you're really here, and that we're making love. I don't want any clothing between us. I don't want anything between us." She meant what she said. She didn't want anything between them, physically or emotionally. Her emotions were open to him, all barriers down, all obstacles gone. There was nothing right now but the two of them, beneath the darkening sky and in the midst of a towering cane field. It was beautiful, what they were doing together, and what she was feeling with Gage. She wanted to feel him, all of him, against her, and she didn't want to wait any longer. She'd waited for this, to be with a man without fear, for as long as she could remember. She couldn't wait any more.

His fingers slipped beneath the tiny straps at both hips, then slid the wet cloth away. Again, the warm breeze from the levee kissed her heated intimate flesh to make her quiver all over.

"I want you inside me," she said. "I need you inside."

"I want that, too—after you come for me." His hands moved up her outer thighs and slid to her bottom, massaging her while he distributed hot, intense kisses to her clitoris, and her entire body trembled with need.

Kayla fisted her hands in his hair and watched in fascination as he thoroughly feasted on her, licking and nibbling and sucking. His hands grabbed her fiercely, pushed her pelvis forward against his mouth, his tongue and his teeth. She sucked in an audible breath and prepared to let go. Gage, obviously knowing how very close she was, pulled her clit between his teeth. Kayla's hips bucked wildly and her climax burst forth in a maddening rush that had her body shuddering uncontrollably.

He cradled her, and lowered her to the quilt. "Now you're ready." Gage kissed her, and tenderly pushed her hair away from her face. "You taste so sweet, Kayla," he said, running his hand down her abdomen, and then dipping a finger into her vagina. Her eyes widened as he brought the finger to his lips, sucked her moisture away, then kissed her again. His tongue teased hers, and the realization that *she* was on his tongue drove her desire even higher.

She'd had enough of waiting—her body was on fire and had to be touched deep inside. Kayla clutched at his T-shirt and pulled it free of his jeans. "I need you. I need you now, and I need to know how it can be, how it's supposed to be."

He brought one hand to her wrist and stopped her from removing his shirt, and Kayla knew she'd messed up. Why had she reminded him that this really *was* her first time, not merely with him, but with any man?

"Gage?"

With his jaw clenched tight, he glanced down at her body, completely nude and ready to be touched, every-where, by him. Her hips moved in slow circles as she waited for him to give her what she so desperately desired.

"Don't stop," she whispered. "Please."

"What if I hurt you?" he asked. "And I'm not just talking physically, but—hell, Kayla, what if I start making love to you, and then you start remembering what happened before? Once we start—once I start—I'm not sure I can stop. I want you too much."

"I don't want you to stop. I won't ask you to." He didn't look convinced, but Kayla was: Gage Vicknair wouldn't hurt her, ever. She knew that deep in her heart, and she wasn't about to go another minute without showing him how much she believed that by giving him what she'd never given any man.

She wiggled her wrist free from his palm and pushed his shirt up his torso, until he had to raise up to remove it the entire way. He tossed it aside, but still looked hesitant about what he was doing, and what they were about to do.

"Don't stop, Gage, please," she urged. "Don't let him do this to us now. He took everything from me back then, my virginity, my childhood, my innocence—everything. And he left me with nothing but fear. Now I'm ready to move on, and I'm starting to. I want more, Gage. I want you completely, and I want to know what that's like, to be with a man—with you—that way. Don't let him win again. Don't let him keep me from having what I want so much."

Gage rolled away from her, and Kayla wanted to cry out in despair. Without even being here, Romero had taken away her chance to make love to a man. Then Gage lifted his hips and in one smooth motion, removed his jeans and underwear. His erection was hard and long and…exactly what she wanted.

"I promise you, Kayla," he said, removing a foil packet

from his pocket, tossing the jeans aside and then rolling back toward her, "I'll never keep you from having anything you want."

She took her hand to his cheek, gently brushed her fingertips along the line of his jaw to the back of his neck. Then she brought his mouth to hers and pulled him on top of her with a deep, probing kiss. The cane snapped and popped as his weight pressed against her, and the reeds pushed harshly against her back through the blanket. But none of that mattered. All that mattered was that she was finally about to experience the wonder of making love.

"You set the pace," he instructed, easing her legs apart with his thighs then nudging her opening with his penis. "Fast, slow, hard, easy. Promise me that you'll tell me what you like, and what you don't. This is all for you, Kayla."

"You trying to tell me you won't enjoy it, too?" she asked, smiling in absolute exhilaration that, within a matter of seconds, Gage Vicknair would be inside of her.

"Hell, no." Those blue eyes were getting darker in intensity in direct correlation to the night sky, converting from ocean blue to indigo as the sun dipped farther. "I'm going to enjoy every—" he pushed the head of his penis into her, then eased it in deep "—stroke."

Kayla bit her lower lip and accepted his length with some effort. She'd realized he was long, but the width of him was something she hadn't prepared for. She could literally feel her body stretching to take him, then he withdrew to the edge of her vagina before slowly moving back in, even farther than before. She looked down her body and saw his ripped abdomen flexing as he apparently struggled to keep the exceptionally slow pace of his fluid strokes. His hands braced against the quilt on both sides of her head, and the reeds beneath them broke loudly with every stroke.

The fact that he was so controlled, that he was being so careful, was driving her mad. This wasn't what she wanted. She wanted to know that her body could let go entirely with a man inside of her, and right now, he was being too cautious, obviously afraid of the past creeping back in.

But Kayla wasn't thinking about the past. It was a mere shadow, a ghost in the back of her mind that she would not let free. She was focused on Gage—she wanted to break down *his* barrier of control and see *him* let go.

"Am—I hurting you?" he asked, beads of sweat forming on his brow as he moved back into her again.

Kayla watched the two of them join, and realized that he *still* hadn't pushed himself all the way inside. "No," she said, and without thinking about the consequences, she rammed her hips upward, taking all of him in one hard slide, then pulled back and surged upward again, this time feeling a delicious pleasure when he touched her deep inside. "Give me everything, Gage. Make love to me. Let go for me. I need this. I need *you.*"

With a fierce growl of satisfaction, Gage claimed her mouth with his tongue and thrust his hips against hers to push his penis even deeper, then, with another growl emanating from his chest, he let his passion take control. Kayla's body literally shook with the power of his thrusts, and she matched his rhythm, pushing against his advances and taking everything he offered.

The cane bruised her back, but the pain only intensified her awareness of what was happening. Gage Vicknair was inside of her, making love to her, showing her that, in spite of the past, she could give herself to a man, give herself to Gage.

His strokes got faster, his breathing got quicker and Kayla realized that he was nearing the edge. Determined to feel every bit of his release, she wrapped her legs behind his back, forcefully pumping her hips to his, and was rewarded with the guttural growl of Gage Vicknair's climax.

Kayla's tears fell, even as his body jerked through the after-shudders of his release, but they weren't tears of pain or of sorrow. She'd given herself, completely, without holding back, and at long last, she knew exactly how it felt to be whole.

11

GAGE BARELY REGISTERED the sheet on his bed lifting slightly as he slept. Even the hand tapping his arm didn't cause him to stir, though it was past noon on Monday. But when the same hand squeezed his bicep, then shook him with enough strength to make his eyelids pop open in the blinding overhead light, he finally paid attention.

"I know you're tired, but you have to help," Lillian insisted, her glowing face set in fierce purpose. "Something isn't right with Shelby."

Still squinting in the light, Gage sat up and tried to get his bearings. Once again, he wasn't at his apartment; he was in his old room at the plantation. And once again, he wasn't alone. To emphasize the fact, Kayla rolled over and moaned softly, then snuggled her head into the pillow and returned to sleep. Bless her heart, she was exhausted from their near-all-night session of lovemaking. Lovemaking that had occurred with the big, bold overhead light glaring throughout, and then remaining on as they'd finally gone to sleep.

Funny, in the past, he'd always been turned on by having sex in the light of day, or night, as the case may be, but with Kayla, he hoped that eventually she'd be comfortable in the darkness of the night.

Lillian tapped the empty condom packages on the bedside table. "Busy night?" Then she shook her head.

"No, don't tell me. I really don't want details, but I'm so happy for Kayla that she has found someone who makes her forget about the pain of her past." She looked up at the light. "Or almost forget."

Gage winced. She was right. Until that light was extinguished during their lovemaking, there would always be a symbol of Wayne Romero in the room when they made love. At least the overhead light hadn't been there the first time, when they'd claimed each other's bodies in the cane field, but then again, it hadn't been dark outside, either, with the last remnants of the setting sun.

"She's making progress, and it's all because of you," Lillian consoled. "You can't expect her to get better all at once. It takes time. And she's been through quite an ordeal over the past two weeks, with him attacking her, and then losing her memory, spending time at the homeless shelter and then learning of my death. The fact that she has become comfortable enough to share her body with you is incredible."

"I know," Gage said, eyeing the beautiful woman in his bed. Her brown hair fanned across the pillow and one arm curled beneath it, hugging it the way she'd hugged Gage throughout last night. He'd been drawn to her in his dreams, had thought the reality couldn't equal, much less surpass, the emotional pull that he'd felt toward this woman. But he'd been wrong. She was a part of him, completed him, and joining with her in the most intimate way had been nothing short of earth-shattering. "I still want her to trust me enough to let me make love to her in the dark, eventually."

"She will, I think." Lillian tugged on his arm again. "But right now, I need to tell you about Shelby. And I need you to call the place where she's staying."

With Lillian pulling on his wrist, Gage followed her out of his room and into the hall. He was thankful that he'd slipped his shorts back on last night before finally succumbing to sleep, otherwise, he'd be giving Lillian an interesting show right now.

She released his arm when they reached the stairs. "Come on."

Gage paused a moment and looked at his wrist, then at his ghost. "You touched me."

Lillian nodded. "I had to. I couldn't get you to wake up, and I don't think we're going to be able to wait until visiting hours to see Shelby."

"What do you mean? And how did you touch me?"

"Mediums can't touch spirits, but there's no rule at all that says we can't touch you."

Gage realized she was right.

"None of your assignments has ever touched you before?" she asked.

"Most of them are just trying to get the hell out of Dodge." Descending the staircase, he heard cussing from the other side of one of the plastic sheets. It was Tristan, but Gage knew his older cousin well enough to know that he was merely working the only way he knew how, with a surplus of colorful language.

"He's okay," Lillian said, grabbing Gage's arm again and pulling him toward the kitchen.

"I know." Gage didn't even slow as they passed the plastic sheets. That was one thing about the Vicknair family: if one cousin had an assignment, the others took up the slack with other family duties and let that medium concentrate on helping their spirit to cross—not that Gage had made much progress there yet. Detective Ingram had called last night saying he still hadn't learned where

Romero had been transferred after leaving the Louisiana pen. Apparently it wasn't a top priority to keep track of convicted rapists in the system.

"I think Shelby's in danger," Lillian said bluntly, taking Gage's attention away from his frustration with the lack of information on Romero.

"What!" They entered the kitchen, where Chantelle was sitting behind Nanette's laptop, staring at the screen. "Is Romero at the clinic? How would he have known she was there?"

"What's happening?" Chantelle asked. "Is Lillian with you?"

"In a minute," he said quickly.

"No, Romero isn't there," Lillian clarified. "And I stayed at her bedside all night, so I'm sure of that. But when she woke this morning, she was upset, and when I left, she had her suitcase on the bed and was flinging all of her clothes inside. That was about—" she glanced at the digital clock on the microwave "—ten minutes ago."

"But her ex said she wouldn't be leaving for a while," Gage reminded her.

"I know that's what he said, but I also know that she sure looks like she's getting ready to go." Lillian picked up the phone from the counter and dialed a number, then handed the receiver to Gage. "Here. Ask them about her status. Tell them you heard she was going home today, or something, and make sure she's still there. Then ask them if you can see her earlier than normal visiting hours."

"You realize I had a cell phone upstairs, by the bed?"

Lillian glared. "I didn't notice it. Just ask them, okay?"

"What's Lillian saying? It's Shelby, right? Is she okay?" Chantelle asked.

"I'm going to find out," Gage assured her.

"Tell me what's happening, as soon as you can."

Gage noted Chantelle's clothing, the same shirt and jeans she'd had on last night, and her hair, messy and frazzled, as though she'd run her hands through it in frustration repeatedly. Her eyes were red and watery, too. "You didn't sleep."

"No, she didn't," Lillian replied. "I sensed her all night, determined to help you get information on Romero. She's been on that computer for hours, but she hasn't found any more than you already did. Bless her heart, she never could sleep when she was upset." Lillian moved from Gage and wrapped a protective arm around her sister.

Chantelle's head tilted toward Lillian's embrace, as though she knew Lillian was trying to hold her, really hold her, one more time.

"I couldn't sleep," she whispered, more to Lillian than to Gage. "I was so worried for all of us, and I still can't get over the fact that you're gone," she ended on a tired whimper.

"I know," Lillian said, stroking Chantelle's hair. "I know."

Gage didn't have to relay Lillian's words to her sister. He knew that the two of them were sharing one last moment of bonding before Lillian crossed, and he didn't want to ruin it. So he remained silent while he waited for someone at the clinic to pick up the phone.

"Slidell Rehab. May I help you?"

"Hello, this is Dr. Gage Vicknair, from Ochsner," he said, deciding to bring in his medical credentials to bypass standard protocol. He knew it probably wouldn't work, but hell, it was worth a try. As Lillian had said, Shelby could be in danger if she left that clinic on her own. "I'm calling to check on one of your patients, Shelby Montana."

"Are you a member of her family, Dr. Vicknair? Because

I don't have you listed on Ms. Montana's list of attending physicians."

So much for using his credentials. "No, I'm not a member of the family. I'm a—friend." Being called to save her life qualified him as a friend, didn't it? "And I'm concerned that Ms. Montana may be in danger and wanted to verify her safety at the clinic."

"I assure you that all of our patients are safe here, Dr. Vicknair," the woman said coolly.

Great. He'd insulted her, and that certainly wasn't going to help him get information. "Oh, I wasn't referring to her safety there. I was concerned that she might leave the clinic too soon."

"Dr. Vicknair, if you are indeed a friend of Ms. Montana's, then you know that she voluntarily checked herself into our facility and, as such, can voluntarily check herself out at any time." Her voice still snapped with an air of coolness, and Gage's heartbeat stepped up the pace. If Shelby was packing, and decided to go…

"Is she still there?" he asked.

"You know I can't give you that information. However, you may visit our clinic during normal visiting hours and request to see a patient. If that patient is still at the facility, and if that patient authorizes your visitation, then you may see for yourself."

"Thanks," Gage said sarcastically, and hung up. He turned to Lillian. "Can you sense her now? Is she still there?"

"I can't sense her at all," Lillian admitted. "That's why I stayed with her last night. I have to actually be with her in order to see what she's doing. I think it's because of her current state of mind. She's so lost within herself. Maybe it's from the drugs. She's obviously going through withdrawal from something. In any case, the only way I can keep up with Shelby is to stay with her, but I'm afraid she's going to try to leave today, and if Romero is out there, near her apartment or her work or wherever, and she returns in her current state, it won't take much for him to get to her and hurt her again."

"I have no doubt that Romero is probably watching Chantelle and Shelby's homes and jobs, and maybe Kayla's, as well, since he's probably still trying to figure out who took her from the alley. Where does Shelby work?" Gage asked.

"The last time I talked to her, she said she'd gotten a job at the Esplanade Mall in Kenner," Lillian said.

"Where does who work?" Chantelle was listening to Gage's end of the conversation. "Shelby?"

"Yeah."

"The Esplanade Mall in Kenner," Chantelle supplied, unaware that Lillian had already said the same thing. "I don't know which store, or if she still works at all, but she did mention the mall the last time I saw her. You could call her husband—I mean, ex-husband—Phillip and ask. He'd know."

"Lillian, you go stay with her and let me know if and when she leaves the clinic. I don't want to risk the chance of her leaving and us not being able to find her before Romero does," Gage insisted.

Lillian nodded, and disappeared.

"What do you want me to do?" Chantelle asked.

"I'm going to take Kayla with me, in case I do see Shelby. Maybe she'll trust me if she's there. Do you want to come—?"

"Yes," Chantelle answered before he finished the question. "I'll get ready while you get Kayla."

Gage took the stairs two at a time, which was a bit difficult due to the warped ones along the way. When he reached his room, he found the bed empty and heard the blow dryer going in the bathroom. He pushed the bathroom door open and saw Kayla wrapped in a towel with both arms in midair, one holding a brush and the other the dryer. She turned to him and smiled. "I was going to come down in a second," she said, then lifted one brow, "and I didn't expect you to leave me sleeping alone."

"Sorry." This was really something, two days of waking up with a woman in his arms. He could really get used to it, particularly if the woman was Kayla Sparks. "But Lillian is afraid Shelby may try to leave the clinic this morning. If she leaves and Lillian isn't there to see where she's going, Romero could find her before we do. But Lillian is with her now."

"Oh, my," Kayla gasped. "We need to get to Slidell then, right?"

"As soon as we get ready. Lillian will keep us informed of whether she's still there, or if she leaves. Chantelle is going with us, too, so Shelby can see the two of you with me and realize that she can trust me."

"I'm almost done." Kayla turned toward the mirror. She tilted her head to the side as she dried her hair, and Gage focused on her back, and a dark bruise peeking above the top edge of her towel.

"What's that?" he asked, moving closer and tenderly touching the discolored skin.

She winced, then forced a small smile. "That cane field was a little rough, even with the quilt."

"Damn." He reached around her and gently tugged at the spot where the towel was tucked between her breasts, pulling it free.

"It's not as bad as it looks," she said, but Gage begged to differ. There were three big bruises on her back, and several small ones in between.

"What was I thinking?"

She flipped the switch on the dryer and turned to face him. The bruises shone brightly in the reflection of the mirror, and Gage shook his head in disgust. Heightening her pleasure? More like hurting her…again. And she'd been hurt enough. "I…don't know what to say."

She reached down and grabbed the towel from the floor, and tucked it back in place. "Well, I know exactly what to say. Thank you. Thank you for making love to me in a place where you never made love before. And thank you for realizing that it would take something unique to distract my mind while I made love, truly made love, for the first time. Something that would bring me to the most amazing climaxes, with you deep inside." Kayla stepped closer to him, rose up on her toes and kissed him softly. "Those bruises will heal," she whispered. "All of my bruises will heal, in fact, and you're the one responsible for making that happen."

Within fifteen minutes, Gage had commandeered Tristan's Jeep, since his own truck was still out of commission due to the shooting, and the three of them were headed down River Road en route to the rehab clinic in Slidell.

"How long will it take us to get there?" Kayla had to raise her voice to be heard over the wind rushing through the open windows. She squinted as her hair whipped around her face and fluttered against her eyes.

"About an hour and a half, if the traffic isn't bad in New Orleans." He glanced at the clock on the dash. "We're in the middle of lunch hour, though, so it could be slow."

"Will we get there by the time visiting hours start?" Chantelle asked from the backseat, while Kayla worked to hold her hair back with her hand to keep it from attacking her eyes. Chantelle had worn her blond waves in a ponytail, so she wasn't having the same difficulty.

Gage withdrew a pair of sunglasses from the glove box and handed them to Kayla. "These will help."

"Thanks," she said, slipping them on. "So, will we be there in time?"

"We shouldn't have any problem getting there by two, but if she leaves early, as Lillian believes she might, we could have a hell of a time finding her."

"But Lillian can tell us where she goes, right?" Chantelle sounded concerned.

"Yeah, she'll be able to watch her leave, but it'd really help if we knew where she was heading if she did." He pulled his cell phone out of his pocket and handed it to Chantelle. "Here. I programmed Phillip Montana's number in. Does he know you?"

"Yeah, he knows me," she said. "I mean, I met him at the wedding, and have seen him a few times since they married, so he should remember me."

"Call him and ask him where she works. If she's still at the mall, find out which store. At least then we'll have two points to watch for her, home and work. Esplanade Mall is right down the street from her apartment, and that'd make it easy for us to be in the general area, whether she goes back home, or to her job."

"Do you really think she'd leave a rehab clinic and head to work?" Kayla asked, while Chantelle punched the buttons on his phone to find Phillip's number.

"I'm actually leaning toward that," Gage admitted. "She's been in rehab for a week, and now it's a Monday and the beginning of a work week, so she may feel the need to go to work and get paid."

Kayla looked skeptical, as though she really didn't think that was something Shelby would do, and maybe it wasn't. She did know Shelby and would definitely have a better handle on her friend's mind-set than Gage. But either way, he wanted to be prepared.

Chantelle was talking to Shelby's ex when Gage pulled onto I-10, and Lillian appeared in the backseat next to her sister.

"What's happening?" he asked her. Kayla leaned forward to listen as Chantelle continued talking to Montana.

"She's telling the nurses that she's going to leave, and they're trying to talk her out of it."

"Do you know where she's going?"

"Just a second, Phillip," Chantelle said, then cupped her hand over the phone's speaker. "Lillian's here? Does she know where Shelby is going?"

"No," Lillian answered, and Gage shook his head.

"No, we don't know where she may go, Phillip," Chantelle relayed. "And I can't tell you why we think she's leaving the clinic, but we do. Sure, I think that'd be a great idea. Okay." She disconnected. "He said he's going to personally check on Shelby at the clinic, though he doubts they'll let him in or tell him anything until visiting hours. Anyway, he's going to call me back if he gets any information, or if he learns anything about her leaving. He also said that the place where she works is located near the food court at the Esplanade Mall. It's a jewelry store."

"How did he sound?" Gage asked. "Did he believe you?"

"I think so," Chantelle said. "I just hope that maybe, if he gets there before she leaves, he can talk her into staying at the clinic. If Romero doesn't know she's there, then that's the safest place for her to stay, until all of this over. I think you're right, that he's probably watching places where he believes we'll be."

"And he's probably pretty ticked that he hasn't found us," Kayla added, and Gage nodded. *Ticked* wasn't the word he'd choose. Romero was probably stark raving mad and hotter than hell. "I really wish she'd stay at the clinic."

"But she doesn't know Romero is after her yet," Gage pointed out, accelerating, then slamming on the brake when traffic came to a standstill past the Clearview exit. "Damn." He shot a look at the ghost in the backseat. "Go see if she's still there, Lillian, and let us know if she leaves."

She nodded, then left.

"I hope she doesn't leave," Gage said. "But if she does, we have *got* to find her first." He leaned out of the Jeep and surveyed the congested traffic ahead. He couldn't even see the reason for the holdup, whether an accident or stalled car or something else entirely. For whatever reason, they were stuck here for a while. He just hoped Shelby Montana stayed put until they could get through New Orleans.

Fifteen minutes later, they'd progressed only twenty feet, and they didn't look to be moving faster anytime soon. The breeze they'd felt on River Road was nonexistent on the heated interstate, and Gage's frustration level was high. They had to get across town, and this interstate was the only way he knew of to do it.

Kayla rolled up her window and turned the air on. Gage knew the air conditioning in the Jeep couldn't adequately cool them when the thing wasn't moving and when the temperature was nearing a hundred, but even a semicool air-conditioning system was better than the blazing heat of New Orleans in the afternoon. He rolled his window up, too, and welcomed what little bit of coolness the vehicle generated.

"Lillian hasn't returned?" Kayla asked.

"No," Chantelle replied, obviously able to sense her sister's appearances now.

"Which is good. If she did, that'd mean that Shelby—" Gage stopped talking when he felt Lillian's distress. Even before she appeared, he knew she was coming, part of the bonding process that occurred between a medium and an assigned spirit. Gage and Lillian's bond had evidently progressed enough that he could tell she was panicked now. "What is it?" he asked.

"Lillian?" Chantelle questioned. "What's going on?"

"Shelby left the clinic," Lillian said frantically. "I have no idea where she's going, but she signed herself out, and she's walking to her car right now. I've got a few minutes, because the head nurse is trying to stop her, but I don't think Shelby's going to change her mind."

"Stay with her," Gage said, "and do your best to let me know what's happening, where she's going, but don't leave her again."

"I—don't know if I can."

Gage realized she was probably right. Even though he could sense Lillian's emotions, he wasn't in tune with her well enough for her to mentally tell him where he should go to find Shelby. "Okay. If you can't tell me without leaving her, then check back with us occasionally, but don't leave her longer than you have to. You have to be there if Romero shows, to stop him."

"Stop him how?" Lillian asked. "I can't kill him." She paused. "Can I?"

Could a ghost kill someone? Gage had never even considered the possibility before. "I'm not asking you to kill him," he said, and Kayla's eyes widened. "Just stop him from hurting her, if he gets to her before we do."

Lillian disappeared, while Gage put on his blinker and prayed that he could make it across four lanes of virtually standstill traffic before the next exit. If Shelby went home or to work, she'd have to travel in the opposite direction and would probably take the Williams Boulevard exit, the same exit Gage took every day when he went to his apartment. He knew the roads there well, and he'd simply find a point halfway between her apartment and the Esplanade Mall and wait until he heard from Lillian about her destination. Then he'd hightail it there and find her before Romero did.

No pressure.

So why did he feel as if his head was going to explode?

"Let me over," he growled, as another eighteen-wheeler crept past him, disregarding Gage's blinker. He looked at the opposite side of the interstate and realized with dismay that there was hardly any traffic heading out of New Orleans, the way Shelby would travel to get to her apartment or job. If he couldn't move over quickly enough, she'd end up ahead of him and would probably arrive at home, or work or wherever before Gage had a chance to catch her.

Would Romero be waiting for her? Or was Gage worrying for no reason at all? Perhaps Romero was staking out Chantelle's house right now, or Kayla's place, and he, Kayla and Chantelle would simply find Shelby and convince her to go to the plantation until they caught the killer.

He finally wedged over one lane between the eighteen-wheeler and an old clunker. The guy in the clunker sat on the horn and waved a fist at Gage when the Jeep's entry made him slam on his brakes. "Get over it," Gage said, and put his blinker on again.

"Why won't they let us over?" Kayla leaned out of the Jeep and waved to a woman in the next lane. "Let us in, please!" she yelled desperately.

"Emergency!" Chantelle screamed, sticking her head out the window as well in a determined effort to help.

The woman slowed her car, and Gage moved over, while

Kayla and Chantelle waved their thanks. "Think you can get us one more?" The exit was extremely close. If need be, he totally planned to stop the Jeep and sit there until one of these idiots stopped and let him in. A woman's life was at stake, dammit, and they were playing King of the Road.

Car.

Gage heard the whispered word at the same time as he jerked the Jeep in front of an SUV to veer up the Causeway exit ramp. "Lillian?"

"Is she here?" Kayla asked.

"No, but I heard her." He surveyed the line of cars in front of him on the ramp. Technically, he wasn't even within the New Orleans city limit yet, but this traffic wasn't letting up. He needed to get to the other side of the interstate, and quickly. "What about a car, Lillian?"

Blue. Neon.

"She's in a blue Neon," he said to Kayla.

Esplanade.

"Esplanade," he repeated.

"The mall?" Chantelle asked. "Is that where Lillian says she's going?"

Gage nodded, focusing his mind on hearing anything else Lillian could offer. He reached the top of the ramp and turned left to cross over I-10, then he got in the turn lane to get back on the interstate and return to Williams Boulevard, merely a block from the Esplanade Mall and three blocks from her apartment.

Esplanade…Road.

"Hell." Gage jerked the car out of the turn lane. "She wasn't talking about the mall," he said, accelerating now that he was away from the city-bound traffic. "She's taking the side route to Kenner." He steered the Jeep past the interstate toward Esplanade Road.

"So she's going home?" Kayla held on to the dash as Gage weaved in and out between slower cars.

"I don't know, but if she's on Esplanade Road already, she probably dodged all of the New Orleans traffic and is ahead of us, whether she's going to her apartment or to the mall." He gunned the Jeep forward, and gave thanks as he beat a red light at the turn onto Esplanade, the Jeep catching a wheel as he yanked the steering wheel left and finally—finally—got on the correct path to finding Shelby.

Esplanade ran parallel to I-10 on the Lake Pontchartrain side and had a broad canal centering the street. Usually, the interstate moved more quickly; however, in the middle of the day, like right now, the side road definitely had its advantages, as Shelby Montana must have known.

Gage praised his luck as light after light was green, and his speed continued to increase. If a cop saw him, moving through the house-lined street at over eighty miles per hour, there was no way he wouldn't get pulled over. Not that Gage had any intention of stopping. Let the police give chase; if Shelby Montana were in danger, he'd need them along anyway. Might as well give him an escort.

"You have that detective's number?" he asked Chantelle.

"Yes, I've got it."

"Call him and tell him what's happening."

She started dialing, then hesitated. "What do I tell him?"

"Hell." Gage wanted the police to help, but Chantelle was right. What could they say? That they *thought* Lillian's killer might be watching Shelby's apartment, or the store where she worked? And that they thought she was heading to one of those places? "Never mind. Wait until Lillian lets us know where she's going, and whether she sees Romero there, *then* call him."

Apartment. Hurry!

"Damn, she's ahead of us, and she's going to her apartment." He punched the gas to the floor, and quickly turned off Esplanade toward Shelby's apartment. There was only a quarter mile of street before it ended at Lake Pontchartrain, so Gage knew it wouldn't take him long to get there. He was thankful that he knew exactly where Shelby's home was, since he and Chantelle had gone to the apartment Saturday, but was Romero there, too?

Phillip. Waiting.

Relief washed over Gage. Evidently, Phillip Montana had wasted no time getting to Shelby. "Her husband—ex-husband—is there, at her apartment," he told Kayla and Chantelle, as he eased up on the gas and turned into Shelby's apartment complex. "Looks like we did the right thing calling him. Maybe with him here, too, it'll be easier to convince her to go with us and get her away from here before Romero finds—"

A bloodcurdling scream ripped through Gage's mind at the precise moment that a gunshot rang out from the complex. Then another shot, and another.

No! Nooo!!!

Lillian's yell sent adrenaline firing through Gage's veins. "Dial 911."

"Hurry!" Kayla instructed, her attention focused on Chantelle's fingers punching the three buttons.

"I am, I am," Chantelle said. "Oh, Shelby, please be okay," she pleaded, then hurriedly gave the information to the operator. "Someone's shooting at—" She frantically searched for an address on the apartment buildings, and spouted the numbers and street name into the phone.

Shelby's apartment was on the last row, near the lakeside exit, and Gage wheeled into the lane in time to see the back of a black sports car peeling out of the lot. Two bodies were crumpled on the ground, and Lillian, glowing madly, wailed in agony over the smallest.

12

KAYLA SAT in Shelby's room at the hospital and held her friend's hand. She turned toward the door as Gage stepped inside, his white lab coat over his shirt and jeans and a clipboard under one arm.

"You were incredible." Her eyes burned from lack of sleep and her back ached from sitting in the hospital chair all night. She'd repeated the statement throughout the night, each time Gage had returned to Shelby's room to check on her condition.

"I'm a doctor," he said yet again, though his tired eyes told her that he really didn't mind hearing the compliment once more. "I was simply doing what I've been trained to do."

Kayla nodded, but was still awestruck at the way he'd controlled the situation outside Shelby's apartment, instructing Chantelle on what to tell the 911 operator so the guys in the ambulance knew exactly what they were facing, and what they should do when they arrived.

Apparently, Romero had been parked outside Shelby's apartment, as they had suspected. However, he hadn't counted on Phillip Montana showing up. Phillip had gone to the clinic, seen that his ex-wife's car wasn't outside and made a beeline to her apartment. Driving like a madman, he'd arrived right after her, but before he could talk her into leaving with him, Romero had pulled up in his car, lowered his window and fired.

Phillip had seen the gun and shielded his ex-wife from the shot. The first bullet hit him in the chest and, according to Gage, it had missed the heart, but shattered a rib and collapsed one lung. The next bullet hit Shelby's clavicle, and the last bullet, thank God, missed both of them entirely, probably due to Romero's haste to flee the scene.

Gage had both of them ready for transport when the ambulance arrived. They were taken to the ER and underwent surgery within an hour of arrival. Shelby's displaced fracture had to be pinned together with a large metal plate and screws, but now she was in stable condition in a regular room, while Phillip was still in recovery.

"How…is he?" Shelby asked from the bed, her voice groggy from the painkillers.

She looked terrible, so pale that the freckles on her nose were even more prominent, and the red spirals of her hair were matted with sweat from the pain. But she was alive, thank God. And thank Gage.

"Phillip. How is he?" Shelby asked again.

"He's going to be okay," Gage promised, and Kayla knew that he would be; Gage wouldn't lie.

"Thank you," she said.

"Yes. Thank you," Shelby repeated from the bed.

"No thanks necessary. And so you'll know, I've told the police the situation with Romero, and they have a guard stationed outside your door."

"Phillip's, too?" Shelby asked.

"Yes, they have one watching Phillip's room, too. Detective Ingram is in charge, and since he is already familiar with Lillian's case, he's the best cop we could have asked for. He's actually talking with Chantelle again right now, and he realizes the link between Lillian and you and Chantelle and Kayla, and is even more determined to learn how Romero got out of prison. He wasn't able to find anything in the Louisiana Department of Corrections records, but he has the state police checking it out now and told Chantelle that he'd let her know when they figure out where he is—or where he was, I should say—and how the hell he got out."

"I thought it was over." Shelby's voice was childlike as she spoke to Kayla. "I thought we'd never have to see him again."

"We won't," Kayla assured her. "Once we find him, we'll make sure he stays behind bars, where he belongs."

"But he got out this time, didn't he?" Shelby said with despair.

Kayla frowned, nodded. "I'm so sorry he hurt you, Shelby."

"He hurt all of us. And this—" she motioned to the bandage covering the majority of her upper body "—this is nothing compared to the pain we went through back then." Her lower lip trembled. "Or the pain of knowing that Phillip got hurt because of me."

"Not because of you," Kayla corrected. "Because of Romero. This wasn't your fault, Shelby, it was his."

"She's right," Gage said emphatically. "And trust me, Phillip did exactly what he wanted to do. He loves you, and he wasn't going to let that bastard take you away from him."

Tears slid down Shelby's cheeks. "He does love me."

"Yes, he does." Kayla grabbed a tissue from the box beside the bed and dabbed at Shelby's face.

"I've been such a fool." Shelby's voice cracked on the last word.

"No, you've been a victim," Kayla told her. "We all

have, but it doesn't mean we have to live the rest of our lives that way. If we do, then he wins, Shelby, and we can't let him win. You deserve Phillip, and he deserves you."

Shelby gave her a weak smile. "Tell him I love him, please."

"I can't go in to see him, but Gage can."

"I'll tell him." Gage gave her a smile that Kayla would classify as the best bedside manner she'd ever seen. "Matter of fact, I'll go tell him right now, before we leave," he added.

"We're leaving?" Kayla asked.

"We've been up for over twenty-four hours. I'm used to that, somewhat, from my shifts at the hospital, but even I'm feeling the need for sleep now. You need to sleep, too, particularly if we're going to do whatever it takes to stop Romero. We can go to my apartment, instead of driving all the way out to the plantation, and get a little rest, then we'll see what the police have found on Romero."

"He's right," Shelby agreed. "You need sleep, Kayla. Thank you for staying all night, but there's a policeman right outside my door to watch over me. I'll be fine here."

Gage nodded. "You will be fine, and I'll go tell Phillip that, too. He's worried about you."

Shelby watched him leave. "He cares about you, the way Phillip cares about me. I can see it in his eyes."

"I know," Kayla said. "I can see it, too." And she could also feel it, with every touch, every look. In fact, she could envision herself having a future with Gage, if that's what he wanted—and *if* they stopped Romero before he killed them all.

"Where do you think he is now?" Shelby whispered.

"Who?"

"Wayne Romero." She eased up in the bed, then grimaced when the movement evidently caused her pain.

"You need this?" Kayla put her finger over the red button that would give her friend another dose of morphine.

"Not yet. I want to be able to think clearly a little longer, while you're here." She bit her lower lip as she tried to situate her body more comfortably. "And…something else about Romero," Shelby said, her speech slow as she pushed the words through the pain.

"What?" Kayla asked.

"Did you see him? When he came after you, did you see his face?"

"No. He wore a hood."

"He had on a hood yesterday, too, and he was in a car, but I turned when I heard Phillip yell, and I saw him, briefly." She frowned. "He looked different."

"What do you mean, different?" Kayla questioned. "In what way?" Had his face changed? Did he have plastic surgery? Did he wear a mask? Kayla had sensed something different about him, too, in the way he'd moved when he ran after her, something about his entire presence that didn't feel right. But she'd decided that it was merely her fear that made her distort the image. Now Shelby had sensed something, too. "What was it?"

Shelby shook her head and frowned. "I'm not sure. Maybe—well, he seemed bigger, taller, somehow. But he was in a car. It could have been the way he was sitting. I don't know. It just—seemed like something was off."

"I know what you mean," Kayla replied. "I felt the same thing, but maybe it's because we were so scared."

"Maybe," Shelby said. "Well, then, where do you think he is? Do you or Gage have any ideas?"

"Not really," Kayla admitted. "We don't even know

where he was transferred yet, or whether he was paroled or escaped or what."

"Chantelle is safe?" she asked.

Kayla had given her a brief summary of what had happened over the past few days. "Yes, she's safe. There's no way Romero would know about the Vicknair home, and the family there, well, they're amazing. They really care about helping us."

The door to the room creaked open, and the guard's head poked inside. "Ms. Montana, there's a man here to see you."

Kayla's skin bristled. "What man?"

"A Tristan Vicknair."

Relief washed through Kayla. "That's Gage's brother," she explained to Shelby.

"Let him in," Shelby whispered from the bed, and then the door opened wider and Tristan stepped through.

"We came as soon as we heard. Gage got there in time, then?" he asked, nodding toward Shelby. "I'm his brother," he added.

"Nice to—meet you," Shelby said, again wincing through the attempt at speech.

"I just wanted to see if there was anything we can do. Nan, Dax and Jenee are here, too, down the hall waiting for Chantelle to finish talking with the cop."

"Thank you for coming." Kayla smiled in gratitude. "I don't know what to tell you to do, though. Maybe Gage will know something. But it really was sweet of all of you to come." Her heart was touched by the Vicknairs and their natural inclination to help others in need, those of the breathing and of the nonbreathing persuasion. They were good people and a strong family. And Gage was a part of it all. No wonder she'd fallen so hard for him.

"Well, let me know if you think of something, and I'll

check with Gage, too. I saw him heading down the hall."
He looked at Shelby. "I'll see you again when you're
feeling better."

Shelby nodded. "Gage has an incredible family," she
said after the door closed behind Tristan.

"Yes, he does."

"We—we missed out on that type of family. But at least
we had each other through those hard times."

Kayla squeezed her hand. "I thank God for that."

"I just wish—" Shelby swallowed. "I wish we could
have helped Lillian."

Kayla nodded. "I do, too."

"We have to figure out how to stop him, Kayla. If we
don't, we're dead."

"But what can we do until the police find something on
him? We don't know where he's been, or where he may be
staying now."

"Have you been back to the Seven Sisters?" Shelby asked.

"The orphanage?" Kayla shook her head. "No. It's been
closed ever since the trial. He wouldn't go back there."

"I don't think he would, either. But Ms. Rosa is still
there, and she might have an idea about where he would go."

Kayla recalled the black woman who lived in the tiny
clapboard house at the edge of the former orphanage's
property. Her mother had been an elderly woman when
she'd started the orphanage, and Ms. Rosa was nearing re-
tirement when she began teaching there. They'd wanted to
provide an alternative to the foster home system that had
children moving every couple of years with no stability
whatsoever. Ms. Rosa's mother had been raised in that
system, and she'd wanted to give at least a few children
something more secure.

She'd never imagined that the man who'd volunteered

his landscaping duties was actually turning that secure environment into a living hell. Shortly after the trial, Ms. Rosa's mother had died, and Ms. Rosa had inherited the orphanage. Unfortunately, the damage had been done, and the place stayed empty.

Ms. Rosa had been a key witness in the trial, testifying that she'd seen Romero on the grounds late at night, and stating that she should have realized what he was doing to the girls, but Rosa wasn't a young woman, and her instincts were rusty; she simply didn't realize that she couldn't trust the man. Both women had only wanted something good to come from the Seven Sisters. They'd done their best to raise the children with love and had no idea what kind of hate lurked in Romero's soul.

"You should ask Ms. Rosa what she remembers about him," Shelby said. "She may be able to tell you where he'd go, now that he's out of prison. She said she knew all of the Romero family, remember?"

"Yeah, I remember." Kayla recalled the woman's statement at the trial.

He's mental. You know, crazy in the head.

Romero's attorney had objected to her opinionated statement, of course, but not before Romero jumped out of his seat and attempted to cross the defense table in an effort to get his hands on Ms. Rosa.

Gage returned, taking their attention away from Ms. Rosa, Romero and that horrible trial. "Phillip said to tell you he loves you, too."

Shelby smiled. "You can push that button now," she told Kayla.

Kayla did as she instructed, then sat beside the bed until her friend drifted back to sleep.

"We can go now," Gage said. "They're both stable,

and we need some sleep so we can concentrate on finding Romero."

"Did Tristan find you?" she asked.

"Yeah. We decided that it'd be best if he took Chantelle back to the plantation when she finishes talking with Ingram and helped her relax and get some sleep."

"She *is* exhausted," Kayla agreed.

"We all are." He wrapped an arm around her as they left Shelby's room.

"Shelby gave me an idea of a place to try. The orphanage where we grew up."

"Why would he go back there?" Gage asked.

"I don't think he would, but there's a woman there who might know where he would go," she explained.

"Well, let's get some sleep first, and that'll give the cops a little time to get us information on where Romero's been and where they think he'll go. If they don't have anything by then to help us out, then we'll go see if that woman can help."

Kayla nodded, too tired to insist they go see Ms. Rosa now. "You're sure she's okay here, with only the police officer outside?"

"That's not all she has," he said. "Lillian is staying with her, and she'll let me know if anything happens out of the ordinary, but I do think Shelby's safe with the guard outside her door."

They left the hospital and, within twenty minutes, arrived at Gage's apartment by Lake Pontchartrain. The complex was extremely neat, with each duplex painted a different beach-toned color. An abundance of well-manicured gardens, rock pathways, fountains and ponds bordered the walk to his building.

Kayla's attention was drawn to one particular courtyard. She recognized those bushes, recognized those roses.

Unable to help herself, she walked toward them, then plucked one large cluster from a branch and held it to her nose. That scent brought back so many memories, some horrible, but others strengthening. These were the roses that they had turned to as a symbol of the way they wanted to be, and the way they finally were when they took Romero to trial. If only he were still in prison, where he belonged.

"Amazing, aren't they?" a male voice said from behind them.

Kayla turned to see an elderly gentleman, his straw hat shielding his face, gardening gloves covered in topsoil. "Yes, they are."

"Don't know why they're blooming now. It ain't their season, you know, but I sure ain't gonna knock it." He motioned toward Gage. "We were admiring them jes' the other day, ain't that right, Gage?"

"Yes." Gage made the introductions. "Vernon, this is Kayla Sparks. Kayla, this is Vernon Medders, the grounds-keeper here."

The old man tipped his hat. "Nice to meet you, specially since you've got a fondness for my roses. We got plenty of them, so take all you want. They make a right nice vase."

"Thank you." Kayla sat on a black wrought-iron bench placed to one side of the fishpond. She watched the fat orange goldfish swim smoothly beneath the water and noticed several rose petals floating on the surface.

"You come back anytime now," Vernon said, then winked at Gage. "I like her."

"I do, too," Gage said, taking a seat beside Kayla on the bench.

"I'll let you two enjoy yourselves in peace." The old man exited the courtyard through an opening in the rose-filled shrubs.

A water fountain produced a bubbling, relaxing cadence as Kayla sat mesmerized by the beauty of the courtyard and the bounty of the roses.

She moved the tiny blooms back to her nose and inhaled the sweet scent again. Then she leaned against Gage and closed her eyes.

"Let's go inside," he said. "Or we'll end up falling asleep on this bench, and I don't think that'd be the most comfortable of sleeping accommodations."

"You have something better?"

"Much better." Then he stood, took her hand and helped her from the bench.

With Kayla still clutching the roses, they continued down the pebbled pathway leading to the next set of apartments.

"That one." Gage pointed to a two-story duplex painted Wedgwood blue.

Nearing the entrance to his building, Kayla paused. "Stop," she said. "Look at me."

Obviously confused, he nonetheless did as she asked. "What is it?"

His eyes were tired, with a tinge of red around the edges. But she saw what she was looking for.

"I wanted to see if your eyes would turn that color of blue when you stand near your apartment building."

One brow arched and he grinned. "And?"

"They do, exactly. It's…very nice." Actually, his eyes were more than nice. They were absolutely breathtaking, and even though she was exhausted beyond reason, she suddenly wanted him, very much.

Gage pulled her close to his side. "Come on." He guided her up the pebbled walkway to his door, withdrew his key and opened it.

Kayla stepped inside. So far, she'd seen him in his

familial element at the Vicknair plantation, and she'd seen him in his working environment at the hospital. But she'd yet to see him at home, and she was eager to get another glimpse into this intriguing man.

The decor was understated yet classy and undeniably masculine, with dark wooden tables and leather furniture the color of caramel. Burgundy and gold were the principle colors for pillows, picture frames and floor rugs. She moved closer to a large entertainment center to view the pictures on display. Vicknairs dominated, and even though the majority of the photos were from their childhood, she still recognized most everyone.

Two photos were larger than the rest. In the first, three girls stood in front of the cane fields by the plantation. The tallest looked around eleven and had black hair, long and straight and well beyond her waist. She smiled brightly, as though she owned the world, or planned to one day. "Nanette."

"Kind of hard to miss that one," Gage said.

Nan had a toddler on her hip, a tiny little girl with pigtails who was rubbing her eyes and frowning. "Jenee?"

He nodded.

The third girl in the photo had big blond curls in ringlets framing a beautiful face with striking gold-green eyes. "Monique?" Kayla asked.

"Yeah," Gage replied. "That's my feisty sister. You'll meet her in a few days, when she gets back from her honeymoon."

"Her honeymoon with the ghost," Kayla said.

"Former ghost," Gage corrected with a crooked smile. "Leave it to Monique to pull that off. You'll like her, and she'll love you, of course."

"Why's that?"

"Just something she said in a recent conversation." He didn't offer anything more than that, so Kayla moved to the next photograph, posed similarly to the first, except with three boys instead of girls. All three of them stood before the cane field looking as though they'd rather be anywhere except in front of that camera. They had on matching outfits, white T-shirts and blue jeans rolled up into thick cuffs, and they all had bare feet.

She pointed to the tallest one, his dark hair so long it practically hid his eyes. "Tristan?"

Gage nodded.

She moved to the toddler of this photo, with his tiny face in a snarl and a nasty scrape on his chin. "Dax?"

"You're batting a thousand."

And then she focused on the boy in the center, his blond and brown hair as streaked as it was now, and his blue eyes the exact color of the sky above the three. Like the other two boys, the young version of Gage Vicknair looked extremely pissed with the situation. "Why were all of you so mad?"

"Our folks told us we couldn't get dirty because we had to get our picture taken," he said. "Or something like that. The fire department was building their Christmas bonfire on the levee right across from the plantation, and we wanted to help. They made us wait until after pictures, and right before this one was snapped, we saw the fire trucks leaving. Not exactly the best way to put us in the mood for a Kodak moment."

She laughed. "I bet you three were a handful."

"We six were a handful," he clarified, pointing to the picture of the girls. "But our parents didn't complain too much, and Grandma Adeline thought we hung the moon, so if we ever did get in trouble, she bailed us out."

Gage took her hand and led her away from the photos, through the living room to the bedroom. "Enough reminiscing. We need to sleep."

She followed him to his bed, king-size with a mattress as thick as her forearm. Unsure how to bring up the subject, she just blurted it out. "I want to make love first."

In a nanosecond he turned, slid his hands beneath her top and pulled it over her head. "I was hoping you'd say that." Gage smiled.

Kayla followed suit, removing his shirt, then she ran her hands over the hard planes of his chest, while he lifted her in his arms and placed her on his bed. Within seconds, they both were nude. He started fondling her breasts, but she shook her head and arched her back, pressing her hot center against his erection. He was hard and thick and…perfect.

"I need you." She didn't want a lot of foreplay this time. She didn't want anything but him, inside of her, a part of her, completing her.

He turned away long enough to withdraw a condom from the nightstand and roll it over his length, then he moved between her legs and held the tip of his penis against her wet opening.

Kayla moaned, so ready she hurt inside. "Please."

Gage kissed her softly, sliding his hand to her waist and then to her clitoris.

She broke the kiss and gazed into those incredible blue eyes. "I can't wait," she demanded, knowing he was trying to bring her to an orgasm before he entered her, or perhaps as he entered her, but what he didn't realize was that all she needed was him, deep inside. So she wrapped her legs around his back, and pushed herself up his length, gasping at the force of his entry and welcoming the delicious sensations that immediately surged to life with their joining. She pushed hard, pulled back, pushed again, pulled back. The friction was exquisite and wonderful and staggering. And even more amazing because it was Gage.

He claimed her mouth with hungry urgency, while his hips matched her thrusts, riding her hard, exactly the way she wanted, until her world spun out of control and she screamed through her release. Two more long, powerful thrusts, and Gage growled through his own climax, his big, muscled body collapsing on top of her, and Kayla thought she would pass out from the weight of him and from her desire for him.

She whimpered softly, and he rolled over to his side, pulling her with him. When she shivered, he grabbed the comforter from the other side of the bed and covered the two of them, then closed his eyes.

Kayla pushed her hips closer to his and smiled in triumph. She would sleep well beside Gage Vicknair. Very, very well.

Then she glanced at the bedside lamp. It blazed brilliantly, illuminating the entire span of the room. Sighing, she reached toward the switch and pressed it. With thick curtains covering the one window, blocking out the morning sun, darkness enveloped the room, but she didn't let it control her thoughts. Comfortable in the knowledge that Gage was there, she closed her eyes.

13

THE RINGING of Gage's cell phone woke him with a start. Kayla's soft body pressed completely against his, so much so that she was curved awkwardly to keep them aligned. He'd woken once, briefly, when he'd inadvertently rolled away from her in his sleep. She'd moaned out as if he had stopped making love to her, and he'd almost taken her again, but then he'd remembered that she needed sleep.

Gage kissed the top of her head, and then realized with sudden clarity what was so different about this than every other time he'd awakened with Kayla. The room was dark. And she was sleeping peacefully…beside him.

He kissed her again and pulled her close. Thank God. She was healing, truly healing.

His cell phone stopped momentarily, waited a beat, then started back up. Someone needed him pronto. Regretfully, he pulled away from Kayla's warmth, rolled over and reached for the phone. Pressing a button to illuminate the display screen, he looked at the caller identification. He didn't recognize it, and he wasn't sure whether that was good or bad.

"Hello?"

"Is this Dr. Vicknair? Gage Vicknair?" the man on the other end asked, while Gage glanced at the clock beside the bed. It was nearly four in the afternoon. They'd slept the entire day, which didn't surprise him, since they'd been up all night, however, that meant Tuesday was nearly over, and that he was down to two days to help Lillian cross…and to save Kayla from Romero.

"Dr. Vicknair?" the voice repeated.

"Yes," Gage said, and Kayla stirred next to him. He climbed out of the bed and moved to the living room to talk without disturbing her. "Can I help you?"

"This is Detective Ingram with the New Orleans P.D." They'd spoken extensively at the hospital, so the fact that he was identifying himself in such a formal manner put Gage on instant alert. Ingram had promised to find out something about Romero before the day was over. Evidently, this detective was true to his word. "Yes, Detective. Have you learned anything?"

"I have, but, well, there's no easy way to tell you this, Dr. Vicknair." He paused. "I've already spoken to Chantelle Bedeau, and she asked me to call you and inform you of our findings. It's not what you were expecting, I'm sure."

The bedroom door opened and Kayla, her eyes puffy from sleep and her body clothed in one of his old LSU shirts, stepped through.

"Who is it?" she asked sleepily.

"The police," he mouthed.

She visibly paled, then moved closer to Gage.

"It seems that Wayne Romero was transferred from Angola to the Apalachee West facility in Florida a year ago. Unfortunately, when he transferred, the corrections department didn't notify the victims. Sometimes that happens," Ingram explained.

"So he was in Florida," Gage repeated. Kayla's brow furrowed.

"He *was*," the detective said. "Until a month ago."

"What happened a month ago?" Gage asked. "Did he escape, or was he paroled?"

"Neither." Ingram's voice was solemn. "I've got to tell you that I have no way of explaining who murdered Lillian Bedeau or who attacked Phillip and Shelby Montana. But it wasn't Wayne Romero."

"What do you mean, it wasn't Romero? How do you know?"

"Because Romero was murdered four weeks ago on the prison grounds. Seems the inmates at Apalachee didn't take too kindly to a pedophile in their midst. Most inmates don't."

Gage's mind reeled. Romero? Dead? "You're sure it was him? I mean, couldn't that have been another inmate, and Romero escaped at the same time?" It sounded far-fetched, even to Gage, but if Romero was dead, then who the hell was after Kayla and the others?

"Believe me, I ran that possibility by the warden at Apalachee before I called you, but he saw the body personally. It was Romero. I'm sorry, Dr. Vicknair, but Wayne Romero isn't the one after your friends."

Gage looked at Kayla. What would they do now? "Will you keep the officers guarding Shelby and Phillip Montana's rooms at the hospital?"

"Sure," Ingram said. "Somebody out there is after them, and it stands to reason that the connection those women had to Wayne Romero is somehow falling into play. Until we figure out who's after them, we'll keep an eye on them."

"Thanks."

"Let me know if I can be of further assistance. And I'll keep you posted on any additional information we receive regarding this perpetrator." He disconnected.

"What is it?" Kayla asked, her brown eyes wide and eager to hear what the detective said.

"Romero did transfer, to Florida."

"And?"

"And he died a month ago, murdered by fellow inmates in prison."

"That can't be right." She shook her head. "I saw his eyes. I know I did. That day, when he had on the hood— I'd know them anywhere. Gray and cold and evil. It *was* him." She paused. "But…"

"But?"

"Something did seem wrong. Shelby and I talked about it in the hospital. He seemed bigger, or maybe younger. We thought it was because we were scared and everything just seemed more out of proportion, but maybe…"

"Maybe it was someone else." Gage sighed. "Well, there's no maybe to it, if Romero did die four weeks ago. That'd have been right when all of this started."

Gage drew Kayla close, wrapping her in his arms. "There's got to be an explanation," he said. "We simply have to find it. But we have to find it soon."

Kayla leaned away from him. "Ms. Rosa! Shelby suggested we go back to the Seven Sisters and find her, see if she knows something that will help us locate Romero. Or locate whomever is after us now."

"Do you remember the way to the orphanage?" he asked.

She nodded. "I go there every Christmas, not to the orphanage itself, but to Ms. Rosa's house, with Chantelle and Shelby and Lillian." She swallowed. "It won't be the same going back this Christmas, without Lillian." Her mouth trembled. "I didn't even call Rosa to tell her about what happened to Lillian. I should have called."

"You can tell her today. We'll go see her now," Gage said, squeezing her closer. "Where does she live?"

"In Chalmette, at the edge of the property surrounding the Seven Sisters."

He frowned, picturing Nan's list of areas undergoing rebuilding after the hurricane. Chalmette was near the top of that list; the entire area had been underwater after the levees broke. "Chalmette took a heavy beating in Katrina. I know, because that's one of the places that has priority over St. Charles Parish, as far as restoration goes. Nanette's keeping up with that, to try to determine how far down our plantation falls on the list. Do you think the orphanage made it through the hurricane?"

"I know it did. It's in bad shape, but it's still there. We went there after the storm to help Ms. Rosa and make sure she was okay. And, of course, we went back at Christmas. It's in a rough state, but it's there."

"Then let's go."

AFTER A good hour's drive, they pulled into the entrance of the Seven Sisters.

Kayla examined the brick columns identifying the place where she used to live. Dead vines covered the brass plate that displayed the orphanage's name, and the earth was rocky and barren along both sides of the stretch of gravel that separated the main road from the brick housing.

"Is this it?" Gage asked.

She nodded.

"Definitely was underwater," he commented, but Kayla didn't speak. She had good memories here, memories of meeting Lillian, Chantelle and Shelby for the first time. They'd been the best of friends, and then the best of confidants when they had to turn to each other for consolation from the violence they all endured at Romero's hand.

"Where is Ms. Rosa's place?" Gage asked.

"Past the orphanage, maybe a quarter of a mile, then turn right," she directed, remembering the dirt road that led to the old woman's home. "She had this huge apple orchard behind her little house. In the summer, she gave us warm fried apple pies whenever we came to visit. She may have been our teacher throughout the school year, but we still wanted to spend time with her in the summer. I guess you'd say she was like our mother back then. I only wish we'd trusted her with what was happening to us sooner. Then maybe it wouldn't have lasted so long."

Kayla remembered running down the dirt road from the orphanage to Ms. Rosa's. Those had been some of the best times at Seven Sisters, and she really wanted to hold on to the good memories. She didn't want every thought of those years to revolve around Romero.

Gage took her hand in his and held it while he drove. "We'll figure out what's happening now, and who's doing this to all of you. It has to be someone that knew about Romero. Maybe this Rosa lady can help."

"She has to," Kayla said simply. "I don't know who else could."

They reached the brick, rectangular buildings comprising the abandoned orphanage. It had seemed so big when she was younger, but she now realized that it wasn't that big at all. Four plain brick buildings. One had housed the girls' living quarters, one housed the boys', another was a large schoolroom and the last was the kitchen and cafeteria. Very small indeed, but in a child's eyes, it was huge. And Wayne Romero was a continual presence throughout.

Like the entrance, weeds had overtaken the structures, and the windows were all boarded up or missing completely. Rocks and debris covered the ground, and the place hadn't seen a rake, or a blade of grass, in years.

Kayla took in the dilapidated structure. "It wasn't in the best shape back then, but...it was nothing like this."

He squeezed her hand. "You okay?"

"I will be, as soon as we find out who's after all of us, and stop him."

Vibrant color to the right of the orphanage caught her eye, and she leaned forward to get a better look.

Kayla's throat tightened. "Oh, my."

Gage stopped the Jeep with a jerk. "What is it?" He followed her line of sight. "No way."

The entire right side of the orphanage was completely covered in dark-green foliage and hundreds of deep-pink clusters of roses.

Kayla shook her head, bewildered by the sight, so similar to the shrubbery enclosing the courtyard at Gage's apartment. Nothing else was growing anywhere near the orphanage, but here was a full-grown hedge, apparently thriving and filled with roses that should be out of season. "What does it mean?" she whispered.

"It has to be a sign from the other side," he said with certainty.

"A sign of what?"

"That we're on the right path." He started the Jeep again down the gravel road. "Now show me the way to Ms. Rosa's."

Kayla took another look at the flowers, even more abundant than they were when the gardens here were tended daily by Wayne Romero, then she pointed straight ahead. "See that big oak?"

Gage nodded.

"Turn there. Her house is at the end of the dirt path."

Sure enough, Ms. Rosa's tiny white clapboard home stood where it always had, its silver tin roof catching the afternoon sun and making Kayla squint.

"Look, there she is," Kayla said, eyeing the woman rocking on her front porch, her two long knitting needles glinting occasionally as they caught a hint of sunlight.

Gage parked the Jeep, and Kayla immediately exited. "Ms. Rosa!"

The woman's dark face split into a knowing smile, and she set the knitting needles into the basket of multicolored yarn at her feet. She wore a pale-blue button-up dress and knee-high stockings that didn't quite reach her knees. Her hair had faded even more through the years, converting from the dark gray Kayla remembered to pale silver. She opened her arms and waited for Kayla's embrace.

"Makayla," Rosa whispered tenderly, kissing her cheek. "I was hoping it'd be you, *chère*." She patted Kayla's back as she spoke, then gently squeezed before releasing her and raising her silver brows at Gage. "And you are?"

"Gage Vicknair." He extended a hand and was surprised when Ms. Rosa brought it to her mouth and kissed it.

"Thank you for bringing her," she said tenderly.

Kayla crouched beside the older woman's chair. She knew they didn't have time to waste, and Ms. Rosa had said something odd upon their arrival. "What did you mean, you hoped it'd be me?"

Rosa moved a shaky hand to Kayla's face and gently pushed a lock of hair behind her right ear. "The roses, dear. I can see them, even from here," she said, turning in the direction of the orphanage. "Those roses told me you girls would need my help. I believe in the signs, *chère,* and those roses, blooming now, when nothing has bloomed here since the storm, they told me you girls were coming. And one of you did." She paused, taking Kayla's hands in hers. "What about the others, *chère?* How are the others?"

Kayla tearfully told her about the killer coming after

them all, about Lillian's death, Shelby's shooting and that Gage had gotten to Chantelle before the killer found her, too. She also told her how they'd believed it was Romero, until this morning.

"What changed this morning, *chère?*" Rosa asked.

"We learned that he died in prison a month ago. It couldn't have been him that came after me, but I *know* I saw him."

"How do you know?"

"His eyes. I saw his eyes, and I was so sure…"

Rosa frowned, shook her head. "But he's dead? The police are sure?"

Kayla nodded.

"We were hoping that you might have an idea of someone else, another man who knew about what happened with Romero and perhaps also wanted to make the girls pay for putting him in prison," Gage said.

Rosa shook her head. "I'm sorry. I—don't know another man. Wayne Romero was the only man who worked here. My mother, she had two ladies who helped her in the kitchen, and then I taught the classes in the school. And then Wayne donated his time to work the grounds." Her silver head shook again. "We shouldn't have trusted him. All we ever wanted was to help kids, to help all of you. It was Mama's dream."

"It wasn't your fault," Kayla consoled her.

"You can't think of anyone else, someone he might have known, a friend, or a brother, someone who might try to follow through with the threats he made to the girls before he went to prison?" Gage asked.

"No. He didn't have any brothers, or any friends that I knew of," Rosa said. "Maybe—maybe it was someone he met in prison?"

Gage frowned, obviously disappointed. He pulled a card

out of his pocket and handed it to her. "We'll ask the police to check that out," he said. "It is a possibility."

Kayla heard the dismay in his tone. True, it was another possibility, but it was a possibility that would take time to research, and they didn't have a lot of time. Lillian only had two more days to cross, and now that they knew the killer wasn't Romero, they had no idea who they were looking for. But one thing was for sure—they were still in danger. Who wanted them dead?

"I'll call you if I think of anything," Rosa promised. "I'm so sorry I've not been any help."

"It's okay." Kayla hugged her. "It was good just to see you again."

"Please come more often, dear. I miss you. And bring Chantelle and Shelby, too, Makayla."

"I will." She didn't correct Ms. Rosa on the use of her given name. Makayla was the girl she'd known, after all, and Makayla was the girl she'd helped. So, if Ms. Rosa wanted to call her Makayla, she could. Kayla kissed Rosa's soft cheek then turned to go, but paused when the woman continued to speak.

"My mother inherited this land from my grandfather, and she wanted the place to be used for good. I know it hurt her when she found out what he'd done to all of you. She'd wanted this to be a place to help children, not hurt them."

Kayla patted Rosa's hand. "You know, what happened back then doesn't mean that this place couldn't be used again to help children, somehow. I mean, it'd take a lot of work," she said, swallowing past the emotion in her words. Rosa and her mother had tried so hard to provide what kids needed, to keep them safe. It wasn't right that Romero had ruined that dream.

Rosa gave her a soft smile. "I'm mighty old to start

fixing up the place, *chère,* but you never know. Maybe something will work out for this place again someday. Maybe something good."

Kayla kissed her cheek again. "Maybe so." They left the sweet woman on the porch and moved toward the Jeep, where Gage picked up his cell phone and started dialing.

"Detective Ingram, please," Gage said into the phone, while Kayla climbed in and waved goodbye to Rosa.

Kayla eyed the buildings as they passed them on their way out. Ms. Rosa was right; the orphanage should be used for something good. That had been Rosa's mother's intention, and letting the place go unused was a waste. Truly. Maybe, when all of this was over, she could help Rosa achieve her dream, to turn Seven Sisters into a place of peace, of safety, the way Rosa and her mother had dreamed of it being. If they found out who was after them...

Gage finished talking to the detective and hung up.

"Anything new?" Kayla asked.

"No." He shook his head in defeat. "Damn."

"She's right, you know," she said. "It could be used for something good, if someone took a mind to fix it up."

Gage's cell phone started beeping before he could respond. "Hold on. This could be Ingram again." He clicked the button. "Hello?"

Kayla watched as his facial expression changed. He pressed the phone close to his ear, as though the caller was soft-spoken or whispering. Definitely not the detective.

"Okay," he said. "I'll ask her." He glanced at Kayla. "It's Rosa, and she wants me to ask you if you remember someone." Gage slowed the car and turned onto the next street, then parked on one side.

"What name?" Kayla asked.

"Aidan Dominic," Gage said. "Ms. Rosa said he was here a lot in the summers and that he was Romero's—"

Kayla's heartbeat increased instantly. Why hadn't she thought of him sooner? "Romero's son." A.D. was Wayne Romero's son, but he wasn't a boy, and he'd always left her, and the other girls, feeling uneasy. He was in his early twenties when she was at the orphanage, though he didn't act like an adult. He'd followed Romero around the orphanage each summer, only in the summer, then left each fall. She'd nearly forgotten about him, because he hadn't been a constant in her life, only appearing three months a year, and never really doing anything to stand out in her mind. He had been quiet, very quiet. In fact, Kayla wasn't certain she'd ever heard him speak. He'd merely existed at the orphanage, as his father's shadow, throughout each summer. But there was something about him…

A.D. was the killer. It made sense, and it made Kayla sick. Aidan Romero had murdered Lillian, and he planned to do the same thing to Chantelle, Shelby…and Kayla.

"She's asking if you think it could be Aidan." Gage was still holding the phone to his ear.

Kayla tried to control the flurry of emotions currently making her skin crawl. "If A.D. blamed us for his father being in prison, then…" She nodded. "Yes, it could be A.D., and it would make sense, too, the eyes. He had eyes like his father's."

"Rosa, do you know where A.D. is now?" He shook his head at Kayla. "No, that's okay. Maybe the police will be able to find an address for us. I'm going to have to let you go and call the detective, tell him about this, Rosa. We really appreciate your help." Gage disconnected and began dialing again. "She said she hasn't seen A.D. since the trial. Tell me what you remember about him while I get Ingram on the line."

Kayla recalled the boy—man—from those summers. "He spent the school years with his mother, or I guess you'd call it a school year. He was in some sort of institution for adults who are challenged. A.D. had a hard time dealing with other people, or that's what I recall. Anyway, he was at that school through most of the year, then he'd show up at the orphanage for the summers." She thought of A.D., so quiet, merely a big body moving in the wake of his father. "I never even talked to A.D., but I do remember how uneasy I felt around him. I thought it was just because he was Romero's son, but maybe there was more to it than that. He was always so quiet. I should have thought of him, but- -" she shook her head "—I'd almost forgotten him completely."

"Well, it looks like he didn't forget you, or the others." Gage held up a finger to indicate that someone had answered. "Ingram? Yes, this is Gage Vicknair."

Kayla listened as Gage told the detective everything they'd learned. A.D. Romero had murdered Lillian. It sickened her to think about it but she realized that it did make a twisted sense. The son vindicating his father's death by murdering the women who'd put him in jail. Evidently, it didn't matter that his father had abused each of them and ruined their lives.

Kayla's hatred for father and son made her skin burn. She didn't care what she had to do; she wasn't going to let another Romero hurt her friends, or hurt her, for that matter. She and Gage would stop him. They had to.

Gage hung up the phone. "He's going to get the last-known address for Aidan Romero and call us back," he said, then cocked his head and looked at Kayla. "Are you okay?"

"No," she replied honestly. "And I won't be until we stop him."

Gage nodded. "I agree. And we will, somehow."

His cell phone started back up and he glanced at the caller ID. "It's Tristan," he said, then answered, "Hey, we've got news on Romero." Within a minute, he'd informed Tristan, and any other Vicknairs who were listening, of Wayne Romero's death and of A.D. potentially being Lillian's killer.

"Chantelle wants to talk to you." He handed the phone to Kayla, then started the Jeep and pulled back out onto the main road, heading toward the interstate.

"Chantelle, are you okay?" Kayla asked.

"Yes, but is it true? Wayne Romero is dead?"

"It's true."

"And A.D.? He killed Lillian?"

"Rosa thought of Aidan," Kayla said. "But it does make sense. Or do you not think it could be A.D.?"

The other end of the line was silent for a moment, as though she was mulling over the idea.

"Chantelle?" Kayla finally prompted.

"You know," Chantelle whispered, "it could be him. I remember how he gave me the creeps. I haven't thought about him in years, and I liked it that way."

"Did he ever talk to you?" Kayla asked, surprised.

"A little, but I tried to keep interaction with him to a minimum. Just a feeling whenever he was around. I always hated it when he showed up in the summer, felt like he was staring a hole through me every time he looked my way. I even caught him gawking through the window to our room once, just standing there at the window staring."

"If it was him, it would explain the eyes," Kayla pointed out. "His eyes were like his father's."

"Yeah, they were. Cold and gray. They bothered me, too."

"What are we going to do? The detective is trying to find

out where A.D. lives now, but what if they don't find him before it's time for Lillian to cross?"

"That's why I wanted to talk to you," Chantelle said. "I think I know a way that we can catch Romero." She corrected herself. "A.D. Romero, now. But even if it is a different Romero that we're looking for, I still think I know how we can catch him."

Tristan's voice echoed firmly behind her. "And I said you're not going to do it."

"I help him build a wall in a day, and suddenly he thinks he can boss me around." She continued talking, but her words were definitely intended for Tristan. "He killed my sister, and I'll do whatever it damn well takes to make him pay."

Kayla swallowed hard. Chantelle had obviously progressed from sadness to anger, and Kayla knew exactly how she felt; she'd felt her own rage churning today. They'd been victimized for way too many years to let the past repeat itself. Lillian was dead, and the murderer should pay for what he'd done. He'd taken away Chantelle's sister and Kayla's friend. And he'd shot Shelby and Phillip Montana. A.D. Romero did deserve to pay, and pay dearly, and if Kayla could help that happen, then she would. "What are you thinking?"

"Jenee went to the homeless shelter downtown today, where you were," Chantelle said. "When she was there, she learned that some guy has been calling and asking about you, where you are, when you'll be back, if they've seen you."

"You think it's A.D.?" Kayla questioned.

"Only guy I can think of, although I had thought it was his daddy calling. Anyway, so far, they've told him they don't have any information, but I got to thinking, what if, when he calls back, they give him my address and say you're staying with a friend? Maybe even give him my name, and then he can kill two birds, or two women, in this case, with one stone? Or that's what he'll think."

Kayla was confused. "We're sure he already knows where you live, Chantelle. The fact that you're at the plantation has been the only thing that's kept you out of his line of sight."

"I know, but if Jenee, or whoever answers the phone at the shelter, tells him that I showed up and took you to my home, then he'll know I'm back. And I can go there, like, you know, bait. But we'll get the cops to come, too, and they can take him down."

Take him down. "You still watch a lot of cop shows, huh?"

"They've always been my favorites." Chantelle laughed. "And it's about time I put what I've watched to use and make Lillian's murderer pay."

"Let me see what Gage thinks." Kayla turned to Gage, who was obviously impatient to find out what was going on.

"Well?" he asked.

"Chantelle thinks A.D. has been calling the shelter where Jenee works and asking about me. She wants Jenee, or one of the workers there, to tell him that she picked me up and took me back to her place, and give him the address."

"As though he doesn't already know it?"

Kayla shrugged. "She thinks he'll come after both of us at her place, and she wants to be waiting there as bait, with the police nearby."

"Not happening," Gage declared. "Or rather, the entire plan isn't happening. Part of it has promise."

"Which part?"

"The part where we give him Chantelle's address and have someone waiting for him when he arrives," he said.

"But that someone isn't going to be Chantelle, or any of you, in fact."

"Who will it be?"

"Lillian." Gage nodded his approval with his own idea. "And me."

14

KAYLA SAT at the kitchen table in the Vicknair plantation late Wednesday afternoon and listened to Gage and Tristan go over the plan to catch A.D. Romero. Jenee had skipped her college classes that day to do extra volunteer work at the Magazine Street shelter in case Romero called asking about Kayla. He did—or they supposed it was him— saying he was a family member trying to reach her. As instructed by Jenee, the volunteer who answered gave him Chantelle's address and said that Kayla would be staying there with her friend.

Gage and Tristan had altered the plan during the day. They decided to keep the cops out of the picture until A.D. arrived at Chantelle's house. As a firefighter, Tristan frequently worked with the police, and he convinced Gage that the cops would never authorize use of a civilian as bait for a killer. Since the time was running out for Lillian to cross over, Gage decided to change tactics.

Now he planned to wait until dark, then drive Chantelle's car to her house. He and Lillian would wait inside for Aidan Romero to show, then Lillian would dial 911 and Gage would use the gun he had gotten from the locked cabinet in the study, if necessary.

Kayla didn't like the plan at all, for a multitude of reasons, but she didn't voice her disapproval. Gage had made up his mind. However, Chantelle was extremely vocal with her opinions.

"This will never work," she said flatly.

"Why won't it work?" Tristan asked.

"Number one-—" she held up her index finger "—Gage is a guy, and much bigger than me. There's no way A.D. Romero would think I ended up that large. And there's this." She pointed to her hair.

"As far as we know, he hasn't seen you yet. You could have cut your hair. And anyway, I'm going in in the dark, and I'm wearing black clothing." Gage indicated his long-sleeved black T-shirt and jeans. "Plus, it's raining, and it's supposed to rain solid until tomorrow, so I'll be in the shadow of an umbrella."

"Number two—" Chantelle popped up another finger "—it isn't all that dark at my house. I picked that particular lot because of the streetlight in my yard. And I also have perimeter lights that come on each night via a timer." She glanced at the digital clock on the microwave. "They'll come on in thirty minutes, well before you could get to my house, even if you leave right now."

"And number three. He hasn't attacked anybody that wasn't the person he was going for. Well, except for Phillip, but that's because he was with Shelby. In other words, he's not going to come barging into my apartment unless he's damn sure I'm the one in there. And if I'm not, he won't show. Which is why *I* need to be the bait. Or Kayla and me."

Kayla decided now was as good a time as any to join in the conversation. "I do want to help," she stated, not quite as forcefully as Chantelle, but she could tell by the way Gage raised his brows that her point was coming across. Still, she really didn't expect Gage and Tristan to hand over the reins easily. "He murdered Lillian, he shot Shelby and he tried to rape me," she continued. "And I want to be a part of making him pay for what he did."

"There's no way in hell that we're going to put any of you in there to wait for that madman," Tristan said, and Gage nodded his agreement.

"I'm not putting you in danger, Kayla." Those blue eyes told her Gage meant every word. Part of her was touched beyond measure, but, like Chantelle, part of her truly wanted to be there to help put A.D. Romero away.

"What about a different female?" Nanette asked. "Someone he doesn't care about?"

"Don't even think about it," Gage warned. "This will work. It has to. Besides, Lillian's requirement for crossing is for her to save Kayla, and if she isn't involved with catching the guy who's after Kayla, then it stands to reason that she won't cross."

"Lillian could go with me." Nanette backed off when Gage's blue eyes turned icy. "Hey, it was just a thought," she said, relinquishing her usual authoritative role to the guys, for now.

And speaking of the Vicknair guys, Kayla realized she hadn't seen the youngest male Vicknair at all. "Where's Dax?"

"Working late," Nanette said. "Again. He had no idea, of course, that all of this would be happening tonight, and he scheduled to work late since the house inspection is tomorrow."

"They moved it up?" Tristan asked.

"Yeah, but we're ready," she told him. "Don't worry."

"I'm not worried. There's too much going on tonight to think about the inspection tomorrow." He turned to Gage. "Sure you don't want me to go along?"

"You're on call, and Chantelle's place is well over an

hour away. You'd never get back in time if there was a fire this side of the spillway. Besides, I really think you and Nan should stay here with Chantelle and Kayla. I'll keep you posted on what's happening."

"I still think," Chantelle started, but stopped when Gage held up a hand and turned toward the stove, where several pots bubbled with spicy Cajun dishes. Lillian was obviously calming herself, once again, by cooking.

"I will." Gage turned back to Chantelle. "Lillian doesn't want you anywhere near that house, and she wants me to tell you that the two of us will get Aidan Romero. She also said you need to work on your stubborn streak," he added with a slight grin.

"She did not," Chantelle argued, then watched a long wooden spoon wave up and down in midair. Her mouth quivered. "Lillian, please. I want to go. He murdered you, and now, it's getting close to time for you to cross. And then— and then—" Tears burst free and tumbled down her cheeks, and Kayla quickly crossed the kitchen to embrace her.

"It'll be okay," she said.

"No, it won't. Right now, at least, Lillian's still on this side, but soon she'll leave completely." Chantelle's voice cracked and a soft sob penetrated the sudden silence within the kitchen.

"Lillian?" Chantelle questioned, taking her head from Kayla's shoulder. Then she smiled through her tears. "I can tell you're holding me, sis," she said. "I'm—I'll remember you forever. I swear. I love you, Lillian."

Gage cleared his throat, but Chantelle shook her head. "You don't have to tell me what she said. I already know."

Kayla moved toward Gage, who wrapped a comforting arm around her and pulled her to his side. "What time will you leave?" A frisson of fear shimmied down her spine.

Why did she get the feeling that if Gage went to Chantelle's tonight, he wouldn't come back?

"Soon," he said. "You ready, Lillian?"

Chantelle sniffed as Lillian apparently loosened her enveloping hug.

"We're about to leave," Gage confirmed, while Kayla's stomach knotted. She peered out the kitchen window. It was getting dark, but not nearly dark enough, even with the rain streaming steadily. "Don't you need to wait a little longer?"

"With this downpour, it'll take us nearly twice as long to get there, and who knows how long it'll be before he shows?"

"I'm telling you, he'll know you're a man," Chantelle reiterated. "He won't show."

"Not under this, he won't." Gage held up an umbrella. "Bought it today, just for this occasion."

Chantelle looked skeptical, then took the umbrella from him, moved to one side of the kitchen and opened it. It was the biggest golf umbrella Kayla had ever seen, solid navy and dome-shaped. She put it over her head, and the dome went nearly to her belly, covering her face and the majority of her body easily beneath its bounty.

"See?" Gage questioned.

Chantelle closed the umbrella. "Okay. Maybe—maybe—it'll work. But I still think that when he figures out it's not me, he's going to blow a fuse. And you'd better be ready. He's already proven how dangerous he is."

"I am ready." His hand inadvertently drifted to the gun tucked beneath his shirt at his waist. Then he turned to Kayla. "Can I see you in the hallway for a moment?"

She nodded and followed him out of the kitchen.

He waited for the swinging door to close, then pulled her against him. "We'll find him tonight. I promise, one way or another, we'll take care of him tonight, and you won't have to worry anymore."

"I don't want you to go," she said. "I've got a terrible feeling about it, and I really don't want you to go."

He put a knuckle under her chin and tilted her face to his. "I'll be fine. I promise. This is the way it's supposed to be, or Lillian wouldn't have received that requirement for crossing. And although I have this along for the ride—" he put his hand over the gun "—I won't have to use it. Lillian is going to call 911 the minute we see him approaching the place. And the police station is two blocks away. They'll be there in nothing flat, and we'll have A.D. Romero behind bars, where he belongs."

"If you aren't going to have to use it, why are you taking it?" she asked, knowing he wouldn't bring a gun if he didn't think there was *some* possibility that he'd have to shoot. "And, don't take this the wrong way, but…you do know how to use it, right?"

Gage leaned down and kissed her, his mouth warm and deliciously inviting. Would he forego this whole thing if she suggested bed?

"I know how to use all my macho accessories," he said, then winked. "Later on, I'll remind you how I use another one. A few times."

"Promise?"

"Definitely." Then his face sobered. "I swear to you, Kayla, I'll come back safe and sound, before the night's over."

She couldn't speak, her throat was too tight and she was afraid she'd start sobbing, so she nodded.

He pushed the swinging door open and said goodbye to his family then left the plantation to catch a killer…if the killer didn't get him first.

Kayla returned to the kitchen. Unlike before, when the

place had been alive with chatter, now the area was like a tomb. Tristan stared out the kitchen window at the rain coming down in sheets. Chantelle had taken over at the stove and was busily stirring the gumbo, which Kayla knew had probably been ready twenty minutes ago. And Nanette sat at the kitchen table, her laptop open in front of her and a stack of papers to grade beside her. But she wasn't looking at the computer screen, and she hadn't scored the first exam.

Kayla sat down across from Nan and, like the others, didn't speak. She just thought. Thought about the fear Wayne Romero had instilled in her and her three friends, thought about the way all of them had been traumatized by his violence so many years ago, thought about him finally getting what he deserved at the hands of those inmates and thought about the last few days with the Vicknairs and how much they had come to mean to her. How much Gage had come to mean to her. She loved him, and she had willingly let him leave to face a killer…for her.

"Why didn't any of you stop him?" she whispered. "Why didn't I?" Tears dripped onto the table, and she stared at the big wet drops. She hadn't wanted him to see her cry, but now, he wouldn't see her tears.

Would he ever?

Nan looked over the top of the computer and frowned. "I know it seems like we don't care about what he's doing, but that couldn't be further from the truth. He's doing what he has to do, based on what the spirits told him in his assignment, and we can't stop him. It's our family duty to help the ghosts cross." Her lip quivered, then she continued, "Admittedly, we've never had an assignment that put any of us in danger. And Tristan and I decided the best thing to do was be strong for Gage, so we were. It doesn't mean we like it that he's facing Romero alone. We don't. But what we have to do now is be patient and wait and pray that everything goes okay."

Tristan, his back still facing both of them as he stared out the window, nodded. "I'm still not sure I shouldn't have gone with him."

"You needed to stay near the firehouse because you're on call," Chantelle reminded him.

"I could have gotten someone else to cover me," he said, "but that wasn't what Gage wanted." He turned to face Nanette. "What if this guy shows up shooting? Gage is a good shot, when it comes to tin cans and target practice, but hell, you really think he could shoot a person?"

"I don't know," Nan whispered, as the "Zydeco Stomp" sang out from the cell phone on the counter.

"Hell, he forgot his phone." Tristan reached for Gage's cellular and flipped it open. "Hello?"

"No, it's Tristan. What's up, Jenee?" he asked. "He forgot his cell, and yeah, he's already headed over there."

The three women in the room hung on every word, and Kayla felt even more ill. Gage didn't have his phone. Was he planning on Lillian using Chantelle's home phone to dial the police? What if Romero cut the phone lines in Chantelle's house? That's what killers always did in the movies. Kayla's stomach roiled wildly. If she had eaten anything at all, she'd probably lose it right now. As it was, she hadn't had more than a couple of bites of toast all day, because she'd been too miserably worried to eat. And that was before Gage forgot his phone.

"Hell," Tristan said. "Well, okay, then. I guess it's happening." He paused. "No. Definitely not. You stay where you are, where you're safe. Don't go anywhere near there, okay?

I'm sure Gage will call all of us when it's over…yeah…love you, too." He hung up, then exhaled thickly. "Jenee just took a call at the shelter from a guy asking about Kayla."

"But Romero called earlier today, right?" Nanette asked. "Isn't that what Jenee told us? That a guy called earlier asking about Kayla?"

"Apparently." Tristan shrugged. "I mean, some guy called earlier asking about her, but Jenee didn't take that call, so she doesn't know if this was the same guy. In any case, this guy was asking about Kayla, too, and Jenee gave him Chantelle's address."

"Maybe he was double-checking to make sure Kayla was still with me, so he'd know how many to expect when he got to my house," Chantelle guessed.

"I was thinking the same thing. He's trying to make sure he's prepared." Nan closed her laptop. "Lord, this is going to be a long night."

Standing, Kayla shook her head. "Well, I'm sorry. I can't sit here and wait and see what happens." She walked to the tiny pegs beside the door and grabbed a set of keys. "These are yours, aren't they, Nanette?"

Nan's eyes widened, and she shot a panicked look at Tristan. "We can't let you go over there, Kayla. He'll kill you."

"Think about it," Kayla said. "Lillian is supposed to save me. *Me*. Her requirement for crossing didn't say she was supposed to catch the man who's after me. It said she's supposed to save me. I don't think Gage saw it that way, because, well, he didn't want to see it that way. But *I'm* supposed to be there tonight, and I'm going."

"Then I'm going, too." Chantelle started for the door, but Kayla held up her hand.

"No. This is up to me, and I'm going alone." Before any

of them had a chance to stop her, she opened the back door and bolted into the rain.

She had to get to Chantelle's…and to Gage.

15

GAGE SAT in a darkened corner of Chantelle's living room, while the television cast a bluish tint over the expanse of the room. He hadn't wanted to turn on the lights, but he hadn't wanted the place to look as though no one was home, either. He and Lillian had arrived about an hour ago, and they hadn't heard or seen anything that remotely suggested A.D. Romero was near.

Upon their arrival, Gage had taken the time to search the house thoroughly, examining every room, every closet, even the attic, but Romero wasn't anywhere to be found.

Gage had even considered the possibility that A.D. might jump him as he walked up the sidewalk to the front door, particularly since Gage was at a disadvantage, under the view-constricting umbrella. But he'd walked through the rain and easily entered the house without even seeing a hint of another human on the street.

"Well, what do you think?" he asked Lillian.

She stood at the window, her body glowing brightly as she kept an eye on the front yard and the street. "Only one car since we got here, and it was somebody next door. Other than that, no cars at all. No one wants to be out in this mess."

"Romero will come," Gage said.

She nodded. "He'd better. I don't plan on being stuck on this side forever."

"I can't believe I forgot my phone," he grumbled. He'd realized he'd left it when they were crossing the bridge between LaPlace and Kenner, but by then, he hadn't wanted to go back.

"It's okay. I've got this one, and I'm ready." She held up Chantelle's cordless phone and smiled. "By the way, in case I don't get a chance to tell you, I really appreciate everything you've done to keep Chantelle safe, and everything you're doing to help me cross."

"No problem," Gage lied through his teeth.

Lillian laughed, obviously thinking the same thing. "Yeah, right. Anyway, I also want to thank you for giving Kayla a reason to smile again."

His chest swelled. "I plan to keep her smiling for a very long time."

"I kind of thought you did," she said. "That's good, because she deserves—" She stopped talking when bright lights filtered through the window behind her. "Someone's coming."

Gage rubbed his fingers over the gun. He truly didn't want to use it. He mainly just had it to scare Romero. Hell, he'd never even shot an animal before. However, if Romero was trying to take his life, then he damn well thought he could defend himself. Hunting wasn't his thing, but he was a good shot.

He'd just never shot at anything that was breathing.

"Well?" Gage asked, as the lights were extinguished and Lillian leaned closer to the window.

"Oh, no," she whispered. "I thought I felt her, but I figured it was because I had her on my mind."

"Who?" Gage thought he knew.

Don't let it be Kayla.

"It's Nanette's car," Lillian said. "She's getting out in the rain."

Nanette? Surely she wouldn't…

"It isn't Nan. It's Kayla." She dropped the phone on a recliner near the window and moved to the door.

At that precise moment, the rain shifted, beating heavily against the front door and window, probably a warning from the powers that be, Gage surmised. Warning him to get Kayla the hell out of here.

He took one step toward the door, then heard Lillian again. "Wait! Something's happening." Lillian stepped out into the rain, her glowing frame obstructing Gage's view of Kayla, then she yelled back. "It's okay, just Chantelle's neighbor. He must have been waiting in his car for the rain to die down before he headed inside." She entered the apartment merely steps before Kayla. "Everything's okay."

But Kayla didn't enter. Instead, she turned toward the other house, and her mouth fell open.

Too late, Gage realized why.

A dark figure grabbed her, the knife at her throat flashing as he shoved her through the door. The neighbor *hadn't* come home, Gage now realized. Aidan Dominic Romero had been next door, sitting in his car and waiting…for this.

A.D. slammed the door behind him as he entered Chantelle's apartment with Kayla held tightly in front of him, both of them dripping wet with rain, and the whites of both sets of eyes visible even in the dim light from the television. Kayla's were wide with fear; Romero's were wide with hate.

"Don't move," he instructed Gage. "Or I'll slice her pretty little throat right here."

Gage nodded. Hell.

Aidan Romero looked to be in his midthirties, though it was tough to tell in the dark room. He had a wide forehead, deep receding hairline and a flat, flaring nose. He gave Gage a triumphant grin, and Gage couldn't believe how quickly things had turned in the lunatic's favor. Why had Kayla come here?

"Now drop the damn gun and slide it over this way," A.D. continued. "We're not using guns tonight." He moved his mouth next to Kayla's ear. "You used a knife on me, didn't you, Makayla? I thought I'd return the favor." He glared at Gage. "Drop the damn gun!"

Gage did as he was told. What else could he do? One wrong move and Kayla was dead. He focused on the knife against her tender neck, at the very spot that he'd kissed thoroughly just last night. At this precise moment, Gage hated his medical knowledge, because he knew exactly what would happen if Romero moved that knife across her throat. If he severed her jugular, which received approximately a liter of blood a minute—and with only five liters of blood in the human body—she was gone. Or if he sliced deeper and reached the carotid, then she would bleed to death after a few beats of the heart. And if he were to hit the middle of the neck, the trachea, then she would asphyxiate.

In short, Gage was completely at A.D. Romero's mercy. What could he do, when any movement of that knife could kill the woman he loved?

Then he saw Lillian. Her ghostly glow had faded when Romero entered, but now she shone brilliantly. She stepped from her spot near the window toward the gun.

Determined to keep Romero from realizing that there were actually four people in Chantelle's home, Gage kept his eyes focused on A.D. and Kayla. His mind, however, urged Lillian on.

Lillian.

Romero gripped Kayla closer to him, the tip of the knife digging into her throat. "This your boyfriend, Makayla?" he hissed against her ear.

"Dammit, don't hurt her."

"Well, don't you sound right tough, for a guy with no gun and a girl at the end of a knife?" Romero said, snickering. "And for your information, I *am* gonna hurt her. I'm gonna hurt her real good, and I'm gonna let you watch. Makayla knows what that's like, don't ya, Kayla? Having someone watch?"

Kayla's brows furrowed, and she didn't speak, until he pressed the tip of the knife into her skin and a thin trickle of blood burst free, only a surface wound, for now, but he was showing Kayla and Gage that he was willing to hurt her.

"Don't you, Makayla?" he repeated.

"I—don't know what you mean," she stuttered.

Romero let out a hysterical laugh. "No? You didn't realize what was happening back then? Seriously? Damn."

"What was happening back then?" Gage asked, while Lillian inched closer to the pistol.

Not the gun! Gage focused on those three words. If Lillian picked up the gun and spooked Romero, then that knife was liable to go straight into Kayla's throat. Gage had to make sure Lillian understood.

She took another step, nearly within reach of the pistol now.

No! Not. The. Gun.

Lillian stopped. "No?" she asked, and Gage was thankful that he was the only one who could hear her voice.

No.

"You really want to know what happened?" Romero said. "Why? You get into stuff like that?" He emitted an evil, hissing laugh and moved the arm that curved around Kayla's waist upward, until his hand palmed her right breast. "Don't move, darling. Or I might just cut you again, in other places." Then he looked at Gage. "And soon, I'll make her pay." He leaned his face around and licked Kayla's cheek. "But maybe we'll have a little fun first, like old times. All we need is a blindfold."

At Kayla's shocked gasp, he laughed again. "Hell, you didn't even know, did you? Daddy rewarded me for staying away all year by letting me have everything I wanted, all summer long. And you, Makayla, were part of everything I wanted. You, and the other three." He scanned the room. "Where's pretty Chantelle? I've waited a long time for her, too."

The phone, Gage thought. Lillian nodded, then turned to get the phone from the chair. Now if he could keep Romero talking while she called 911.

"Why now?" Gage asked. "Why did you wait all these years, and then come after them now?"

"Daddy was going to get out." Romero's voice suddenly converted to that of an adolescent. "And when he got out, we were going to get our revenge. Kill every damn one of them, together. And then those bastards murdered him, and it was just me again. It was up to me to make you pay for all his years in that place, and all of mine waiting for him to get out. Daddy took care of me. Gave me everything I wanted." He looked at Kayla. "And I gave all of you what you wanted. You really wanted it, Daddy said so, and he was right. I could tell. You're filthy whores, just like my mother, and you wanted it. Every time. And every time, we gave it to you." He grinned. "Tonight, I may give you another taste in front of your boyfriend, before both of you die. That'd make Daddy happy."

Behind Romero now, Lillian picked up the phone.

Kayla stared at Gage, and he shifted his eyes from her to Lillian, hoping like hell that she understood. She made a subtle movement with her eyes that told him she hadn't forgotten the ghost's presence in the room.

Romero was still ranting about everything he did back then, and everything he'd do again.

"Grab the knife?" Lillian asked, looking at Gage.

Call first, he silently responded, and prayed that what he was planning would work.

Lillian nodded, and Kayla kept her eyes focused on Gage, evidently prepared to do whatever it took to help Lillian, whenever the spirit was ready. Lillian pressed the talk button, and the dial tone was faintly heard over the rain beating against the window.

Romero's head turned slightly, but his attention wasn't completely averted until Lillian pushed the three buttons and the 911 operator's voice came loudly through the line.

"Nine-one-one. State your emergency," the woman said. The volume was turned up loud enough on Chantelle's phone that everyone in the room, including A.D. Romero, heard her.

"What the hell?" He stared at the phone falling from midair as Lillian tossed it to the chair, then grabbed Romero's arm and yanked the knife from Kayla's throat. Gage had never been more thankful that spirits did have the ability to touch…and grab. She yanked Romero's arm with as much strength as any breathing male could have.

Kayla, ready for the attack, twisted out of Romero's embrace and kneed him solidly in the groin, while Gage dove for the gun.

Romero's knees buckled and he dropped to the floor.

"I didn't miss this time," Kayla snapped, then she

kicked him there again—as hard as she could—for good measure. "Bastard."

Gage aimed the gun directly at Romero's face, while sirens blared loudly in the distance. "It's over, Romero." He looked at Kayla and repeated, "It's over."

"Lillian?" Kayla questioned, looking at Gage to find out where her friend was within the room, but he shook his head.

"Not here anymore," he said. "But believe me, she's okay where she is."

Tears welled in Kayla's eyes, but she nodded, obviously realizing that once she'd been saved, truly saved, from Romero, Lillian had moved on.

Police cars pulled up outside Chantelle's house and officers quickly covered the place. After Gage tended to Kayla's neck, which—thank God—was merely a surface wound, he answered all their questions, as did Kayla. Then another vehicle pulled up behind the cop cars.

Tristan, with Chantelle and Nanette at his heels, quickly hurried to hug Kayla and Gage in relief. The police had already taped off the front entrance, so everyone stood in the rain and watched them do their job.

"You okay, Kayla?" Chantelle asked, eyeing Romero as the police unceremoniously put him in the back of a squad car.

"Yeah," Kayla reassured her. "I am."

"And—" Chantelle looked past Kayla to Gage "—Lillian?"

"She crossed over." Chantelle's lip trembled.

Kayla wrapped an arm around her and let her cry. "Oh, God, I'll miss her," Chantelle said.

"I know," Kayla answered, rubbing Chantelle's back as she spoke. "I will, too. But you know that she needed to cross, right?"

Chantelle nodded. "And now she knows that he didn't get away with what he did to her." She glared at the cop car that held A.D. Romero.

"Come on, Chantelle," Nanette said. "Let's get out of the rain." She led her back to the car, away from her house and away from Romero.

Tristan waited until they were safely out of earshot, then asked, "Hell, Gage. What happened here?"

"I'll tell you everything later. Right now, I just want to get out of this rain, go home and go to bed." He glanced at Kayla. "If that's okay by you."

"It's more than okay," she said, grabbing him and holding him tight, while the rain soaked them completely. "It's perfect."

16

KAYLA MOVED easily around Gage's kitchen. It had been four days since A.D. Romero had been taken into custody at Chantelle's place and three days since the plantation inspection had gone off smooth as silk, without any glitches whatsoever, due to all of Dax and Tristan's work on the first floor. She and Gage had spent the majority of the next two days in bed. He'd left this morning for the hospital, and Kayla had busied herself making plans for her future.

She could hardly wait to tell him what she'd decided, and had cooked a celebratory dinner. She heard the door to his apartment open and knew he was finally home. Amazing how much she missed him when he was gone, but if her plans went through, then she'd soon have plenty to keep her busy throughout the day. She added a teaspoon of liquid crab boil to the cheesy mixture on the stove, coughing as the spices overpowered the steam. Then she turned to see Gage, his eyes ultra vivid today, set off by the royal-blue scrubs he wore.

He dropped his hospital badge and pager on the dining room table, then entered the kitchen smiling. "Okay, should the fact that you're coughing like that while cooking our dinner alarm me? Because there's a great little Italian place down Williams called Mama Nez's, and they've got the best stuffed eggplant…"

She smacked his chest with a wooden spoon. "Very funny. For your information, Lillian wasn't the only one who learned how to cook when we grew up. Ms. Rosa taught us all a thing or two in her kitchen." She stirred the cheese, then spooned a little out and held it toward his mouth. "See what you think, but be ready—it's spicy."

"I live for spicy," he said, grinning, then sampled the sauce. "Mmm, remind me to thank Ms. Rosa next time I see her."

"Funny you should mention that." She grinned back. "Seeing Ms. Rosa, I mean."

"Uh-huh." He didn't sound surprised at where this conversation was headed. "You ready to tell me about it?"

She moved the heat down to low and turned to stare at him. "Tell you about what?"

"Your plan to help Ms. Rosa reopen the orphanage as a sanctuary for kids who've been abused," he reeled off, without batting an eye.

"How did you know?"

He pointed to his pager. "Amazing how much time my youngest cousin can find to call me throughout my workday, particularly when she's excited about something."

"Jenee?" Kayla asked with a laugh.

"Did you really think you could tell her about her dream job, and how you would love to work with her to make that place a reality, and then she wouldn't want to tell me about it? She's been calling all day with plans for landscaping, for renovating the buildings, for raising money from doctors at the hospital, you name it. And she told me that you've decided to go back to school and get a degree in social work, so you can officially help girls who have been through what you went through."

"I always wanted to go back to school," Kayla admitted. "But I was afraid."

"And you're not afraid anymore?"

"No, I'm not. Jenee sounded pretty excited about the idea, so I'm actually looking forward to school, and to learning what it would take to get that place fixed up and actually doing something good with it. And if we do make Rosa's dream come true and turn that place into a safe home for abused girls, then we'll have something positive to show for Lillian's sacrifice. Lillian will watch over that place and the girls that stay there. I know she will."

"I'm sure you're right," Gage said. "And Jenee is more than pretty excited. She's over the moon." He wrapped his arms around her and softly kissed her. "And I am, too, for that matter."

"Why's that?"

"Because, if you're planning to go back to school and help Jenee reopen that place, and take on all the responsibility that goes with running it, then that means you're planning on sticking around New Orleans for a while."

"Did you think I'd leave?" She was surprised.

"I knew you didn't have the best of memories here, and yeah, I wondered if now that both Romeros were taken care of, you wouldn't want to move somewhere else and start over. But I'm glad you're staying here."

"Why's that?" she asked, hoping he'd tell her what she wanted to hear, that Gage wanted her to "stick around" for him.

"Well, not that I couldn't work somewhere else, but I do like my position at Ochsner. And then there's the family, and the spirits. My assignments are delivered to the plantation, so naturally, I need to be close enough to get to them."

"Funny. I thought we were talking about me sticking around, not you."

"Same difference," Gage said smoothly.

"Run that by me again." She rubbed her hands over his behind, then curved her body against him. She knew what he was implying, but she wanted to hear him say it.

"I'm saying that you're stuck with me, Ms. Sparks, for as long as you want." He leaned away from her and reached into the pocket of his scrubs. "That is, if that's what you want."

Kayla's mouth opened but no words came out as Gage withdrew a small, velvet-covered box.

"Open it."

She did, and beheld an exquisite square diamond in an antique setting. "Oh, it's incredible."

"It was my great-grandmother's." He placed a finger beneath her chin and brought her eyes to meet his. "Kayla, marry me."

She laughed. "That wasn't exactly a question."

"It only needs to be a question if you're planning on declining." He gave her a look that was extremely smug.

"Fairly sure of yourself, aren't you, Mr. Vicknair?" she teased.

"I'm thinking it's with good reason. I've waited for you for a long time, and dreamed of you before I ever saw you. I don't want anyone else, Kayla, and I don't want to spend another minute without you. My life was meaningless before, but now I've found what I'm looking for, and I'm going for what I want. You." He gave her that adorable crooked grin that made her insides quiver. "What do you say?"

"Yes," she whispered, then gasped when he picked her up, swung her around the kitchen and kissed her thoroughly. Kayla's entire body melted against his, and she knew that she'd never in her entire life felt so…right.

The doorbell buzzed loudly, but Gage didn't stop his celebration dance.

Kayla giggled. "I think someone needs to see you."

"They'll come back," he said, running his hands up her shirt and over her breasts while she moaned, and the doorbell continued to sound.

"I don't think they're leaving," she said breathlessly, and, as predicted, the buzzing continued.

"Hell, I'm thinking you're right." He released her, adding, "But we're continuing this as soon as I get rid of them." He kissed her again, then went to answer the door.

Kayla's knees were wobbly as she followed him.

Gage opened the door, and Kayla viewed a nice-looking guy, she'd guess early twenties, holding his finger flush against the doorbell and grinning guiltily.

"Were you busy, big brother?" he asked, shifting his head to the side to move brown wavy hair out of his hazel eyes.

"Dax?" Kayla said, shocked. She hadn't seen his chin all week; it had been covered with a scruffy untamed beard. She hadn't seen his eyes, either, for that matter.

He laughed and gave her a grin that she'd bet had the power to melt many a Cajun female's heart. It was good to see him smile, particularly since he'd been so sullen ever since they met.

"Monique and Ryan got back this afternoon. She took one look at me and drug me to her shop. Before I knew it, she had me cut and shaved and *presentable* according to her." He shrugged. "I did need to get cleaned up. I've got a little girl coming to visit, I believe."

"You've been hearing a ghost?" Gage asked.

"Yeah. Should get an assignment any day," Dax said. "And Monique was right. That *look* I had going would scare a kid."

"You do look much better cleaned up," Kayla agreed, smiling. "So, does that mean you're feeling better about things?"

"You mean about the fact that I seem to have fallen for a ghost that's already crossed?" He shrugged again. "Hell, I guess I've decided that all the Vicknairs aren't meant to be lucky in love."

"And speaking of Vicknairs in love—" Gage lifted Kayla's left hand and held the ring out for Dax's view.

A shadow passed over Dax's handsome face, then he nodded as though he'd expected nothing less. "Welcome to the family, Kayla."

"Thanks."

"So, what brings you to my place?" Gage asked.

"These." Dax handed him a set of keys.

"My truck keys?"

"Yeah. Tristan picked it up from the shop today and was going to drive it over, but he didn't have time before he went to work. So being the good brother that I am, I brought it to you."

"Good, and modest," Gage said sarcastically.

"Well, there is that." Dax smiled. "Plus, I like driving his Jeep, and I'm supposed to bring it back to him."

"And there's the real reason you volunteered to bring the truck." Gage reached in his pocket and pulled out Tristan's keys. "What's wrong with your Beemer?"

"Nothing. Every now and then, though, you just want the rowdiness that goes with a Jeep."

"You trying to get rowdy?"

Dax chuckled. "Actually, I'm trying to get out of this damn funk. Nan's still celebrating at the house over the inspection going so well, and I'm not really in the mood to celebrate much of anything. I just want to drive, and I decided I wanted to drive the Jeep."

Kayla searched for some words of comfort. "Maybe things will get better soon."

Dax shook his head. "Only if I can get her off my mind, or if she comes back. And I haven't been a medium all that long, but I haven't seen or heard of a ghost crossing *all* the way over and then heading back this direction. I believe I'd have to get some sort of miracle."

"I've become a believer in miracles." Kayla rose on her toes to kiss Gage's jaw.

Dax smiled. "And I'm glad that it worked out for you, Kayla. And you, too, bro," he said, tossing Tristan's keys in the air, then catching them. "Now, I'm going to head on back to the house, in case my little ghost comes calling." He turned and walked away.

Gage pulled Kayla back inside the apartment. "How about an early dinner, and then to bed for dessert?"

"You know," she said, "that sauce could simmer a while before I add the shrimp."

"Shrimp? What are you making?"

"Shrimp fettuccini."

"You plan on cooking like that every night?" he asked hopefully.

"Not every night," she admitted, "but most. And I expect you to help out. Actually, I'm expecting you to help tonight."

"With what?"

She pulled him toward the bedroom.

"The appetizer. Now take off your scrubs, Dr. Vicknair."

"With pleasure."

* * * * *

*Want more of the Vicknair family and
their ghostly counterparts?
Turn the page for a
sneak preview of Dax's story,
SHIVER AND SPICE, also by Kelley St. John.
On sale September 2007
wherever books are sold.*

CELESTE BEAUCHAMP hadn't expected to be so drawn to Dax Vicknair, but she was, and she'd spent the majority of her time in the middle trying to determine how to get back to him. But that path, his path, was closed. *That* was the path she wanted, and *that* was the only one that never seemed to grant her access. She wanted to forget those voices to the right, forget that light in the middle, and head left…to Dax.

How could she get back to him, if she couldn't find her way through?

"I want him," she whispered.

A loud creaking penetrated the silence, and to Celeste's complete bewilderment, the blocked entry to her left eased open, and an elderly woman, her glowing silver hair long and flowing around her shoulders, leaned out from the darkness and crooked an elegant finger toward Celeste.

"Come, *chère,*" she said. "Dax needs you."

And that was enough for Celeste to follow, no further questions asked.

* * * * * *

Every Life Has More
Than One Chapter™

Award-winning author Stevi Mittman delivers another hysterical mystery, featuring Teddi Bayer, an irrepressible heroine, and her to-die-for hero, Detective Drew Scoones. After all, life on Long Island can be murder!

Turn the page for a sneak peek
at the warm and funny fourth book,
WHOSE NUMBER IS UP, ANYWAY?,
in the Teddi Bayer series,
by STEVI MITTMAN.
On sale August 7.

CHAPTER 1

"Before redecorating a room, I always advise my clients to empty it of everything but one chair. Then I suggest they move that chair from place to place, sitting in it, until the placement feels right. Trust your instincts when deciding on furniture placement. Your room should "feel right.""

—TipsFromTeddi.com

Gut feelings. You know, that gnawing in the pit of your stomach that warns you that you are about to do the absolute stupidest thing you could do? Something that will ruin life as you know it?

I've got one now, standing at the butcher counter in King Kullen, the grocery store in the same strip mall as L.I. Lanes, the bowling alley cum billiard parlor I'm in the process of redecorating for its "Grand Opening."

I realize being in the wrong supermarket probably doesn't sound exactly dire to you, but you aren't the one buying your father a brisket at a store your mother will somehow know isn't Waldbaum's.

And then, June Bayer isn't your mother.

The woman behind the counter has agreed to go into the freezer to find a brisket for me, since there aren't any in the case. There are packages of pork tenderloin, piles of spare ribs and rolls of sausage, but no briskets.

Warning Number Two, right? I should be so out of here.

But no, I'm still in the same spot when she comes back out, brisketless, her face ashen. She opens her mouth as if she is going to scream, but only a gurgle comes out.

And then she pinballs out from behind the counter, knocking bottles of Peter Luger Steak Sauce to the floor on her way, now hitting the tower of cans at the end of the prepared foods aisle and sending them sprawling, now making her way down the aisle, careening from side to side as she goes.

Finally, from a distance, I hear her shout, "He's deeeeeeaaaad! Joey's deeeeeaaaad."

My first thought is *You should always trust your gut.*

My second thought is that now, somehow, my mother will know I was in King Kullen. For weeks I will have to hear "What did you expect?" as though whenever you go to King Kullen someone turns up dead. And if the detective investigating the case turns out to be Detective Drew Scoones…well, I'll never hear the end of that from her, either.

She still suspects I murdered the guy who was found dead on my doorstep last Halloween just to get Drew back into my life.

Several people head for the butcher's freezer and I position myself to block them. If there's one thing I've learned from finding people dead—and the guy on my doorstep wasn't the first one—it's that the police get very testy when you mess with their murder scenes.

"You can't go in there until the police get here," I say, stationing myself at the end of the butcher's counter and in front of the Employees Only door, acting as if I'm some sort of authority. "You'll contaminate the evidence if it turns out to be murder."

Shouts and chaos. You'd think I'd know better than to throw the word *murder* around. Cell phones are flipping open and tongues are wagging.

I amend my statement quickly. "Which, of course, it probably isn't. Murder, I mean. People die all the time, and it's not always in hospitals or their own beds, or…" I babble when I'm nervous, and the idea of someone dead on the other side of the freezer door makes me very nervous.

So does the idea of seeing Drew Scoones again. Drew and I have this on-again, off-again sort of thing…that I kind of turned off.

Who knew he'd take it so personally when he tried to get serious and I responded by saying we could talk about *us* tomorrow—and then caught a plane to my parents' condo in Boca the next day? In July. In the middle of a job.

For some crazy reason, he took that to mean that I was avoiding him and the subject of *us*.

That was three months ago. I haven't seen him since.

The manager, who identifies himself and points to his nameplate in case I don't believe him, says he has to go into *his cooler*. "Maybe Joey's not dead," he says. "Maybe he can be saved, and you're letting him die in there. Did you ever think of that?"

In fact, I hadn't. But I had thought that the murderer might try to go back in to make sure his tracks were covered, so I say that I will go in and check.

Which means that the manager and I couple up and go in together while everyone pushes against the doorway to peer in, erasing any chance of finding clean prints on that Employees Only door.

I expect to find carcasses of dead animals hanging from

hooks, and maybe Joey hanging from one, too. I think it's going to be very creepy and I steel myself, only to find a rather benign series of shelves with large slabs of meat laid out carefully on them, along with boxes and boxes marked simply Chicken.

Nothing scary here, unless you count the body of a middle-aged man with graying hair sprawled faceup on the floor. His eyes are wide open and unblinking. His shirt is stiff. His pants are stiff. His body is stiff. And his expression, you should forgive the pun—is frozen. Bill-the-manager crosses himself and stands mute while I pronounce the guy dead in a sort of *happy now?* tone.

"We should not be in here," I say, and he nods his head emphatically and helps me push people out of the doorway just in time to hear the police sirens and see the cop cars pull up outside the big store windows.

Bobbie Lyons, my partner in Teddi Bayer Interior Designs (and also my neighbor, my best friend and my private fashion police), and Mark, our carpenter (and my dogsitter, confidant and ego booster), rush in from next door. They beat the cops by a half step and shout out my name. People point in my direction.

After all the publicity that followed the unfortunate incident during which I shot my ex-husband, Rio Gallo, and then the subsequent murder of my first client—which I solved, I might add—it seems like the whole world, or at least all of Long Island, knows who I am.

Mark asks if I'm all right. (Did I remember to mention that the man is drop-dead-gorgeous-but-a-decade-too-young-for-me-yet-too-old-for-my-daughter-thank-god?) I don't get a chance to answer him because the police are quickly closing in on the store manager and me.

"The woman—" I begin telling the police. Then I have

to pause for the manager to fill in her name, which he does: *Fran*.

I continue. "Right. Fran. Fran went into the freezer to get a brisket. A moment later she came out and screamed that Joey was dead. So I'd say she was the one who discovered the body."

"And you are…?" the cop asks me. It comes out a bit like who do I *think* I am, rather than who am I really?

"An innocent bystander," Bobbie, hair perfect, makeup just right, says, carefully placing her body between the cop and me.

"And she was just leaving," Mark adds. They each take one of my arms.

Fran comes into the inner circle surrounding the cops. In case it isn't obvious from the hairnet and bloodstained white apron with *Fran* embroidered on it, I explain that she was the butcher who was going for the brisket. Mark and Bobbie take that as a signal that I've done my job and they can now get me out of there. They twist around, with me in the middle, as if we're a Rockettes line, until we are facing away from the butcher counter. They've managed to propel me a few steps toward the exit when disaster— in the form of a Mazda RX-7 pulling up at the loading curb—strikes.

Mark's grip on my arm tightens like a vise. "Too late," he says.

Bobbie's expletive is unprintable. "Maybe there's a back door," she suggests, but Mark is right. It's too late.

I've laid my eyes on Detective Scoones. And while my gut is trying to warn me that my heart shouldn't go there, regions farther south are melting at just the sight of him.

"Walk," Bobbie orders me.

And I try to. Really.

Walk, I tell my feet. *Just put one foot in front of the other.*

I can do this because I know, in my heart of hearts, that if Drew Scoones was still interested in me, he'd have gotten in touch with me after I returned from Boca. And he didn't.

Since he's a detective, Drew doesn't have to wear one of those dark blue Nassau County Police uniforms. Instead, he's got on jeans, a tight-fitting T-shirt and a tweedy sports jacket. If you think that sounds good, you should see him. Chiseled features, cleft chin, brown hair that's naturally a little sandy in the front, a smile that…well, that doesn't matter. He isn't smiling now.

He walks up to me, tucks his sunglasses into his breast pocket and looks me over from head to toe.

"Well, if it isn't Miss Cut and Run," he says. "Aren't you supposed to be somewhere in Florida or something?" He looks at Mark accusingly, as if he was covering for me when he told Drew I was gone.

"Detective Scoones?" one of the uniforms says. "The stiff's in the cooler and the woman who found him is over there." He jerks his head in Fran's direction.

Drew continues to stare at me.

You know how when you were young, your mother always told you to wear clean underwear in case you were in an accident? And how, a little farther on, she told you not to go out in hair rollers because you never knew who you might see—or who might see you? And how now your best friend says she wouldn't be caught dead without makeup and suggests you shouldn't, either?

Okay, today, *finally,* in my overalls and Converse sneakers, I get it.

I brush my hair out of my eyes. "Well, I'm back," I say. As if he hasn't known my exact whereabouts. The man is a detective, for heaven's sake. "Been back awhile."

Bobbie has watched the exchange and apparently decided she's given Drew all the time he deserves. "And we've got work to do, so…" she says, grabbing my arm and giving Drew a little two-fingered wave goodbye.

As I back up a foot or two, the store manager sees his chance and places himself in front of Drew, trying to get his attention. Maybe what makes Drew such a good detective is his ability to focus.

Only what he's focusing on is me.

"Phone broken? Carrier pigeon died?" he asks me, taking in Fran, the manager, the meat counter and that Employees Only door, all without taking his eyes off me.

Mark tries to break the spell. "We've got work to do there, you've got work to do here, Scoones," Mark says to him, gesturing toward next door. "So it's back to the alley for us."

Drew's lip twitches. "You working the alley now?" he says.

"If you'd like to follow me," Bill-the-manager, clearly exasperated, says to Drew—who doesn't respond. It's as if waiting for my answer is all he has to do.

So, fine. "You knew I was back," I say.

The man has known my whereabouts every hour of the day for as long as I've known him. And my mother's not the only one who won't buy that he "just happened" to answer this particular call. In fact, I'm willing to bet my children's lunch money that he's taken every call within ten miles of my home since the day I got back.

And now he's gotten lucky.

"*You* could have called *me*," I say.

"You're the one who said *tomorrow* for our talk and then flew the coop, chickie," he says. "I figured the ball was in your court."

"Detective?" the uniform says. "There's something you ought to see in here."

Drew gives me a look that amounts to *in or out?*

He could be talking about the investigation, or about our relationship.

Bobbie tries to steer me away. Mark's fists are balled. Drew waits me out, knowing I won't be able to resist what might be a murder investigation.

Finally he turns and heads for the cooler.

And, like a puppy dog, I follow.

Bobbie grabs the back of my shirt and pulls me to a halt.

"I'm just going to show him something," I say, yanking away.

"Yeah," Bobbie says, pointedly looking at the buttons on my blouse. The two at breast level have popped. "That's what I'm afraid of."

Silhouette

Desire

REASONS FOR REVENGE

A brand-new provocative miniseries by *USA TODAY*
bestselling author **Maureen Child** begins with

SCORNED
BY THE BOSS

Jefferson Lyon is a man used to having his own way.
He runs his shipping empire from California, and
his admin Caitlyn Monroe runs the rest of his world.
When Caitlin decides she's had enough and needs
new scenery, Jefferson devises a plan to get her back.
Jefferson *never* loses, but little does he know that
he's in a competition....

Don't miss any of the other titles from the
REASONS FOR REVENGE trilogy by
USA TODAY bestselling author **Maureen Child.**

SCORNED BY THE BOSS #1816
Available August 2007

SEDUCED BY THE RICH MAN #1820
Available September 2007

CAPTURED BY THE BILLIONAIRE #1826
Available October 2007

Only from Silhouette Desire!

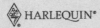

HARLEQUIN®

Mediterranean NIGHTS™

Glamour, elegance, mystery and revenge aboard the high seas...

Coming in August 2007...

THE TYCOON'S SON

by
award-winning author
Cindy Kirk

Businessman Theo Catomeris's long-estranged father is determined to reconnect with his son, so he hires Trish Melrose to persuade Theo to renew his contract with Liberty Line. Sailing aboard the luxurious *Alexandra's Dream* is a rare opportunity for the single mom to mix business and pleasure. But an undeniable attraction between Trish and Theo is distracting her from the task at hand....

ATHENA FORCE

Heart-pounding romance and thrilling adventure.

A ruthless enemy rises against the women of Athena Academy. In a global chess game of vengeance, kidnapping and murder, every move exposes potential enemies—and lovers. This time the women must stand together... before their world is ripped apart.

THIS NEW 12-BOOK SERIES BEGINS WITH A BANG IN AUGUST 2007 WITH

TRUST
by Rachel Caine

Look for a new Athena Force adventure each month wherever books are sold.

REQUEST YOUR FREE BOOKS!

2 FREE NOVELS PLUS 2 FREE GIFTS!

HARLEQUIN®

Blaze®

Red-hot reads!

HARLEQUIN®

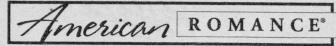

American **ROMANCE**®

TEXAS LEGACIES: THE CARRIGANS

Get to the Heart of a Texas Family

WITH

THE RANCHER NEXT DOOR
by
Cathy Gillen Thacker

She'll Run The Ranch—And Her Life—Her Way!

On her alpaca ranch in Texas, Rebecca encounters constant interference from Trevor McCabe, the bossy rancher next door. Rebecca becomes very friendly with Vince Owen, her other neighbor and Trevor's archrival from college. Trevor's problem is convincing Rebecca that he is on her side, and aware of Vince's ulterior motives. But Trevor has fallen for her in the process....

On sale July 2007

HARLEQUIN®

Blaze™

COMING NEXT MONTH

#339 HARD AND FAST Lisa Renee Jones
She's been in and out of locker rooms her whole life. Now Amanda Wright is there looking for the inside scoop to take her column to the big leagues. When pitcher Brad Rogers offers a sexy time in exchange for an interview, her libido won't let her refuse!

#340 DOING IRELAND! Kate Hoffmann
Lust in Translation
A spring that inspires instant lust? With the way her life's been going, Claire O'Connor is ready to try anything—even if it means boarding a plane to Ireland. But once she arrives, she knows there has to be *something* to the legend. Because all she had to do was set eyes on gorgeous innkeeper Will Donovan, and she wanted him....

#341 STRIPPED Julie Elizabeth Leto
The Bad Girls Club, Bk. 2
Lilith St. John is a witch—really! And she hasn't been too good lately. (It seems using a spell to make Mac Mancusi totally infatuated with her was a big no-no. Who knew?) But that doesn't mean she deserves to be stripped of her powers. Especially now—when Mac's suddenly back in her life, looking to rekindle the magic...

#342 THE DEFENDER Cara Summers
Tall, Dark...and Dangerously Hot! Bk. 3
Theo Angelis puts the "hot" in "hotshot lawyer," but savvy, sexy Sadie Oliver's simple handshake sets him aflame. Her brother's facing a murder rap, their sister is missing and Sadie is in terrible danger. Her only way to be involved in the case is to pose as a man. But the heat in Theo's eyes never lets her forget she's *all* woman....

#343 PICK ME UP Samantha Hunter
Forbidden Fantasies
Do you have a forbidden fantasy? Lauren Baker does. She's always wondered what it would be like to have sex with a total stranger. And now is the perfect time to indulge. After all, she's packed up her car and is on her way to a new life when she spots a sexy cowboy stranded by the side of the road. How can any girl resist?

#344 UNDERNEATH IT ALL Lori Borrill
Million Dollar Secrets, Bk. 2
Multimillion-dollar lottery winner Nicole Reavis has the world at her feet, but all she wants is hot Atlanta bachelor Devon Bradshaw. The Southern charmer has plenty to offer and plenty to teach Nicole about the finer things...including the route to his bedroom. But she's got a secret to keep!

www.eHarlequin.com